For information contact :
Makin Books Publishing
http://www.makinbooks.net

Cover : Christian Connett
ISBN 13: 978-1-945663-15-4

Second Edition: September 2016
Printed in the United States of America

10 9 8 7 6 5 4 3 2 1

*I'd like to dedicate this to my parents
Bruce and Wanda Henderson,
whose love for each other grows stronger each day.*

While writing this column the rain was falling down hard on my roof like it was trying to break in. As I heard the thunder I thought about that song "Can You Stand The Rain" originally sung by New Edition and later splendidly redone by Boyz II Men. I heard that song many times, but I never really listened to it. I walked out of many relationships because I couldn't stand the rain. I just wanted sunny days and I realize that I wasn't being realistic. In every relationship you're going to have your storms. It's when you can make it through those rainy days that you appreciate the sunshine even more

~Choose This Day column by Ruben Wells of SA Prevalent~

1

Spoiled Life

Everything begins with a choice. My life changed in a second because of a choice.

Straight and narrow is the way I've always walked never easily distracted from doing what's right.

My only problem in life, which is ironic, is having a hard time telling people no.

A moment of compromise has put me in the middle of a quagmire. The one thing everybody has in common is that everybody encounters trouble.

I felt aghast, as sweat sprinted down my face while someone held a gun to my head. My hands were in the air shaking like I was having convulsions. My stomach was turning as if I came off a rough roller coaster ride while my heart was beating uncontrollably like I ran a marathon.

One wrong choice I made has me staring at the barrel of a .357 magnum. From my point of view, it was like staring back at a mortar. Surely this isn't the end of Ruben Alexander Wells.

If I could possess one superhero power, it would be invisibility. Or better yet indestructibility.

Choices are a gift. They are bestowed to everyone every day. I hope that I'm given a chance to make many more choices for a very long time. If I could choose how I die it would be by natural causes or just very, very old age.

Instead this person with a steady hand is going to choose how I die with a single bullet to the head or multiple shots to the chest.

If this masked individual pulls the trigger that means no more access to pre-screenings to offer my criticism of a film, goodbye Comic Con, no more opportunities to visit South by Southwest Festival or Sundance Film Festival and let people know what to look forward to on the big screen, and most importantly no more living.

Prior to looking down the barrel, I often pondered if my life were to be a movie what would the studio executives choose to label it?

It's had moments of comedy. Maybe not the kind that makes an audience roll on the floor laughing and tears fall down their face due to mirth, but it could bring a chuckle. A little bit of adventure, but not like Indiana Jones or James Bond that would leave a child in awe. A touch of suspense, but not enough to be an R rated film that leaves a woman keeping the lights on when trying to sleep at night. Although having a gun pointed at your head is suspenseful.

Overall my life would be labeled a drama. It's been filled with conflict, sorrow, heartbreak, and loss.

Ambivalent is probably how people would feel viewing my life. Would I be like Matt Damon's character from The Talented Mr. Ripley? Would an audience sympathize or pity me or would they wish for me to receive a comeuppance? Like Adam Sandler's movies you would either love me or hate me. There's no gray line for what people's opinion of me would be. An audience will either love or hate me.

The majority of my life I've been a Christian and I would try to live right. And I heavily emphasize the word "try." I'm as humanly flawed as the next man, but I'm not corrupt nor am I a saint. Recently in my life I've done wrong by a few people who didn't deserve it.

Perhaps my aberrance has led me here, judgment day.

It's always been difficult for me to trust people. That's why all my relationships have failed, then again with the majority of them I didn't care if they succeeded or failed.

Most women pray for a knight in shining armor and they get me, a knight in tarnished armor.

All my ex-girlfriends told me I never knew when a good thing was standing in front of me. When it comes to relationships I can admit I'm a bit fastidious. For those that don't understand the word fastidious, I mean persnickety or particular. Still don't know what I'm saying, it means picky. Wow even in my possible final moments I'm being condescending.

I know that nobody is perfect, but I know what I want. If it's the rest of my life I'm thinking of spending with someone I believe I have a right to be particular or as I like to put it selective. I'm particular to the point where I come off as judgmental, which makes things difficult for others. I don't settle for mediocrity. Even in relationships I expect excellence. Relationships are difficult, but they change people.

When a man is single the girls look at him as a pleasant man to be around like Ghandi and wonder how on earth he is still single. When a man becomes a significant other it seems no matter what he does a girl will have nothing good to say because they see him as terrifying or repulsive as Hitler.

Deciding on whom to spend my life with is almost like taking a multiple-choice exam. There are so many options standing before me, but it is difficult making the right choice. Sometimes I want to go with the obvious answer, but I wonder if it's a part of a trick question, so I have made different choices in women that turned out to be the wrong ones. I came to a point in my life where I chose to invest in temporary companionships instead of long-term relationships.

Pardon my morose view on relationships, but that's how the wheels have turned for me.

In a way I seem to sabotage myself getting involved with someone that I know I shouldn't be with. It's convenient to be with someone when I don't feel like being alone. I like being single, but nobody enjoys being alone all the time. Perhaps I make things more complicated than they need to be.

I would love to have a long-term, permanent relationship that involves sacrifice, communication, and desire one day, but I don't see it happening anytime soon; especially if this individual easily squeezes the trigger with that steady finger.

Having my hammer would have been handy.

As the gun was staring me in the face, all I could think about was the life I spoiled.

Destiny is no matter of chance. It is a matter of choice. It is not a thing to be waited for, it is a thing to be achieved

~William Jennings Bryan~

2

PYT (Pretty Young Thing)

March 2009

This is the best place to begin where everything makes sense.

I was enjoying some of the finest cuisine at the Bishop Minor Experience. It was actually called BMX Lounge. I guess that title made it more marketable to a younger and hip clientele.

Bishop Minor was a retired professional football player that was a high school legend in San Antonio as a star tailback at John Jay High School. After attending Baylor University, he was drafted by the Oakland Raiders where he played for seven seasons. He spent the beginning of the second half of his 14-year career with the Washington Redskins and his last two seasons with the Dallas Cowboys.

After he retired from the NFL he returned to San Antonio and opened a few restaurants or nightclubs as well as the Minor Community Center on the east side of San Antonio and a charter school entitled Bishop Minor School of Excellence. BMX Lounge was his latest restaurant that had been open for six months. And of course Thursday night through Saturday night after eleven o'clock it would turn into a nightclub.

I was with my friends Scott and Shiloh.

Scott got out less than a groundhog because he was married with children. I never met his wife, but he was out tonight because his wife was having a girl's night out while his mother-in-law was at their house watching their two kids. Of course he promised that he would be home early to relieve his mother-in-law of her babysitting duties.

Shockingly enough, Shiloh White was still single. I'm shocked because he was a Boris Kodjoe lookalike that was tall, light skin, and handsome. I'm secure in my sexuality to say that. Trust me I got nothing, but love for the ladies.

Anyway those were the reasons we gave Shiloh the nickname Turkish Delight. Plus, he was born in Turkey as his mother was Turkish and his father was black. He was fluent in Spanish, Turkish, and German. He was currently learning French. He would be voted into People magazine's "50 Most Beautiful People in the World" if he was a celebrity.

We were sitting in some tall chairs that surrounded a very wide square bar. There was smooth jazz music being played that wasn't hindering our conversation.

"Tell me this," Scott said. "Would you ever consider being with a single mother?"

"Ah Hades to the no," Shiloh emphatically replied.

"What about you Ruben," he asked not able to contain his laughter.

"I have to concur with Shi on this one," I replied.

"Why is that?"

"A single mother is just too much drama to handle my friend. It's an aneurism just waiting to happen."

"Not only is there a child or children to deal with, but you also have to deal with the baby daddy or ex-husband and let's be honest that is not a walk in the park I'm willing to take," Shiloh said. "Ruben you feel me on this right?"

"Amen to that brother," I replied. "Let me ask you a question Scott."

"Okay, give it to me," Scott said.

"If your wife ever cheated on you could you honestly forgive her and forget about it. That means from the moment you forgive her you never bring it up, no matter what. You move on and never hold it against her. Could you do that?"

"That is a good question," Shiloh interjected.

"I thought so."

"I can't wait to hear the response to that question."

"Let the man answer."

"That's a tough one," Scott replied. "Honestly I could forgive her, but I couldn't forget it. I would have to divorce her. It would be hard for me to trust her again, even stay in love with her."

"I wouldn't blame you."

"I think you would have to be a fool to stick around," Shiloh replied.

"Well let's pray I never have to make that kind of decision," Scott said.

"Amen to that," I replied.

At the moment Scott was a distinguished gentleman in the lounge, as he was the only white person in attendance. Scott and I became really good friends while taking core real estate courses together. Sometimes after sitting in the classroom for eight hours we would kill some time going to a barista and getting us some smoothies. He was a 32-year-old clean-cut redhead with blue piercing eyes. In a crowded room he could make someone feel like they were the only person in the room because he always looked people in the eye not just so they would know they had his attention, but also as if he was searching for something. He was a real health fanatic because he was always eating fruit or vegetables as well as tuna sandwiches in class and was anal about drinking eight to ten glasses of water a day.

He graduated Summa Cum Laude from Texas A&M with a degree in engineering while he was being all he could be in the Army.

Shiloh and I actually met last weekend. We met after an Alicia Keys concert while we were both waiting in line to get a picture with the renowned artist. And after the concert we went to a club where the ladies seemed to take a natural liking to him. It was as if he had a natural ease in talking to women like chewing gum and walking at the same time. I know that he is an aspiring actor and maybe it comes with ease because he possibly puts on an act or approaches everyone as a character. He's an aspiring actor, but trapped in a cubicle like millions of other Americans waiting for a dream to become a reality.

"Hey, I've got a gig I need to head out for," I said placing a five-dollar bill on the table for my tip.

"Where are you performing tonight," Shiloh asked.

"I'm playing at Club Nocturnal. You guys should come and check it out."

"I can't make it tonight. I have to get in bed early.

"It's Saturday night."

"I have to get up at 6 to be on the road by 7:30 to be at a nine o'clock film audition in Austin."

"If you get a role, would you get paid?"

"Oh yeah, that's the only reason I'm going out there so early in the day."

"What about you Scotty?"

"No I have to get back home and take care of the kids," Scott replied.

"Now this is your mother-in-law that is watching the kids, right?" Scott nodded his head. "So why doesn't your wife come back home early since that's her mother?"

"I love my wife and my kids and I want to see my kids."

"Oh I know what it is…you're whipped."

"Shut up," he laughed. "One day you'll both understand when you get married."

"I'm not going to lie, but I would rather stay in tonight and get some sleep since daylight savings time kicks in tonight. But I could use the extra money."

"Yeah, you do what you got to do. Besides I do have to pack some clothes."

"You're anticipating your wife kicking you out," Shiloh replied.

"No, you jerk," he laughed. "I will be out of town all this week for work and I'm leaving tomorrow evening."

"I guess I'll see you around again when your wife gives you permission to get out," I said motioning my hand like I was handling a whip and made a whipping sound making Scott and Shiloh laugh.

"Ha ha that's very funny," he replied sarcastically.

* * * * *

I've always wanted to amaze people with what I can do. Now I can't dance like James Brown or even hit a high note like Michael Jackson, but I have the ladies mesmerized tapping down the ebony and ivory keys of a piano or strumming the strings of a guitar like my fingers were magical.

Tonight, I should have stayed home and rested because I have to get up early for church and lead praise and worship. But I'm making a few extra dollars breathing life into the trumpet. I was at Club Nocturnal playing with a Latin group called Azul Luna.

Even though I'm a black man playing in a band with nothing, but Puerto Ricans and Dominicans I felt at home. Plus, I can fluently speak Spanish and I love Latin women. There were so many of them filling up the club tonight.

As I was playing the trumpet during my solo my eyes were fixed on a woman wearing turquoise. She was as attractive as a gazelle strutting with confidence going to a small round table. Only she didn't walk; it was more like she glided to her table. With her beauty she could be like a mannequin and not have to do anything to get attention. She was so beautiful that Halle Berry and Sofia Vergara would have to slap me to get my attention.

She sat down with her legs crossed in a white skirt with a turquoise blouse on along with minty white open toe heels. She had a cinnamon complexion and seductive eyes that had me in a trance. One of her hands was holding a wineglass that was almost empty, while the other hand was running through her long, curly brown hair.

I was blowing hard into the trumpet like I was trying to save someone's life. In my solo while some couples continued dancing, I could hear some girls cheering, but my eyes were still locked on the woman with the cinnamon complexion. Wanting so badly to impress her, I fell down on my knees. I felt like I was working out because as I continued to blow my abdominal muscles were tightening up and I could just feel my veins popping out. As I drew near to the end of my solo I noticed the potential Mrs. Wells put her wineglass down and she was clapping with a little smile on her face. That's all I needed to know that I had her attention. It's on!

* * * * *

We played a couple more songs before we were finished for the evening. The rest of the night DJ Perro would be spinning some of the biggest hits in salsa, merengue, bachata, or reggaeton.

"Hey Wells, man I didn't know you could blow like that on the horn," said Buster Foster who had a light skin black woman with him. "I thought it was Miles Davis reincarnated."

"I don't know about that, but thanks for the compliment, I appreciate it," I replied.

"Oh this lovely lady here is Stella."

"Oh hello, glad you came out."

"You did really great," Stella replied shaking my hand.

"Well, we're going to go on ahead and step out of here," Buster said. "I'll see you around Wells."

"Alright Buster and Stella, be safe out there."

That's typical Buster, arriving to the club by himself, but always leaving with a lady…sometimes two.

Someone snuck up behind me and covered my eyes with their hands asking "Guess who?"

"Oh gee I wonder who it could be," I said not amused. I grabbed the silky smooth hands and turned around to see Rosa Barnes, my girlfriend. Dang I forgot I had a girlfriend.

Rosa was the kind of woman that guys would give a second or even third look to. Part of it was because she resembled Milla Jovovich from when she starred in The Fifth Element with Bruce Willis. She was the only white woman I ever dated. Her skin was immaculate and her green eyes were piercing, as if they once belonged to Cleopatra. One of the things that annoyed me was that it looked like her head was covered with a mop. She was originally a redhead, but two weeks ago she dyed it black with a moptop that The Beatles made popular. Instead of Fifth Element, now she looked like Milla Jovovich in the dud Ultraviolet. I wasn't very fond of it. Her hair I mean. Oh the movie was also dreadful.

We've only been together 45 days so it's understandable I would forget that I was in a relationship. I have been meaning to break up with her, so no better time than the present. We made out a lot, but I don't know if we would be defined an official couple by society's standards because we never slept with each other.

Another thing that bothered me is that she wore black a lot. Seriously was she going to a funeral every day? Don't get me wrong she was looking exquisite in her strapless black dress showing off her muscular shoulders and she had some firm legs that were helping her stand tall in some four inch black heels. Dang, maybe I should hold off on this break up. No, no, I need to break up with her. I hate that her toes are covered with black nail polish. It's spring time for crying out loud. Wear some other colors like other women sporting yellow, orange, or pink.

She was going in for a kiss, but I backed away.

"What's wrong bae," she asked.

"Do you not know that bae is Danish for poop," I replied. "I hate it when you call me that."

"Okay I'll stop calling you that. Now give me a kiss." She leaned in, but I pulled away.

"Come on Rosa, you know I'm not big on public displays of affection."

"What's wrong with you?"

"This isn't working for me anymore."

"What do you mean this isn't working for you?"

"I mean I'm breaking up with you."

"Is it because I wouldn't sleep with you? Remember you told me that you wanted to take your time and wait."

"No it has nothing to do with that. I just don't want to be with you."

"It's because I'm white isn't it." Her face was turning as red as her hair once was.

"No, that is not the reason why I'm leaving you."

"Oh please, give me a break. You don't want to kiss in public, only in private, and you won't even hold my hand when we're walking through the mall. Please, you're ashamed of me because of my skin tone."

"No, that has nothing to do with it."

"Whatever. I bet if I was black you would fornicate me." Now for the sake of keeping this story kind of PG-13 rated, she didn't say fornicate. She said the other "f" word that is followed by a vowel and two other consonants.

"No I wouldn't."

"So just like that it's over." I didn't say anything, as I felt I got my point across. "Fine we're done. I'm feeling grown and sexy tonight so I won't have a problem getting with someone tonight." She started walking off.

"Glad you understand."

She threw up the middle finger and stomped her way through the crowd.

At least she was being mature about this.

* * * * *

Now that I was officially done with Rosa I was looking around the club for the cinnamon complexion woman I saw earlier. I didn't have to search long, as she was still sitting at her table. Her female friend, that was tall enough to be mistaken for a WNBA player, had left her alone as she went to dance with someone.

I couldn't take my eyes off of her. She had a gorgeous figure. She wasn't a full figured girl, but yet she wasn't trim. Athletic was how she looked, which was just right for me. Her skin complexion blended in with her long brown curly hair. She had a mountain of curls. People would have mistaken her for a celebrity, as she closely resembled Paula Abdul. She was my childhood celebrity crush ever since she asked "Straight up now tell me is it going to be you and me together." In my world we would be together forever.

As she looked at me, I breathed in and exhaled as the music got louder and the floor was getting raided with a stampede. The volume was pumped up louder and the music moved quickly, as Pitbull was spitting out The Anthem, but for me everything was silent and moving slowly. If I was a director of photography the camera would zoom in on her and focus on her angelic face blurring the background. At the moment I had tunnel vision focused on this woman.

Her eyes greeted me and stayed on me for more than a few seconds. I smiled and in return she gave me an incandescent smile that illuminated the room.

She brushed her hair back that moved in slow motion like she was in a Telenovela. Her hair was thick and beautiful like the mane of a lion. I decided to attempt to impress her by speaking some Spanish.

"Vienes aqui seguido," I asked while walking up to her as she remain seated. Saying "come here often?" in Spanish, just sounds so much better. It backfired on me, as she looked more confused than impressed.

"I'm sorry, but I don't speak Spanish," she replied.

"Here I thought I was being smooth."

"Trust me; you don't have to speak Spanish to be smooth. The way you were playing that trumpet was smooth enough."

"Well thank you. My name is Ruben Wells. And you are?" I stuck my hand out.

"I'm Bianca Jones," she replied shaking my hand.

"You probably get this a lot, but I think you're very lovely."

"You'd be surprised, but I don't hear that enough."

"Really, that's shocking." She laughed.

"Actually, I never grow tired of hearing that."

"That sounds a little more honest." I smiled maintaining eye contact.

"You have a very nice smile."

"Thank you. I've been told I should smile more often."

"You should, don't let it go to waste. You play that trumpet really well."

"Thank you."

"Are you Puerto Rican?"

"No."

"Where are you from?"

"I'm actually from Atlanta."

"Oh okay."

"Bianca would you like to dance?"

"I would love to."

With her back to me she shook her hips horizontally wrapping my hands around her waist like I was her seatbelt. She was comfortable with me touching her, as if I was frisking her. She had an intoxicating aroma that was inescapable. As we gyrated with the music I ran my hands across her stomach. She had a little fat in her belly, but I still liked the feel of her stomach. She grabbed my hands and ran them down the inside of her legs as she opened them a little wider.

Lord I need your help to remain pure.

She turned around and pulled me in closer to where we were within kissing distance.

"Ruben Wells," she said. "Sounds like it should be the name of an actor or musician."

"Hey I hope to be famous one day. Don't meet a lot of Biancas, it's a pretty name. Jones is your last name so does that mean that you're mixed?"

"No, I'm one hundred percent Mexican. The last name is just a long story."

"Okay."

This woman must have walked out of the house of mirth because she wouldn't stop smiling. Even though her smile was priceless there was something mysterious about her. It kept me wanting to know more about her, thus desiring her more.

She was killing me slowly with her looks while I was trying to do my best LL Cool J impression slowly licking my lips, hoping that I was taking her breath away. Hopefully no one has made her feel sexy the way I've attempted to. I hope the way I touch her or talk to her makes her feel cherished. The way I hold her, I hope she has been longing for, because she seems like she hasn't been held in a long time.

As the song ended a merengue song came on and people were leaving the dance floor, but we continued dancing. We danced a couple of merengue songs and then segued into a salsa dance, as Celia Cruz was being played. I was turning Bianca like a record being spun.

As we danced I could see Rosa dancing with another guy wearing a tight pink v-neck shirt and jeans so tight they could have fit him like spandex. If her eyes were lasers they would vaporize me. That's how perturbed she looked, but I didn't pay her any mind.

After dancing circles around Bianca she needed a break. I sat at her table with her. Her tall friend was still dancing.

"Where did you learn how to dance," she asked.

"Well I just learned by watching other people," I said. "I also took some ballroom lessons."

"Really, you did ballroom dancing?"

"Yeah, you learn to dance to different rhythms. You just learn to feel the rhythm and you dance with the music."

"Are you sure you're not Puerto Rican?"

"I'm sure I'm not."

"Are you sure?"

"I think I know my own ethnicity." She laughed. "You're not the first to ask me that, but I am black."

"Well you sure do move like a Puerto Rican."

"Really, how do they move?"

"You move real smooth and under control and also very sensual."

"Am I making you horny baby," I said impersonating Austin Powers making her laugh. "What do you do for a living Bianca?"

"Right now I'm getting my masters at Incarnate Word."

"What's your degree in?"

"I am studying psychology."

"Really, I know that has to be interesting?"

"Yeah and I'll be graduating in May."

"So what will you do when you graduate pursue your Ph.D. next?"

"I thought about it and I'd like to go into children's counseling."

"Well that's nice. Wait, are you psychoanalyzing me right now." She laughed.

"When I'm not in school I work for the Northside Independent School District in the Public Information department. What is it you do for a living Mr. Wells?"

"I work for a newspaper."

"Really, how long have you been doing that?"

"It's going on two years. I should have stayed in public relations."

"So you don't enjoy it that much?"

"It has its pros and cons, more cons than pros though."

"I know that industry is taking a beating at the moment, with some publications shutting down."

"Yeah there was one in Seattle that shut down operations and a couple weeks before that there was one in Denver that shut down."

"Does that concern you at all?"

"Of course, but it's out of my control. So I just do the work I'm supposed to do while I still have a job." She seemed to be impressed, as she smiled.

"Which paper do you work for?"

"I work for Alamo City Times and I also do some freelance work for the S.A. Prevalent as a columnist."

"What do you do at Alamo City?"

"I cover the arts, entertainment, and culture section. We focus on what's current in that industry. Every once in a while, I'll write in the religion section as well."

"Yeah, yeah I get that paper every day. I've also checked out Prevalent too. I've probably read some of your stuff."

"Oh so you're the one," we both laughed.

"Now I remember your name. You recently did a story on Bishop Minor's newest restaurant BMX Lounge."

"Yeah I did. I was there earlier tonight with a couple of my boys for dinner."

"You should have done a story on those five kids he has from five different mommas."

"It's actually three kids from one woman and two kids each from two different women. That's why he's opening up so many different kinds of businesses. He's got a lot of child support to pay. But that's off the record." Bianca laughed, as I winked.

"You did a story on that new jazz club and restaurant Tucker Magee's that has an atmosphere like something you would see in New York or Chicago."

"Yeah and whenever I want to go there he hooks me up for free because he liked the story I did on him. Sometimes I play there as well."

"So do you just play the trumpet?"

"I can play almost every instrument, but my main instrument is the piano."

"Oh, I bet you have some magical fingers."

"Well I don't like to brag, but I do what I can."

"Well with all these hook ups from working for the newspaper how come you don't like it?"

"Don't get me wrong I enjoy writing and I've always wanted to work for an arts and entertainment section, but journalism is a dying industry. I won't be surprised with all the turbulent times in the economy if some newspapers get shut down in San Antonio. As was mentioned earlier there's been a few shut down in other states and cities. If Alamo City does get shut down it will give me time to pursue what I'm really passionate about."

"And what is that?"

"My real passion is music. Writing is just something to pay the bills. So why do you want to counsel children?"

"I have a passion for children. Plus, kids nowadays challenge you."

"And you always like a challenge."

"Yes I do."

"You always like to go where no one else wants to go."

"Exactly."

"Well dealing with kids is probably the route to go."

DJ Perro segued into a bachata song by Aventura called El Perdedor. We both looked and smiled at each other as Romeo Santos crooned. She held my hand as I led her back to the dance floor. It felt so good to be holding another person's hand. Her hand with my own was a perfect fit that would never slip away.

I kept eye contact while we danced. She bit her bottom lip. As she moved in closer to me and held my hand a little tighter my heart was racing faster.

I wrapped my arms around her and tucked her in. I don't know if she was feeling how sculpted I was, but she held me tighter like we were going to take flight.

As I looked at her I knew what I wanted to do next, but what if I looked like a fool wanting to kiss her when she didn't want a kiss. I didn't want to embarrass myself closing my eyes and puckering up just kissing air.

I've never been big on public displays of affection and I've never been quick to fall in love. Normally I don't kiss a woman after knowing them for only a few minutes, but I knew that I really liked Bianca. I didn't care that less than a couple of hours ago I broke up with another woman. I wasn't on the rebound, but at this moment I really wanted to kiss Bianca because there wouldn't be another opportunity like this. I believe in being efficient.

I was looking down at Bianca while she smiled and her eyes narrowed in on me. Take it; don't ask for it. Her lips looked tasty.

"This may sound a little strange," she said, "But you have some nice looking lips." I pulled her in closer. "They're not too big or too small, but just right. They look like they would feel soft." I softly grasped the back of her neck. "I wish I was a couple inches taller so I could..."

I knew where this was going and I cut her off by softly kissing her lips. She grabbed the back of my head and rubbed it while she pulled me in. Doves were let out of their cages while a church choir in white robes sang "Hallelujah." Her thin moist lips felt like paradise. Her kiss was sweet like the feel of rain pouring down your head after a drought. As we looked at each other after we kissed I was in a daze like I had too many drinks while Bianca was smiling licking her lips. A dentist would have found her impeccable, pearly white teeth flawless, very much like her kiss.

The lack of planning on your part, does not constitute an emergency on my behalf

~Anonymous~

3

Wanna Be Startin' Somethin'

Staying home tonight would have been a better alternative. It was near four in the morning and I was only going to get maybe three hours of sleep having to get up early for church, but it was worth it because I got an attractive woman's phone number and a sweet, moist kiss.

I slid a hammer underneath my sleeve while getting out of my vehicle. I carried it for protection whenever I got home late at night. A lot of vehicles and apartments were broken into where I resided. A hammer may not be useful in a gunfight, but if I can hit someone between the eyes it should be effective. It's the only thing I had close enough to a weapon.

I hit the lock button on my key and the alarm was on. Even though I heard it go off I had to do it a second time just to be sure. The alarm beeped again.

For the last couple of weeks, every time I came home late at night I always saw this gray cat sitting on some steps outside my apartment. Most stray cats seem to run whenever humans come near them, but this one never ran away.

I've never cared for cats, but I call this visitor Ash.

When I walked in my apartment I went into the kitchen, grabbed two little plastic bowls, and poured some milk in one of them. I grabbed a can of pineapple chunks from the fridge and after opening it dropped the chunks into the other bowl. I was hungry and needed a little late night snack. As I walked outside towards the cat with a bowl full of milk he was ready to run, as if I was going to hurt him, but I placed the bowl down. He cautiously walked towards the bowl and looked at me suspiciously with those deep green eyes. He took a sip of the milk to make sure it was edible. After a couple of cautious sips, he dug into the milk like a dog drinking water from the toilet.

He continued to enjoy his milk, as I sat near him enjoying my pineapple.

Pineapple was my favorite fruit. At the risk of coming off as pretentious the interesting thing about the pineapple plant, ananas comosus, is that it is a native of South and Central America and looks rather like a small yucca tree. It has large, blade-like leaves and a fleshy edible fruit that is actually made up of the flowers fused together into a compound whole. It got its name because it's shaped like a pinecone. While on his second voyage to the West Indies in 1493, Christopher Columbus first discovered pineapples at Guadeloupe in the Caribbean.

Bodybuilders go through a lot of training to get the perfect physique. I guess you could say I train my mind to gain intelligence. Looking up the meaning of words or names and their derivation is one of my hobbies. Some of them, like pineapples, have interesting stories as to how they got their name. The spiritual connotation of the name Ruben is wondrous recognition.

I took in the silence of the night and luminous stars that filled the darkness, like a blanket covering the sky.

The Palermo, a nice gated apartment complex, is where I lived. The scenery of the complex was beautiful. The architecture of the facility had a classic exotic Mediterranean style to it. I lived on the third floor in a rich looking 964-square-foot two-bedroom apartment. Along with it was a luxurious oval garden tub, step saving island kitchen, and a fireplace with a decorative mantle. My walls were dressed with pictures of lions hanging throughout as well as paintings or photographs of jazz musicians.

As much as I despise cats, they are unique with their own abilities and limitations. Every cat is its own individual. We either have to accept the cat as it is or not try to fight its innate behavioral tendencies. People tend to expect things from their cats, hoping that they'll conform to some kind of cat image they have in their minds. It doesn't always happen this way. Just like people. You either accept them for who they are or don't try to fight their peculiarities.

I went back inside my place. Before taking a quick shower I turned the lock on my door three times. You can never be too careful when you are protecting yourself from intruders.

After drying myself off I put on my black pajama bottoms, white socks, and a white t-shirt to sleep in. Even while going to bed I would dress conservatively. I poured myself a nightcap, which is glass of milk for me. Placed my pillow on my couch and fell into my couch with a thick beige comforter covering me.

My place always looked new. One of my friends said that it was so cold and immaculate that he would have mistaken it for a museum. I cleaned it every day because I'm a neat freak, but sometimes I felt like I suffered from an obsessive-compulsive personality disorder. If I don't keep my apartment clean germs will invade my space and I can't allow that.

I'm so protective of the carpet that I treated it like it was worth millions. When people walked into my apartment I made them take off their shoes because I didn't want them to get my carpet dirty. Besides the carpet is so soft that it felt like wool was rubbing against your feet. I supplied them with slippers, as I had seven pairs of slippers. There was always a cinnamon aroma in my apartment simply because I sprayed that everyday throughout my apartment.

I didn't have many visitors. The only time I threw a little party was the night of the Super Bowl, Grammy Music Awards, or the Oscars.

I didn't have a roommate, but I had a second room that I called the studio because that's where I kept all my instruments and sound equipment. To add inspiration, I had pictures of Michael Jackson, Miles Davis, John Coltrane, Nat King Cole, Tito Puente, Sade, and Alicia Keys hanging on the wall. A futon was set up in my studio just in case anyone ever wanted to stay over for the night.

I not only played the piano, but I could also play the acoustic guitar, lead guitar, bass, drums, violin, and the trumpet. The piano was the first instrument I learned to play at the age of five.

Every writer or musician remembers that moment that inspired them to pursue their profession.

It was on March 25, 1983 that my life changed. Of course I didn't know it because I was barely two years old, but my parents remember that day I was immobile in front of the television set watching Michael Jackson perform on *Motown 25: Yesterday, Today, Forever*.

Forty-seven million viewers watched him on the stage dressed in his signature black pants, silver socks, silver shirt, black-sequined jacket, and a single sequined glove. It was while singing "Billie Jean" the unthinkable moment occurred that would leave millions breathless. With widespread public attention millions gasped, amazed at the creation of…the moonwalk. Reporters were calling it an act of illusion, as it was surreal.

My parents recorded the special and a couple years later I watched the video. After watching the "King of Pop" perform that was the moment I knew that I wanted to be a musician.

My top ten favorite artists are Michael Jackson, Miles Davis, John Coltrane, Mint Condition, Arturo Sandoval, Marc Antoine, Boyz II Men, Sade, Alicia Keys, and Thelonious Monk. Honorable mentions go to Gypsy Kings, Dave Brubeck, and Chick Corea.

I was never much into hip-hop except for maybe artists like Fugees, Outkast, Roots, Mos Def, Talib Kweli, Lupe Fiasco, Common, and Kanye West before he went on his ego trip after Late Registration. The lyrics that would flow from these artists was an illustration of real hip-hop and brought a unique sound to what they did. I was into salsa music and really grew accustomed to bachata music. I especially enjoyed listening to Hector LaVoe, Antony Santos, Luis Vargas, Aventura and Monchy y Alexandra. Growing up in the church and living in a Christian home I listened to gospel music. Some of my favorite gospel oriented artists are Fred Hammond, Kirk Franklin, Israel Houghton, Tonex, Kenoly Brothers, Salvador, Yolanda Adams, anything by or acts associated with Cross Movement, GRITS, and anything by any of the Winans.

I loved playing music in clubs, parties, or church and just mesmerizing the people with what I could do. When I was on the stage performing I kept people in wonder making them ask, "How does he do that." I also got a chance to put a smile on someone's face that had a terrible day.

As far as sports, I was good in basketball and soccer. I was great in high school and I only played basketball my senior year at ORU. I finally made it as a walk on. They might as well have not signed me up because I didn't see that much playing time. But I got to travel and I got my #41 jersey framed so I won't complain. When I wasn't playing ball or when my head wasn't buried in the books I was working on my music.

My couch served as my bed because I got up quicker whereas it was hard for me to get out of my bed because it was too comfortable and I always got up later than I wanted to. My couch was made for one and my bed was made for two, so it seemed convenient for the moment to sleep in my couch. I didn't feel like having all that open space in my bed to myself. I hated staring at my bed because there was no one there for me to hold. Sometimes I wondered if I would ever lie with a woman. Sleeping in my couch took my mind off of those thoughts.

Before going to sleep I was reading my bible. I would read my bible and pray first thing every morning. At the end of the night before I went to sleep the last thing I did was read my bible. I was reading 2 Chronicles 35 and 36 getting close to reading the book of Ezra. For the last couple of years I was reading every book of the bible. All 66 books I had been reading over and over again learning something new every time I read from the good book.

After getting done with my daily reading I chugged down what was left of my milk, turned my lamp off, and stretched out on my couch. As I was falling asleep my last thought was of Bianca Jones. I was hoping to have a chance to get to know her better.

Before I fell asleep I saw that my phone was blinking a red flash. I must have gotten a call or text while I was taking a shower. I saw that I got a video texted to me from Rosa. It was probably her venting to me and she was probably pissed that I kissed another woman. I was shocked to see that she sent me a video of her having a sex with the guy that had on the tight clothes tonight. They were in the back seat of a car. I wasn't upset, but I also wasn't a pervert so I deleted that video.

I saw that I had a voicemail message. It was from Bianca. When she spoke she sounded confused and somber. I imagined her standing in front of me while I listened to the message.

While she spoke I could hear James Blunt singing "You're Beautiful."

"Hey Mr. Ruben Alexander Wells," she said in her voicemail message "I know that I've only known you for a few hours, but I was feeling a strong connection between us, that I think you were feeling too. I really like you Ruben and I really want to get to know you. Not just because you're a great kisser, wow those lips of yours are very soft, but I think you're just a wonderful person to be around. Not a bad kisser as well. Sorry I already mentioned that." There was silence for a moment. I thought my signal had faded, but I heard her breathing. "This is so difficult to say and it shouldn't be." Sweat was running down my face, as I was afraid she would tell me she was once a man. Dang it! What if she's a prostitute or a porn star? Or worse, what if she has herpes? Boy, the thoughts that run through my mind. She took a deep breath and then she spoke. "I'm married Ruben." When she said that I got up from the couch, as my jaw dropped to the floor and my eyes were raised to the ceiling. "I've been unhappily married for 12 years. I have two children, a boy and girl, 7 and almost 2. I love the way you looked at me. The way you touched me hasn't happened to me for years. It's been awhile since I've felt wanted or needed by a man. It's been so long since I felt secure in a man's arms. I really loved being around you tonight and I would like to be around you even more. I'll understand if you don't want to talk to me, but know that I really do like you and want to know you even better. Well that's what I had to say. You have my number. Hopefully you'll give me a call. Good night."

Just when I thought things were going well. For some reason the whole night I was around Bianca the song "Me and Mrs. Jones" was running through my mind.

Her last name made sense now. I couldn't believe she was married.

Me and Mrs. Jones have a thing going on.

We design our lives through the power of choices

~Richard Bach~

4

Beat It

"Come on everybody put your hands together," I said while playing the piano in a church congregation filled with over 1,500 members. I was a member of the choir at Covenant Center. I was singing Israel Houghton's "I Am a Friend of God" while majority of the church members were standing up clapping their hands, and singing along. *"Who am I that you are mindful of me, that you hear me when I call,"* I sang.

I reluctantly joined the choir a year ago as a tenor. Word spread around the church that I could sing thanks to my voluminous best friend, Alejandro Padilla. He would never win the quiet game because like the energizer bunny his mouth kept going on and on. I didn't want to join because I knew the commitment that it required being a part of the choir, but it wasn't so bad. It wasn't Madison Square Garden, but it was fun being on stage.

I was trying to keep my mind focused on the service, but as I was pounding the ebony and ivory keys I couldn't help, but feel guilty for kissing a married woman. Was it wrong for me to do that even though I didn't know she was married at the time that it happened?

What if she was at my church right now just trying to show that Christians can't be trusted?

I was thinking way too much. I needed to stay in the moment and prepare to hear a good message.

* * * * *

After 20 minutes of praise and worship, Pastor Harper stepped to the podium and presented a message. He was a Southern white man that didn't have a gray hair in sight of his long black hair, a thick horseshoe mustache, and preaching style that if blind people heard him they would think they heard a black man speaking.

He placed his black bible that was as thick as an encyclopedia on the podium while holding a microphone in his other hand. He opened his bible and asked the congregation to stand and turn to Genesis chapter 3 and verse 6.

"When the woman saw that the fruit of the tree was good for food and pleasing to the eye, and also desirable for gaining wisdom, she took some and ate it," Pastor Harper said reading from his bible. "She also gave some to her husband, who was with her, and he ate it." He stepped away from the podium. "Today I will be starting a four-week series entitled The Realities of Sexual Sin. This first part of my series is called Bitter Sweet. Please take a seat."

Watching Pastor Harper preach was like viewing a tennis match, as he paced back and forth on the stage while speaking. "None of us are immune to being tempted. We're all going to be confronted with temptation. When the devil tempts he's not going to tempt you with something you can easily reject, but he will tempt you with something that would be a struggle for you to resist. It will be something that is desirable. We all know that sex is desirable. So when Satan tempts an unmarried couple with sex, he makes it seem like it's something that they need, like it's an antidote that they won't be able to live without because it's an ultimate desire that they have not given into. Satan will make them feel like they are empty without it. Sex is desirable and can be pleasurable, but let me ask you something church." He stopped walking and bent down a little. "Is that pleasure worth disobeying God?" Some people yelled "Oh" or gave some grunts. Pastor Harper started walking back and forth again. "Let me tell you what temptation does to your church. Temptation will have you focus on the things that you don't possess, which you desire most and this causes you to lose focus or neglect what God has already given you." There were some people saying "Oh," letting Pastor Harper know they understood his concept. "Oh yeah church it's going to get heavy today."

* * * * *

After the Sunday morning church service ended I purchased a copy of the message. Because I'm involved with the praise and worship group I could purchase it half off regular price. While I was waiting to receive my copy of the message I was speaking with Mari Castillo, assistant manager of the bookstore. She was a very attractive woman, but unfortunately for all the single brothers out there, she was already taken.

She almost aged like an actress, as she looked like she was in her late 20's, but I believe she was in her late 30's or early 40's. Either way she was a beauty. Her mother was the manager of the bookstore. Mari's younger sister had a crush on me, as Alejandro told me who heard it from Mari's husband who heard it from Mari's mother. Mari and her husband had two daughters that had their mother's looks. Besides beauty, Mari was a very sweet woman always greeting every customer with a smile. While waiting to receive my copy of the message from this morning Mari and I engaged in some small talk.

"So how was your weekend," she asked.

"As usual it flew by," I replied.

"Isn't it funny how the week is long, but the weekend is always a blur."

"Tell me about it. Although the weekend isn't over yet, we still have the rest of this day to enjoy or relax."

"That is true." Dang she was lovely. I hope this doesn't happen, but if she ever gets a divorce brothers will be lining up to win her heart. More so they would want to jump into her pants first before trying to win her heart, but that's crass of me to say.

"Hey Ruben, how are you today," asked Brenda, Mari's little sister.

"I'm doing fine Brenda, how are you?"

"You certainly are fine," I thought I heard her mumble.

"Pardon me."

"I'm doing fine."

Mari handed me a CD with a smile on her face. As I walked off I felt like Brenda had sniffed me. After purchasing myself a copy of the message I was waiting for Alejandro so that I could talk to him about what happened the other night. He's a social butterfly. He could have been a greeter because he spoke to everyone that walked in his direction.

"Hey how you doin' brother," he said shaking an older white man's hand that looked at him strange. "Hope everything is good with you."

"Who are you," asked the older white man.

"Come on man how many times we got to do this. You know me, I'm Alejandro. Good seeing you brother."

"Who was that," I asked.

"I have no idea."

I'm originally from Atlanta, but I moved to San Antonio when I was fifteen. Alejandro was the first person I met when I moved here. We met during the summer playing in an AAU Summer Basketball league. We were both going into our sophomore year of high school playing for William Howard Taft High School's junior varsity basketball team.

Alejandro had a butterball face that made him look like a pretty boy Latin singer. His gaze was dark, but he kept a bright smile on his face. His beard covered his face like a chinstrap. He always wore a big flashy silver belt buckle that had his initials on it. Urban is how he looked having both ears pierced walking in Stacy Adams or Timberlands along with baggy jeans and a nice bright colored button shirt hardly ever tucked in and a sports coat covering his squared shoulders along with a fedora covering his ebony curly hair.

When Alejandro sang he sounded smooth like Marvin Gaye. He was also a tenor in the church choir and sometimes he would fill in on bass guitar.

He also wrote some terrific poems, but he had never read them aloud to anyone. I found out he was a poet because I stumbled upon one of his poems when I visited his place one day. He needed to let other people hear his words; otherwise, he was depriving the world of enlightenment.

We were in a band called The Foundation. It was a quintet with Alejandro playing the bass guitar and myself on the piano. The other members of the band included Gill Moore on the lead guitar, Julian Stevens on the saxophone, and Roland Welch on the drums who was the leader of the band. All the members of the group could sing, but we were looking for a girl who could sing that could be the lead.

Being half-Dominican, half-Italian Alejandro was the only one of the group who wasn't black. He wasn't much of a great dancer, but turn on some music and he is the first one on the dance floor. Sometimes it was painful to watch him dance because it looked like he was trying to stretch out a cramp in his leg.

We were both music lovers with dreams of coming out with our own CDs that would go platinum and winning Grammys. Alejandro was one of the few people I could trust with anything.

We were sitting outside the church at one of the small roundtables on the patio. Alejandro was drinking some sweetened iced tea and eating a bean and cheese taco.

"Look Alejandro I need to talk to you about something," I said putting on my sunglasses, as the sun was blinding me.

"Yeah sure, what's goin' on," Alejandro responded looking as if he was all ears while sipping on his iced tea.

"Rosa and I broke up."

"What happened?"

"I just wasn't feeling her. Plus, I couldn't stand that mop top look of hers."

"Oh Lord."

"Anyway, last night I went out to Club Nocturnal and you know I met a few girls and got a few numbers," I said with my head hanging down, but my eyes were looking up at him.

"Yeah, you're a free man" he said shoving a piece of the taco in his mouth.

"Well there was this one girl I came across that I just kicked it with the rest of the night. Man, she was something else."

"Oh yeah, so you recovered quickly," he smiled.

"On a scale of one to ten she was an eleven."

"Oh dang, the girl had it together like that chico. What's her name?" He took another bite out of his taco.

"Bianca."

"Ooh I like I like," he said getting on my nerves smacking his mouth like a cow chewing alfalfa, as he was talking with his mouth full.

"Don't talk with your mouth full. That's disgusting!"

"Sorry," he replied while still chewing, "but I like this Bianca already, so tell me more."

"She was not only beautiful, but she was intelligent and knew how to hold a conversation. She was a sexy dancer that she didn't have a problem following my lead. I'm probably exaggerating when I say this, but she was making love to me with her eyes."

"Esta loco," he laughed. "You are a fool man."

"We couldn't take our eyes off of each other." I couldn't stop looking behind my back having that feeling that someone was watching me.

"She sounds cool man," he smiled while finishing up his first taco. "So did you get her number?"

"No."

"No...why not?" He took another sip from his drink. "Don't tell me, because you were afraid that you would later find out she was someone you wouldn't want to be with just because she didn't like Boyz II Men's very first album or she didn't like to drink Root Beer."

"Hey Boyz II Men let the world know that they would be making a huge impact in the music industry breaking society off with that CooleyHigh Harmony," I said passionately as if I was William Wilberforce wanting to free the slaves. "And Root Beer is the most refreshing soda available. Not everybody in Texas prefers Big Red. But it was nothing like that. I gave her my number."

"You did what? Man she ain't ever gonna call you."

"Por el contrario mi amigo. She happened to call me last night or this morning."

"Okay that's all good, so why do you look like you received news that a family member passed away." My head was hanging down while my eyes fell to the ground.

I was biting my lip hesitant to tell him why, but I lifted up my head. Alejandro was looking at me with a curious look while eating his taco. I leaned in a little closer because I didn't want any church members to hear what I had to say. Sad to say, but it seems like church is the one place you can't share your darkest secrets because some church members have a bad habit of gossiping and trying to condemn people. "She told me she was married and has two kids," I whispered.

Alejandro was about to take another bite of his taco, but when he heard Bianca was married he stopped eating, as if there was a hair in his taco. He put the taco down on his plate and looked at me while he was wiping his hands. "Look man I'm your best friend, so don't take this the wrong way, but it always seems like in relationships that you're quick to settle. Like it defines your value or whether you're whole or not. It's almost as if you suffer from OCD."

"What do you mean by that?"

"I don't mean obsessive compulsive disorder, but I mean obsessive compulsive dating. In other words, you'll just date anyone or settle for whatever comes your way."

"Don't be ridiculous."

"It's a little soon to be dating someone. It sounds like after breaking up with Rosa you literally hooked up with another lady within an hour."

"That isn't true."

"You just date one woman after another and drop them when you get bored. And hey that's fine when they're available, but you know you can't be messin' with a married woman, that's like goin' on a suicide mission, you're just lookin' for trouble. Besides what if you're not the first guy she's hooked up with that she met in a club."

"No she's not like that."

"Ruben we go way back. You like to think that you can read people, but when it comes to women you suffer from myopia hombre. Your desire for compassion makes you unstable and your judgment gets cloudy. In the last year you've been in four different relationships that were supposedly serious, most of them lasting for less than two or three months. Before they even started you felt they wouldn't last, but you went through with the relationships anyway. While in those relationships you would try to find some reason to break up with them. Some would describe your view on relationships as neurotic." I was going to cut him off, but Alejandro raised his hand. "Tell me if I'm wrong. You broke up with Amber just because she didn't like the movie Good Will Hunting." I leaned back in my chair and folded my arms like a stubborn child.

"Hey that was a groundbreaking film and we both know that's my second favorite film right behind Heat. Anyone who doesn't believe Matt Damon convincingly portrayed a troubled genius; I have to question their intelligence. She thought Robin Williams was a disappointment because he didn't make her laugh. First of all it wasn't a comedy and second he's not Mork anymore so get over it. He gave an Oscar worthy performance. Now Ben Affleck has fallen off as a leading man, but everybody agrees that was his best role ever. Every actor hits a roadblock and I'm sure like others that he will bounce back. Weak character, my size 13 shoe breaking someone's tail! The movie was spectacular and I can't be with someone who doesn't value praiseworthy entertainment. Don't get me started on how I would try to avoid seeing terrible comedies where she would be the only one laughing in the theater. She would be an awful comedian's cheerleader. And she was also spending more time with her family than she did with me."

"Mary was fine and I don't understand what happened there."

My right leg was violently shaking. "Hey she was always wearing a mask."

"Do what?"

"With all that makeup she had covering her face it might as well have been a mask. In that two months we dated I don't think I ever saw her real face. The only time we saw each other is when it was dark. With makeup she looked like Vanessa Williams and without it she looked...man let me stop I don't want to say anything mean about her because she was a very nice girl."

"And let's reflect back on Vicky, just because she didn't want to grow her hair."

I unfolded my arms and pointed my finger at him. "You and I both know that women with long hair are more attractive. All she had to do was grow her hair longer and things would have been peachy, but no she had to be an independent woman of the 21st century and keep the G.I. Jane look. And last I remember Vicky wasn't in the military. Matter of fact she was against the war in Iraq. Talking about she was trying to look like Halle Berry. Halle Berry didn't look atrocious with short hair. For crying out loud she almost looked like a Vulcan from Star Trek. I was tempted so many times to tell her to live long and prosper."

"And let's not forget India. You broke up with her just because she didn't enjoy dancin'."

"A black woman that didn't enjoy dancing, that's just an oxymoron. That's as ridiculous as a black man saying he doesn't like fried chicken. That relationship was as boring as watching grass grow. Besides she was 42 and it was bound to come to an end at some point. I want to grow with the wife of my youth not a wife who has already outlived her youth. And I'll never date a woman who is more than ten years my senior because sometimes the cougars can be too needy."

"How is that?"

"India wanted me to spend every spare minute I had with her and I didn't have the energy for that. Don't get me wrong, she was a good, devoted woman, which is hard to find. She was so loyal and committed that if I told her to go to hell she probably would have gone. It wasn't meant to be. Sad to say, but I miss her dog more than I do her. That was such a cute little Pomeranian."

"All these relationships didn't last because they could all never compare to Monique."

"We were together for eight months."

"I thought for sure y'all would be meeting each other at the altar having a bonita blanco boda."

"She had a personality that was contagious because everyone she came across was drawn to her."

"She was the only woman you loved, but things happened that were out of your control. It was good actually seeing you happy with someone. She was your perfect match." My head was hanging down. "I say all that to say this, you're in a vulnerable position right now and you're probably just feelin' lonely. Since Monique I don't think you've figured out what you want. I think you're focusin' on all these women's outer shells, but not what lies inwards. And maybe you're lookin' for someone that is just like Monique. I think you've been searchin' for significance, but you're lookin' in the wrong places."

"You're out of your mind," I said in disbelief knowing Alejandro was right.

"It would be nice to see you in a serious relationship. I'm still waitin' for that day I finally get to be the best man of your boda. But do you really want to try to pursue being with a married woman." I was feeling guilty for seriously contemplating pursuing Bianca. "I strongly advise against you pursuin' her because that's somethin' you don't want comin' back on you."

Alejandro was not overstepping his boundaries in saying that. A couple of years ago he had gotten involved with a married woman. Their many nights of secret rendezvous lasted for a couple months. I was the only one Alejandro confided to about that.

We're best friends. Unlike everybody else, he knew that I didn't have it all together. Besides my parents he was probably the only one who could see I wasn't this perfect little Christian boy that is set in all his ways with no room for compromise. A lot of people I encountered thought that I was bulletproof and incapable of doing the worst.

Alejandro was a great friend, even if he told me what I didn't want to hear.

"I know you're right Alejandro, but what if I just become a really good friend to her? What if it was meant for us to know each other, but it wasn't an affair?"

Alejandro looked at me as if I asked the dumbest question in the world with a scowl in his eyebrows while his chin rested on his fist. "Here's what I want you to do. I want you to sit in a pool with your clothes on and see if they don't get wet. Or better yet walk on some hot coals and see if your feet don't get scorched. Do me a favor and be the driver in a bank robbery. If you get caught, try to see if you get off by explainin' that all you did was drive." I looked at him like he was mad. "There's no way this can work out for the good. You met her at a nightclub at a time when she should have been at home with her husband and children havin' some quality family time. You're a grown man and you'll do what you want to do, but trust me when I say that no man goes unpunished for sleepin' with another man's wife. I know God has forgiven me, but I still deal with the consequences." Alejandro's eyes were watering up. He pulled out his wallet and showed me a picture of a girl that from what he told me was almost two years old. "The consequence I have to face is that

I will probably never get a chance to meet my own daughter because her mother wants to stay in a marriage that is going nowhere fast." A tear ran down his face. "I wanted her to leave her husband, but she was never gonna do it because she had it made as an army wife." More tears ran down his face.

"I never did ask you this, but uh, what uh, was the girl's name that you got involved with?"

"Her name was Olga Garcia, that's if it was her real name."

"What did she name your daughter?"

"Our daughter's name is Angela."

"She's your little angel."

"Yeah, but you keep your Johnson on lockdown until you get married so you don't have to go through what I'm experiencin'. I think some of us men abuse the benefits of having a penis. All I wanted was something meaningful, but what I got instead was sex. There's nuttin' wrong if that's all you want, but its best when it's not abused." He wiped the tears off his face. "Listen to me, talkin' like a chick," he laughed. "I need to get ready to go." Alejandro was getting up from his seat taking a last bite of his taco.

"We're still on for some soccer later today right?"

"You're never goin' to come around to callin' it football are you?"

"You know I will never give in. Besides that's what we call it in America my Dominican Italiano amigo."

"Uncompromisin' son of a gun, that's what I like about you. Yeah it's on today. I'll see you."

We both pounded our fists together and went our separate ways.

As we separated after talking about my ex-girlfriends it was ironic that I had just received a call from India Redd, the older woman I had dated. Not wanting to hear her begging me to take her back, I ignored her call and continued walking. While walking I saw Brenda leaving the child care building with her two nieces. She waved and I waved back probably making that the highlight of her day.

As I was walking to my car, I remember Alejandro mentioning Monique and how she was my true love. I thought about the first time that I met her, which was exactly three years ago. Man, 2006 was a great year.

*　*　*　*　*

It's crazy that I remember the time because it was a quarter till eight and I was at Woodlawn Lake Park sitting on a bench watching the sunset.

It was on a Thursday evening that I was watching the sunset. I had this adoration for sunsets.

Anyway Monique walked passed me while I sat on a bench. We both greeted each other with a kind hello and a smile. I told her I liked her shirt and she thanked me while giving me a smile. Her red shirt read in the front "Eyes Up Mister" I found it quite amusing. She continued to walk on while I continued to watch my sunset. Her dark hair was pulled back into a ponytail and along with her red-shirt she was wearing white Adidas with tight black sweat pants cut off at the calves.

Probably ten minutes later a chubby fellow walked passed me talking on his phone.

It was strange, but after passing me, five minutes later he comes to my bench needing to tie his shoelaces. After tying his shoes, he decided to sit on the other end of my bench and interrupt me in being one with nature.

He looked rough as he had tattoos covering his whole body and a wild afro like Howard Stern, but he sounded feminine, gay, in other words, but I didn't want to judge him. Maybe he was real masculine, but just had a feminine voice.

This guy I had never met or ever seen tells me this story of his brother being caught masturbating by their father. Why was he talking to me about this? Was he making a pass at me? When I spoke he told me that he thought I had a beautiful voice and loved how deep it was. It was at that point that I was ready to beat this guy down with my fists if he didn't walk on, but Monique was walking around the corner where we were, so I had to improvise.

"Baby there you are," I said to Monique, as I wrapped my arm around her and mumbled to her just play along and help me. "I've been looking all over for you. Why didn't you wait for me by the basketball court like I asked you to do?"

Monique looked stunned at first, but she must have known what the situation was, so she played along. "Well, babe you kept me waiting for about 15 minutes and I couldn't wait any longer, I needed to start my walk because we have that charity ball tonight we have to go to and I wanted to get my walk in as soon as possible."

"Well I apologize for being late, I just got caught up with this song I was putting together and you know how I am when I'm creating something." I mouthed to her thank you.

"Yeah you're in another dimension," she winked. She smiled and looked at the guy. "Who's your friend here?"

"Oh I'm sorry man this is my girlfriend…"

"Monique."

"Yeah this is Monique. And I never did get your name, what is it?"

"Tyrone, as in I'll be leaving you alone," the chubby man said walking off very fast like someone was chasing him.

Monique and I stayed behind at the bench I was sitting at. I took my arm from around her.

"Thank you for bailing me out," I said. "That guy was hitting on me talking about masturbation. I was pretty close to beating him down."

"You are aware that attractive men can't be alone at a park." Usually I would have something to say, but as I really looked at Monique I was left speechless. "You'll have to beat these guys off with a stick if you come here alone again."

"So you think I'm attractive?"

"Did I say that," she replied acting coy.

"I think you did."

"I think you may need to get your hearing checked because I don't recall saying that."

"Alright Monique, it is Monique right?"

"Yes and you are?"

"I'm Ruben, Ruben Wells." We shook hands.

"Well, Mr. Wells I'm Monique Valdez."

"Thank you again for playing along."

"Don't you know this park is known for homosexual activity especially in the evening?"

"I had no idea. I thought that was just the Ortega Basin Park. I know not to come here alone."

"You know you owe me right," she smiled.

"What can I do to repay you?"

"I really do have a charity ball to attend. My friend that was going to go with me canceled on me due to a family emergency, so maybe you can take his place. You just need to have a suit on. You didn't have any plans tonight did you?"

"Well it looks like I do now. Where is this ball taking place?"

"It is taking place downtown at La Villita. There will be a live band and they will also have a casino set up, so you can play cards or craps if you like."

I noticed that she wasn't wearing a wedding ring. "Well, Ms. Valdez, it is miss right?" She nodded her head. "I don't normally go out with someone I've only known for less than five minutes, but I have a good feeling about you."

"I feel the same way about you. I love your accent by the way."

"Thank you. So shall I meet you downtown or would you mind if I pick you up?"

"You're not a crazy person or the stalking type are you?"

"I guess you'll just have to trust that I'm not."

"You can pick me up. I'll give you my address."

"You hardly know me and are already giving me your address. Maybe you're crazy."

"My therapist says I'm making some progress."

"Oh you've got jokes," I laughed.

"What do you mean by that?" She gave me a serious look, as if I had offended her. "What did I say that was so funny?" She placed her hands on her hips and pressed her lips together.

"I'm sorry; I thought you were just playing around."

"Yeah, I am I just wanted to mess with you," she laughed. "I'll have lots of fun with you. Here's my address."

I walked Monique to her car after we met. I liked her from the beginning because she carried herself like a lady with dignity. She also had a great sense of humor, which is very attractive. Monique was definitely a one in a million. She was unforgettable like the Alamo.

Monique was half-black and half-Cuban. She had light caramel skin with beautiful eyes that almost made her look mixed with Asian. Her eyes weren't hazel, but more light brown.

I remember the night I took her to the charity ball she let her hair down. She had long curly black hair with highlights. The Lord blessed her with a slim athletic frame, as she was perfectly chiseled. I was in love from the moment I saw her in a black dress that went down to her knees with open toe black stilettos showing off her manicure toes. The dress exposed her coke bottle figure. I thought it was sexy that she had a ring wrapped around one of her toes and a bracelet around her right ankle.

When I escorted her at the charity event I felt like I was with a celebrity. Almost everyone in the room knew her. She was one of the board members of the non-profit organization, Child Advocates San Antonio, sponsoring the event. Wherever I was at with her people showered her with kindness, but she wore kindness like it was a necklace. She always had a heart for giving to others. She was affable, as she had a heart for anyone she encountered. Maybe that's why everyone loved her.

Mo, that was my nickname for her, was the most unique woman I had ever known. She was always beautiful, but what attracted more people to her was the way she could light up a room, not just with her natural beauty, but a personality that could make anyone feel as if she was their best friend. Her attitude was easy going, which made her a joy to be around. Even if she had a bad hair day and was dressed down in sweat pants, devouring a hot dog like a tiger consuming a goat, she was still alluring.

She could have been a beauty queen if she wanted. I found out that a couple years before I met her she was named the Hottest Latina of San Antonio in 2004. Much like Mo my relationship was clear and simple, there was nothing complicated about it. We may have had difficult times, but we worked through them. I loved that she was outgoing, spontaneous, energetic, and optimistic, which I found to be her greatest characteristic. When most people would face something impossible and say no, she was the one that would be willing to give that impossible task a try. She was always into taking on a challenge. Maybe that was part of the reason she dated me.

It was easy to love her because she was loveable. She was so loveable that if I didn't, it would have been as lethal as breaking one of the Ten Commandments. Happiness is what I felt with her because I felt wealthy with her. I know it may sound like a cliché, but she was more profitable to me than silver or gold could ever be. She helped me grow like a tree producing fruit. She's the first girl, no wait, woman I ever loved.

She was the champagne to my caviar. I think we could have been a legendary couple like Ossie Davis and Ruby Dee or Paul Newman and Joanne Woodward, when couples stayed married forever despite the hardships they encountered. Not like married couples now. It seems it's more convenient to get divorced than to stay married and work through the hard times. But I digress.

Sometimes when I think about Monique I feel like a basketball team losing a close game after they had a huge lead only to see so many things fall apart that led to their loss. The thought of knowing they had the game won, but lost is a terrible feeling. And yes I am talking about the San Antonio Spurs.

I miss Mo. It hurts knowing that everything came to an end when we were so close to starting a life together.

There are two standards for living; one set by society and one set by God.
Which do you choose?

~Anonymous~

5

Dangerous

After going home and changing clothes I went to my parent's red brick house. They lived five minutes away in a gated community called Elm Creek. I couldn't wait to sink my teeth into juicy ribs and spicy chicken legs that my father was barbecuing.

I pulled up into the last open space in the driveway of my parents' 6,000 square foot home. The driveway was filled with cars that belonged to all my family. We were celebrating my Aunt Stella's birthday and all our family members that lived in San Antonio came over.

I rang the doorbell. My cousin, Byron, opened the door. He was Aunt Stella's 13-year-old son who was so used to getting whatever he wanted that he could get away with murder.

"What's going on Byron," I said shaking his hand that was flaccid like a dead fish.

"Hey Ruben," he replied nonchalant.

"Boy, give me a firm handshake. You're six foot six; you gotta have a handshake that's as big as you are." He squeezed my hand a little tighter. "That's what I'm talking about. How's school going?"

"Its fine I guess."

"As long as you're passing your classes that's what matters right?"

"Yeah, as long as I'm passing I'm happy."

I walked through the living room that was the size of my apartment where Uncle Terrell, his wife Shanice, Uncle Pete, Aunt Stella, and my cousin, Raquel Barker, were watching the Spurs play against the Houston Rockets.

"What's going on nephew," said Uncle Terrell as we gave each other a fist bump. At the age of 54, Uncle Terrell was a year younger than my mother. If he dyed his gray hair black, he would look a lot younger. It was funny seeing him with those gray hairs braided. His braids did look good though, as his wife braided his hair.

"What's happening Uncle Terrell," I replied. "How are you Shanice," I asked hugging her. Aunt Shanice, oh wait, she just wants me to call her Shanice because calling her Aunt as her first name makes her feel old. She's 39, so I understand where she's coming from.

"So you come alone to another family gathering huh Ruby," said Uncle Pete, as he gave me a hug. "Boy when are you going to get married and have some kids?" This was something he was always asking me every time I saw him, which if it was not every other month maybe every quarter.

"I haven't met the right girl Uncle Pete. Besides what's the hurry. You want me to go through three divorces like you."

"Hey that first one was an annulment. Only the second marriage ended in a divorce. I'm just in a separation with wife number three. She'll come around and see things my way." He took a sip of his drink. Uncle Pete was from my father's side of the family. He was the second oldest out of six. My father was the fourth oldest, but with the way he lived and how mature and responsible he was he could be mistaken as the oldest.

"How's the game?"

"Oh it's a close one. I'll be surprised if the Spurs can pull this one off." I couldn't help, but cover up my nose. Sometimes I wanted to wear a mask or bag over my head whenever I spoke with Uncle Pete because his breath smelled like spoiled milk. I love my uncle, but the sad thing about that is he's an orthodontist so I can only imagine what his patients have to go through. They have no way of escape. Wearing one mask won't do his patients justice. His lack of oral hygiene could be the reason why he's had more than one marriage.

"Now Ruby, your Uncle Pete does have a point," Shanice said. "It's not right to be single after the age of 25. If not marriage you should already have a child on the way."

"You make it sound as if my biological clock is ticking," I replied. "In order to have a kid, I need to get married, not just get into a relationship. It'll happen for me when it's meant to happen. Before donating sperm I want to give a woman my last name first." Everybody was laughing. Whenever the whole family got together it seemed like they ganged up on me wanting to know when I'm going to bring a girl with me for them to meet that has wife potential. To them it was unorthodox to still be single after 25. Most of my family thought by 25 you should be married and within a year a child should be arriving. While the rest of my family was trying to push me into a relationship, my parents would tell me to take my time. "Besides whenever I get engaged y'all won't meet the future Mrs. Ruben Wells until the wedding reception."

"Wedding reception?"

"That's right the wedding reception. I don't need her to back out before vows are exchanged." The whole family laughed again. Except Aunt Stella who was yelling at the television screen because one of the Spurs players missed an easy layup. She got up from the couch and gave me a hug. "Happy birthday Aunt Stella."

"Oh thank you," she whispered. "And thank you for not blocking me from Buster."

"Yeah we're family we have to look out for each other."

"He was something else. I see why he's called Buster."

"Oh Aunt Stella, glad to hear you got your groove back."

"Come on y'all let Ruben go at his own pace," said Raquel. "I'm sure he knows what he's doing."

"Yeah exactly."

"OH COME ON SAUL," she yelled at the screen as well after seeing Spurs player, Saul Russell, miss a shot. "YOU'RE WIDE OPEN FOR A THREE, YOU GOTTA MAKE THAT BABY! Sorry, but he should have made it." Raquel was 26 and currently dating NBA superstar, Saul Russell. They had been dating each other since their senior year at The University of Texas in Austin, so they've been together four or five years now. She was my cousin from my dad's side of the family. Her mother was his twin sister, Aunt Shelley. He was older than her by three minutes. Raquel was born and raised in Atlanta as well.

"Where are the owners of this house that I call my parents? Is Kat here?"

"We're in the kitchen," I heard my mother yell.

My mother was pulling some pieces of corn on the cob out of the oven and placed them on a countertop, while my little sister, Kat, was filling cups up with ice.

My mother greeted me with a hug. Most people had mistaken her for being Latino because her skin was lighter than most blacks and her hair was golden brown. When some people spoke Spanish to her and she told them that she's not Latina they thought she disowned her Hispanic heritage. I got my skin complexion from her side of the family. Everybody on her side of the family looked like they could pass for anything, but black. Anyway she's the oldest of three brothers and three sisters, but she looked fifteen years younger than her age.

"Hey mom," I said while hugging her. "Need help with anything?"

"No, we're pretty much set," she replied. "We're just waiting on your dad to finish grilling a few more meats."

"So how was church today?" We went to different churches. They recently started attending Common Union Church. A church that was a little different from Covenant Center in that it had a predominantly white congregation, but that didn't bother my parents.

"It was really good. Pastor Bill was speaking a message you probably would have enjoyed hearing," she said.

"Oh really what was it on?"

"Singleness, as a matter of fact I bought you a copy of the message."

"Oh thanks." This is just what I need to hear. Another message on how just because you're single doesn't mean God can't use you. Or "value can be found in singleness." And my favorite, "don't be discouraged in your singleness because you're not nobody, but somebody." I've heard it all before, so it's probably nothing new.

"And it's not what you think it is, but it has a much different approach that will surprise you."

"We'll see."

"Yes you will. How was your church?"

"It was fine."

"What did Pastor Harper speak on?"

"To be honest with you I don't remember."

"Ruby." That was my parents', as well as the rest of the family, nickname for me.

"Well I had a late night last night. I only got about three to four hours of sleep."

"Still that's no excuse."

"Yeah, but I went and isn't that what really matters?"

"Yeah you did, but you have to do more than just show up. There are people who don't attend church that are closer to God than regular church attendees."

"Mum, please I've already heard a sermon."

"Yeah, one you can't remember."

"Actually Pastor Harper was talking about sexual sin. Matter of fact he's doing a series on it. He started it with Adam and Eve and how they gave into the forbidden fruit."

"Alright, alright, I'll stop."

"See, I actually do listen."

"So what did you do last night?"

"I played the trumpet last night at a salsa club."

"Really," she said with a smile. My mum always enjoyed dancing. She especially enjoyed watching salsa dancing. She was just amazed at the things dancers could do. "Did you have a good time?"

"Yeah," I smiled just thinking about Bianca. It was a guilty pleasure.

"What?"

"Oh, nothing."

"Could you set the plates on the table please?"

"Sure."

"Hey brother, how are you," Kat asked.

"I'm doing alright sis," I said hugging Kat. "Did you go to church this morning?"

"No I didn't."

"You heathen," I jested.

"I didn't go because I went yesterday."

"Ah you got me there." Kat was a spitting image of our mother. They had the same light complexion that was as golden as honey. She had light brown eyes like my mother and she also had long curly ebony hair with golden highlights.

"Hey son could you go see if your father needs some help," Mom said.

"Sure."

While my mom and Kat were talking about women stuff I joined dad in the backyard while he was sporting his red apron flipping some patties on the grill and just taking some of his spicy chicken off the grill.

My parents have been married for 22 years. My last name was Green until I was five years old. Ruben Wells has a much better ring to it than Ruben Green doesn't it? It's strange, but Sheldon, my stepfather, I call him dad and my biological father, Alton, I call him by his first name…of course I didn't call him very often. Sheldon, dad, has loved me my whole life, as if I were his own seed.

My mother and Alton got married right after she finished high school. He was a couple years older than she was and he was in the Navy. Three months into their marriage he was to be stationed in London, England. So my mum and Alton moved to London. After five years of living in London and raising two children Mom decided to attend the University of London and major in Accounting. She was tired of being a housewife. It was at the university that she met my soon-to-be second father who was a construction worker, but also a student at the university majoring in Architecture. He met Mom when she couldn't find her way around campus.

My father was English, but one day he had dreams of moving to America and starting his own business. He now has his own architectural firm that is making millions in revenue.

Alton didn't have a problem raising his voice or pulling my mother by the arm in public. Of course that was just a warm up session for him. Behind closed doors he made her bleed or left bruises on her body.

One day after one of his tongue-lashings while my dad was coming to their house to help my mom with a research paper he comforted my mother literally giving her a shoulder to cry on when Alton decided to drink his problems away in a local pub. From that point on my parents were very close.

She started dating my dad six months before she and Alton got a divorce. Sheldon married my mother when I was five and for the last 22 years my mother has been filled with joy. All this time she's been with a man who loves, respects, and believes in her. He never insults or looks down on her, but admires her. Now they have their disagreements like any other couple and they may berate each other at times, but they have never stopped loving each other. They are business partners, as she's the chief financial officer of their business, while he serves as the chief executive officer of Revelations Architecture.

A while back I asked her what she saw in Alton and she told me it was because he was a football player when he was in high school. And when I asked her about what attracted her to dad, she said it was because she liked that he was thoughtful and made use of his mind because she had never met a black man who did that. Most of the black men she knew solved problems by slugging it out, but my father would talk things out before resorting to violence. Of course my father had no problem getting violent when someone couldn't settle an argument in a civilized manner.

I was the middle child. From my mother's first marriage I have an older sister, Lauren, who's 31 with three kids. In the divorce I stayed with mom and I don't know why, but Lauren stayed with Alton. My younger sister is from my mother and Sheldon. Kathrina, who everyone called Kat, just turned 21.

Kat was in her junior year at UTSA majoring in engineering and had a 4.0 GPA. She also had an internship at my parents' office. They called it Revelations because they're making dreams come true for their clients. This world could use more minorities in the field of architecture. According to a survey by the American Institute of Architects only 15 percent of architects are minorities.

It cracked me up sometimes when people would say I look like my dad, when the only way we look alike is by our skin complexion. One time I was shocked that an older woman thought my dad and I were brothers. Maybe she wasn't wearing her glasses. Other people would say I looked more like my mother, as I had her smile and eyes.

My dad had always been proactive and tenacious, which is why he has been successful in architecture. If he wanted something he went after it. If he hadn't told my mother, he loved her they probably wouldn't be together right now. Shoot I wouldn't have a little sister to look out for. Three things would have happened with my mother if he didn't say those three powerful words. She would be miserable, or in jail because eventually she would have killed Alton, or lying six feet under.

I love my mom and respect her even more for having the courage to leave because most women wouldn't do that.

The memories I carry of Alton are rather unpleasant, but if my mother hadn't gotten with Alton than I wouldn't be here. That's the only good thing I could say about him.

"Ay ay," I said.

"Hey, there he is," dad said with his thick British accent. We gave each other a hug.

"Nice day for a barbecue."

"Hey it's a beautiful day, so why not. Plus, it's been awhile so I thought I'd break out the grill."

"Well I can't blame you. I'd probably do the same thing."

"So what's new son." Every week I visited that's something my father always asked me.

"Same ol' same ol'." This was always my response to his question.

"So you mean to tell me nothing new happened in your life this week. You avoid change like it's a virus."

"I have to stick with the same routine or else everything is just out of order."

"That's going to be your new excuse to use," he laughed. "Besides you know that insanity is doing the same thing over and over again expecting a different outcome. How was the salsa dancing last night?" He knew I did that a lot lately almost every weekend.

"It was fun. Actually something rather exciting did happen last night."

"What happened last night?"

Before I spoke I took a deep breath and exhaled. "Well I met this girl last night."

"That happens to you a lot, I thought something else may have happened," he laughed while flipping some patties.

"Well when I finish this story it will have a different ending."

"Okay, please continue."

"So this girl I met she was beautiful and intelligent. Conversation we carried was just flowing. She reminded me of Paula Abdul and we know how much I love Paula Abdul." My dad nodded his head. "Things were going well until she told me that she's married." My father remained silent. "She decided that she still wants to stay in contact with me. So dad is it wrong that I want to stay in contact with her even if we just stay friends?"

"I think you know the answer to that. If you have to justify or try to compromise you know the answer."

"Is it really wrong though if I just want a friendship? Besides it's not like she has a happy marriage."

"That makes no difference."

"But mom was in the marriage from hell and you got involved with her while she was still with Alton."

"Yeah I know, but that was a different time and a different situation. First of all, what woman could resist a black British." He laughed. "Seriously for one we were a lot younger and you really don't know what this young lady's situation is. I witnessed some of the things Alton did to your mother. Back then we weren't Christians. We were just young, naïve, and in love. It was a situation your mother needed to be out of. Now this girl you met, she could give you a story that would make a big R&B hit to make you sympathize with her and would probably make a great TV movie for Lifetime network. Make you feel like you can save her when she probably isn't the one that needs to be saved. Her husband could be the one that wants to be set free. She could be the one frequently practicing infidelity while her husband stays loyal to her by keeping his tail at home like she should be doing. And even if she left her husband for you how do you know she won't do the same thing to you? The thing you need to ask yourself is if you were married what would you want your wife to do?"

I never thought of it that way. In some relationships there are things spouses don't disclose to one another, but a relationship, platonic or otherwise, outside the marriage should never be kept a secret.

And Bianca probably did more than go behind her husband's back, but she probably also emasculated him by insulting him with words. Who knows what's going on in that marriage? My father's right. I do need to leave her alone.

"Son, you may like to put on this front that you don't want to be with anyone and you're satisfied with being single. I know how much you desire a relationship, but this is one you don't need to get into. You don't want to share the story of how you and your wife ended up together and it being that to be with her you had to violate a marriage she was in. Now your mother and I know we weren't right for what we did, but sometimes things happen. That's a part of life. I know God has forgiven me for everything that happened because I've asked for forgiveness. The consequence we faced was that feeling of distrust, but after a while, a very long while we both learned to trust each other and believe that neither one of us would be disloyal to the other. That was my past and I don't dwell on it, because all I have to look forward to is the future. And with your mother by my side and no one else, I'm highly anticipating where the Lord is leading us in this journey together. You're a grown man. You don't have to take my advice because you can make your own decisions. Just be careful. Remember that you always have a choice to make."

"Dad, how much longer is it going to be," Kat said with her head sticking out the door.

"They'll be ready in a few more minutes. Are they about to go crazy in there?"

"Well no they got the nachos to hold them over, but Uncle Pete is almost ready to finish off what's left. If the food isn't ready by that time, you may have to buy new furniture."

"Your Uncle Pete knows better. Besides he's going to take care of his teeth and not eat too much crunchy foods."

As we continued on were talking about how happy Aunt Stella was. As if she just won a million dollars.

"And I thought she was going to be depressed about turning 50," my father said. "She's taking it a lot better than I thought she would."

My friend Buster that I saw last night at Nocturnal is 25 years old. Knowing Buster, he would have asked how we knew each other and I didn't want to mess with whatever kind of chemistry he built with my aunt. My aunt looks young for her age as well, but if Buster found out her real age he probably would have left her alone and my aunt would have blamed me and I didn't want to deal with all of that drama.

Actually, this is Buster I'm talking about. As long as a woman is 21 or older he doesn't care. Buster and my Aunt Stella are not the serious relationship type, so they both must have got what they wanted only for the night. I'm betting that Buster had something to do with the joy my aunt was feeling today. He probably gave Aunt Stella another spring in her step. Oh just thinking about that almost made me vomit in my mouth.

To live is to choose. But to choose well, you must know who you are and what you stand for, where you want to go and why you want to get there

~Kofi Annan~

6

Enjoy Yourself

My family and I ate like royalty consuming a well-balanced meal of chicken, burgers, hot dogs, ribs, potato salad, corn, and baked beans.

Quality time with my family today consisted of watching basketball games and playing a game of spades or dominoes. Kat and Raquel joined me at the South Texas Medical Center Park to catch up with Alejandro for a game of soccer. Kat was meeting with a friend of hers to jog a few miles while Raquel and I played.

She was the only girl who ever came out here to play with us burly men. Raquel has always roughed it up with the boys. Even if it was tackle football she could hang with the best of them. Scraped knee or bruised arm was a badge of honor to her.

It was a beautiful day outside and it wouldn't be getting dark until 8:30 in the evening thanks to daylight savings time. There was a nice breeze calmly swaying the trees as sheets of cloud spread across the sky, but not enough to keep the sun hidden. Other people were making use of the baseball field, tennis courts, and sandy volleyball courts.

There were about 20 other guys stretching out, covering their shin guards with high knee socks, and tightening their laces on their cleats getting ready to play a nice friendly competitive game of football.

Soccer was a hobby Alejandro and I picked up for a few months. Throughout high school and college we both had hoop dreams. We had dreams of making it to the NBA and become rivals that sports commentators would talk about for many generations like Jordan vs. Bird or Magic and Isaiah. When we got into the real world and started working real jobs those dreams faded.

"Remember back in the day when we thought we would be hoop stars," Alejandro asked as he was covering up his shin guards with some high knee green socks to match his green jersey.

"Yeah and then reality hit hard," I replied. After college we would still play some street ball, but we soon felt it was a waste of time because there weren't any NBA scouts looking for street ballers.

"Did you ever think we would gain an interest in golf, tennis, and now soccer?"

"Well I knew I would because I'm sophisticated and cultured," I joked making Alejandro laugh. Growing up I used to play soccer a lot, but I grew an interest in basketball as I got older. "Golf was relaxing and tennis offered a great workout."

"The thing I used to hate about soccer was that you couldn't use your hands. Without using your hands it just feels like you're limited."

"I can understand that. With the game of soccer there might be little contact, but you can possibly collide with someone when trying to kick the ball away from an opponent. You could trip somebody on purpose, but still make it look like an accident."

"I know it's such a beautiful thing."

I turned around and was shocked to see Torres Russell pop up behind me. "Ah dang, Torres, you almost gave me a heart attack sneaking up on me like that."

"I didn't see you coming either Torres."

"Yeah, you never see him or hear him coming," Roland said walking up behind Torres.

"I guess in another life I could have been a ninja," Torres replied with his cleats and shin guards on ready to play. And as usual he was carrying a pen and notepad with him like cops carry their badge and gun.

Torres was Saul's cousin. He was half-black and half-Puerto Rican. With his head shaven and thick goatee, he had a striking resemblance to LL Cool J. Sometimes he would joke that he couldn't believe some people thought I was Puerto Rican, maybe he would believe Mexican, but not Puerto Rican.

It's a small world because he lives in the Elm Creek area with his parents. Our families are one of the few minorities that live in the opulent area.

He was a difficult person to read not showing a lot of emotion, as if he constantly walked around with a poker face. Don't get me wrong he was one of the nicest guys in the world, but he's someone I wouldn't want to see upset because I bet it would be like seeing Bruce Banner get angry. In case you don't know who Bruce Banner is, he's The Incredible Hulk. I'm kind of a geek.

Torres was so righteous that he could glow in the dark. When it came to sports he was a completely different person. Normally he was placid and exercised the double d's, being demure and using decorum, but in sports he was competitive and vocal almost to the point where he was antagonistic.

For a long time, we both knew each other by our writing, but we met each other a year ago at a media mixer for all minority journalists and broadcasters throughout San Antonio. It wasn't exclusive to only minorities, of course white people showed up. It was open to anyone involved in any aspect of media. People just came for the alcohol.

Anyway, Torres was a freelance reporter for the San Antonio Chronicles, a weekly business newspaper. He worked full-time for the government, working in the City of San Antonio's Housing and Community Development department. He was excellent in writing like Michelangelo was in painting. He may have been a man of very few words, but when he wrote he was multiloquent. The pen would probably be his weapon of choice on a battlefield. Definitely a writer at heart, as he always carried a pad and pen because his head was floating with ideas. I won't be surprised to see him come out with a novel one day.

"What no suit Roland," I teased.

"Man please," he laughed.

It was funny seeing Roland not wearing a blazer or a sports coat because he always wore one like it was his uniform. He's the reason I started wearing a sports coat more often. He had his head covered with a white bandana and he was also showing off his muscles wearing a wife beater. This guy was so suave that he could probably stay cool in a sauna. He was so cool that he could give ladies goose bumps the moment he entered a room. I've never seen him lose his cool.

As we were stretching we were in our own circle joking around about some phrases that we thought were oxymoronic. Is that a word?

"Now my favorite one is when somebody says it's cool as hell or funny as hell," I said.

"Oh I know what you mean," Torres said. "If hell is so cool than why is that the place everybody tries to avoid visiting."

"Well have you ever been," Roland said.

"Hey have the people that made up the phrase ever been there. Now remember Dante's Inferno was just a work of fiction. And last I heard there's nothing funny about hell." We all laughed. "Besides you know how hot it is in Texas during the summer. For me, this might as well be hell."

"If hell is hot as Texas during the summer then take me to Heaven," Alejandro replied.

While we were joking around Raquel was humming a song. It caught Roland's interest since he was looking for a lead singer for our band.

"Hold up Raquel, why didn't I think of it," he said.

"What," she asked.

"I can't believe I didn't bother to ask you if you wouldn't mind singing for our group. You can be the lead singer for The Foundation."

"Are you serious?"

"Yeah girl I'm as serious as a heart attack. Ruben, Alejandro she's got some pipes on her doesn't she."

"Yeah," I said. "I can't believe I didn't think of that either and she's my cousin."

"You should be ashamed."

"I am."

"Raquel we'll have to talk after we get done playing a little soccer here okay."

"Okay," she said.

Someone blew the whistle for us to begin our friendly competitive game of soccer, oh I'm sorry, and I mean football.

"Let's get it on," Torres yelled running onto the field like he had one too many Red Bulls.

* * * * *

After playing for almost an hour and a half the sun was setting. I decided to take a break while everyone else continued to play. While I was sitting on the fluffy grass watching the sun beginning to slip away Kat came up to me with I her friend she met up with.

"Hey Ruby," Kat said walking up to me. "I want to introduce you to my friend…"

"Deanna Cortez," I said with a smile on my face, as I was getting up. "Good to see you again."

"Good seeing you again as well Mr. Ruben Wells," Deanna said shaking my hand.

"How do you two know each other," Kat asked.

"Oh, we met awhile back at a media mixer." Her eyes stayed locked on me. "You're a lot taller than I remember you."

"How come we never met up for lunch," I asked.

"You never called me."

"You do have a good point there, but I sent you a friend request on your Facebook and I'm still waiting for a confirmation on that request."

"So I guess we both need to learn to follow up." We both looked at each other and just laughed. Deanna was half-Puerto Rican and half-Mexican who looked like Rosalyn Sanchez.

"That's a nice tattoo."

"Thank you."

Deanna had a small tattoo of a Puerto Rico flag and Mexico flag crossing each other on her stomach that was flatter than mine. She looked like she was a professional runner not having a piece of fat on her. Her neck was long and slender like a swan. She almost looked Native American with her straight jet-black hair that other women wouldn't mind wearing as a wig or as weave. Her belly button was pierced.

She was like a flame because she was beautiful to look at, but dangerous to touch. Like fire, women with her beauty were so hot that wherever they walked they quickly captured people's attention. She came across as the kind of woman that felt she could get any man she wants and from any man she could get whatever she wanted whenever she wanted it. But as I got to know her at the mixer she was actually a confident woman who didn't have to use her looks to get what she wanted.

Kat watched the boys play soccer as Deanna and I spoke like old friends.

Deanna wasn't just a pretty face, but she also had brains. We both found it stimulating that we shared the strange habit of studying the origin of words. For example, I was breaking down the origin of Adam 's apple.

"Everybody knows that the Adam's apple is the name given to the projection of the largest cartilage of the larynx at the front of the throat in men," I lectured. "It is a translation of the Hebrew tappuah haadam…"

"Say that for me one more time," Deanna interjected.

"Tappuah haadam," I repeated, as she nodded her head. "And refers to the belief, that when Eve gave Adam the forbidden fruit or apple to eat, a part of it got stuck in his throat. That's how we got the term Adam's apple."

I was blown away, as Deanna gave me the origin of the word barbecue.

"It's actually a Haitian word that came into use in the English language," Deanna said. "Now this is something because not many Haitian words have come into use in the English language, but this is one, probably the most widely used spoken everyday by millions of people. Anyway the Haitian Creole word barbacoa denotes a framework of sticks set upon posts, in other words our barbecue grill.

The original intent of the word was applied only to the framework itself, on which an ox or sheep would be roasted whole. Later barbecue came to be applied to any open-air feast of this kind, particularly large-scale ones. It isn't a recent addition to the English language, but has been used for a very long time because it is used in the present sense in the work of Alexander Pope, the English poet who lived from 1688 to 1744."

"That's fascinating. I never knew that."

Isn't that interesting? I guess it is if you're fascinated on discovering the origins of words or phrases.

In getting to know her I realized that she had a lot to offer. My interest in her really soared when she mentioned she didn't have kids and was never married. We were already off to a fresh start.

I loved how she looked at me. Sometimes she would look at me like I was her equal. The same way Monique looked at me.

* * * * *

If People Magazine were to name Ruben the Bachelor of the Year I like to think they would say not only does he have a face that grants him favor with the ladies, but when he speaks he makes them sweat because of his deep voice that sounds very authoritative like a commanding officer in the military. He was as tall and lean as a tower. Not like Yao Ming, but he was a lot taller than me and it's a plus when a man standing next to me doesn't need a stoop to stand on to look taller than me. He had square shoulders that looked as though they could bolder through a wall. I wipe some sweat off my forehead imagining his physique that would have people think he stepped out of Homer's epic poem The Iliad.

He had an unnecessary bald fade. I say it was unnecessary for him to shave his head because he wasn't losing hair. Sometimes shaving your head is unnecessary like wearing glasses when you don't need them. He has a mustache and a goatee that compensates his temporary baldness.

If there's only one flaw he has it's that his nose is kind of big. If he was in a race against Usain Bolt and it came down to a photo finish, Ruben would literally win by a nose because it is pointy and sticks out there. But like Richard Gere, even though he has a big nose, you still find him handsome and charming.

I was conspicuously looking at Ruben from head to toe. I wasn't ashamed if I was giving him an erotic look. He maintained eye contact with a beautiful smile on his face. "I know I've said this already, but you do have a lovely voice," I said.

"Thank you."

"Born in Atlanta moved to England for a little bit, then back to Atlanta before moving to San Antonio correct?"

"That's right."

"See I was listening when we last spoke."

"You have a good memory. And now you lived in New York for a while, correct?"

"That's right."

Deanna and I were both in the Public Relations Student Society of America UTSA chapter. I was the president of the club, while Kat served as the treasurer of the club.

I'm 28 and looking forward to graduating from college. After finishing high school, I went straight into the Army. While in the Army I was stationed in San Antonio at Brooks City Base. After doing that for four years I went back to New York and did some modeling for a couple years. While that was a fun ride, eventually modeling can take its toll on you. I remember San Antonio being more calm than my beloved New York, so I returned to the Alamo City and started attending UTSA three years ago. I'm finishing a little earlier since I did school year around. With the exception of maybe taking a month off near the end of the summer as well as holidays I never took a break from school once I started. I was afraid that with all that time off during the summer I wouldn't want to go back to school. So I took courses during the summer.

"What do you think of San Antonio," I asked.

"I've lived here a very long time and its home to me," he replied. "I am open to the idea of leaving San Antonio if an opportunity comes my way."

"Would you be open to moving out of state or out of the city?"

"Either one, doesn't matter. If I stay in the state I wouldn't mind living in either Dallas or Austin."

"Why isn't Houston an option?"

"Houston is a lovely city when you're a tourist, but it's not a place I would want to be a resident. Especially since hurricanes are always visiting that city. Plus, I can't stand the traffic that seems to be happening all day, every day. And don't even get me started on the copious toll roads. Plus, Austin is the music capital of Texas, so I wouldn't mind living there just to get noticed in music. Dallas seems to have people who are on the fast track and all about handling business. That's my kind of city."

"I feel that." He was definitely thoughtful.

"Plus they're the home of the greatest team in the NFL, the Cowboys."

"Oh is that what you think."

"Oh I most definitely know that."

"The Giants are America's team. Forget about Dallas being that team, they lost that title a long time ago."

"We'll see about that."

* * * * *

I was so wrapped up in my conversation with Deanna that I hadn't realized it was dark outside. I grabbed my cell phone and saw a text from Kat that she and Raquel caught a ride with Alejandro. When I saw the time on my cell, I couldn't believe how fast time had flown by.

"Dang I didn't realize it was getting late," I said.

"What time is it?"

"It's a little after nine o'clock."

"Oh dang, we should get going."

"Yeah, I'll walk you to your car."

As we were walking to the parking lot all I could think about is kissing Deanna. I don't know if it was seeing her dressed in some pink daisy dukes showing off her bronze legs that many women try to get in tanning salons, but I was wondering if I should just ask her if it would be inappropriate for me to kiss her or just take it like I did with Bianca. The thought of feeling Deanna's lips gave me some tingling feelings. We got to her vehicle, which was a big crimson Toyota Tundra.

"Dang you like them big huh," I said.

"I'm not your typical girl," she replied. "I've always liked trucks more than the luxury cars."

"That's alright. With this vehicle you fit in just fine with Texas where shotguns and pickup trucks are the norm."

She laughed while she opened the driver side door to her truck. "Well you have my number so give me a call some time," she said rattling her keys. "I mean it I really want you to call me."

"You like origins of words or phrases. Do you know how a kiss got its origin?"

"No how?"

"Some people want to give credit to the Romans for the erotic kiss and then some want to say it even started with Solomon from the Song of Songs in the Bible. So I guess a lot of people have their theories. Some even say it started in the prehistoric times. It was important at that time, not for romantic purposes, but I guess it could be more scientific. It was a way to select a mate with a good immune system to further the species with. So apparently our ancestors would taste each other's saliva in order to find a healthy prospect."

"Eeewww, gross," she laughed.

"I know, so instead of the indulgence or joy of the kiss, our predecessors were using a smooch as a like a health screen to test their partner. Somehow their nervous system was able to recognize a suitable match purely through the exchange of spit." She was still laughing. "Turns you on doesn't it." We both laughed.

"And you're telling me this because…"

"It was a feeble attempt to kiss you." She stopped laughing when I said that. As she bit her bottom lip, her eyes narrowed in on my own. "Pueda le beso?"

"Besame."

She speaks Spanish, we have a keeper folks. I walked up closer to her and touched her face gently pulling her towards me. When our lips met I closed my eyes and at first contact I was glad I asked if I could kiss her. One of her hands was rubbing the back of my head. As we kissed I could feel the wind blow through her hair. As I softly touched her neck, she tightly grasped one of my biceps. As I leaned into her on her truck we both seemed to get into some heavy breathing. Before it got real intense I backed away.

"Woo," I said.

"Mmm, that was something else," she said with a smile on her face. "I liked that. I'm going to uh get going." She almost stumbled walking into her truck.

"Whoa, watch your step there."

"Give me a call some time."

"I will do that. And whenever you log onto Facebook confirm my friend request."

"I'll be sure to do that."

Deanna got in her truck and slowly drove away, as I was walking to my car touching my lips wishing the kiss could have lasted even longer than it did. I couldn't help, but wonder if what I had done was wrong since I kissed two women within 24 hours. It's not like Bianca was my girlfriend because she's married. So it wasn't wrong for me to kiss Deanna after only knowing her for a few hours, right?

…With relationships come very many choices that have to be worked out between two people. Choosing to stay or leave. Choosing to love or hate. Part of the reason I'm single is because I hate having to consult with someone instead of just doing what I feel needs to be done.

Some people would probably say that I'm selfish and they're right because presently I choose to do what's best for me. Now don't get me wrong I would love to be with someone, but right now I've chosen to be single. So at the moment the only person who can love me is myself. I know that one day someone will love me, but the real question is will I choose to accept the love that person has for me

~Choose This Day column by Ruben Wells of SA Prevalent~

7

The Girl Is Mine

Mondays, Mondays, Mondays…you got to love Mondays. I'm being facetious of course. In the office there's nothing, but chaos as we were fighting to get the paper out to the printers.

I wish I could say I took heed of my father's words of wisdom, but it's as if I stabbed my ears with q-tips because I didn't stop speaking to Bianca.

I hadn't seen her since that night at Nocturnal, but we spoke with each other this morning for an hour. This girl already has me acting immoral making a personal phone call, as I was acting like I was doing a phone interview just scribbling on a notepad. I actually was writing down some questions to ask in case there was a moment of awkward silence. This connection wouldn't have resumed if she didn't send me an e-mail.

The email she sent me said:

Good morning Mr. Reporter. I really enjoyed being with you at Nocturnal. It's rare to come across gentlemen like yourself. I was impressed with how proper you were. You're a great dancer. I really enjoyed being close to you, not just physically, but intellectually as well. Nice to meet a man who doesn't carry only good looks, but a brain as well and knows how to carry a conversation. I hope you'll stay in contact with me. I can understand if you don't, but please know that I would really like to get to know you better. If you don't have my number, it's 865-0992. Call me!

Love, Bianca

After reading that email I immediately dialed her number pressing rapidly on the dial pad as if it were the code to dismantle a bomb.

I discovered that she was the second oldest of four siblings with an older brother ahead of her and another brother and sister behind her. They were raised by their mother because her father passed away when she was eleven years old. Her family, as well as her husband, called her by her middle name Olga. Whenever she met new people she would introduce herself as Bianca, since it was her first name. No offence to women named Olga, Bianca sounded much sexier than Olga did.

"You're different from most guys," Bianca said.

"Oh really, how am I different from most guys," I asked.

"Other guys don't see me being married as a big deal. I know it bothers you, but I'm glad you're still talking to me."

"So you've spoken to other guys?"

"Well other guys have spoken to me. When I tell them I'm married they're nonchalant about it. Maybe they get an adrenaline rush from talking to a married woman."

"Most men don't mind talking to a married woman because they don't have to worry about being tied down, since a married woman is already tied to another."

"So is that why you're talking to me?"

"Well, no. Normally I don't talk to married women, but I don't know there's something about you that's irresistible."

"You're smooth." I did feel like patting myself on the back. "We should get together some time."

I didn't immediately respond because I was shocked at how forward she was. "Really, you think so?"

"I have a thesis due next week and since you're a reporter maybe you can help me with it. Just edit it and make minor adjustments so that it makes sense."

"Why is it that since I work for a newspaper people think I'm a grammar and composition specialist? There's a reason I'm just a reporter and not an editor."

"You're being modest. Anyway my husband is out of town all week on business and won't be back until next Monday." While we were talking my pants were feeling tight particularly in the groin area. Sex wasn't mentioned in our conversation, but the thought of being that close to her built my anticipation thus made me more alert than a cup of coffee could. "On Wednesday night I was thinking about checking out this jazz group at Tucker Magee's. Maybe you can join me."

"And even if we're just friends how would your husband feel if he saw us together at a club."

"He wouldn't like it."

"What time were you thinking of going to the club?" What am I doing?

"I'll probably go around ten o'clock."

"Maybe I'll see you there."

"I would like that."

"Well I got this meeting to attend, so I'll talk to you later."

If I didn't have to attend this meeting I would probably still be on the phone with her. Instead of work all I was thinking about was seeing Bianca later in the week.

I hated working at a newspaper. A reporter's life is spent getting overworked and underpaid. My profession is one that is not highly valued by the public. I enjoy writing and I'm good at it, but to be a great reporter it takes dedication...dedication that I don't have. For me it's all about the paycheck, not about the love of creative writing.

I'm surprised that I stayed in the industry for so long because it has taken a beating. Journalism isn't highly regarded as it once was. More people are asking what we need journalists for. Bring the truth, but too many have a hard time doing that.

Print publications are struggling to stay alive as more people catch the news by watching television or browsing the Internet for information. People hardly ever listen to the radio anymore because now people can download songs in their iPods or iPhones. Advertisers are taking their business to electronic outlets or nationally publicized publications like Time, Rolling Stone, or People. But we're still around because we continue to entertain, educate, and inform, thus giving a reader something to think about.

Journalism isn't as big in San Antonio as it is in New York City and we may have a high illiteracy rate, but it's still needed.

At Alamo City News, on average we have a little over 110,000 readers every week. Fifty-three percent of our readers are male. Of all our readers 48 percent have purchased three books from a bookstore in the last year, and 25 percent of our readers exercise at least three days a week in health clubs as we have issues available for purchase at all the Gold's Gyms in San Antonio. They are one of our biggest advertisers.

The best part of my job was being able to get out of the office. It was almost like being set free from prison; of course I wouldn't know what that feels like because I've never been arrested or imprisoned. Getting out of the office was the best part of my job because I was getting a chance to meet other people and tell their stories either through words or a photograph. Sitting in front of a computer all day isn't something I was born to do. Every minute being spent seated in front of the computer I felt like I was losing a small piece of intelligence and gaining another pound every hour.

My job wasn't the greatest job in the world, but it paid the rent and never left me starving. Besides having medical coverage and 401K benefits are very beneficial.

While at work instead of hearing other people's conversations I listened to music off of iTunes, browsed my Facebook page, and watched some tv shows or films online. I only watched videos when I had some free time or nothing to do, but it's rare that happened.

Growing up journalism was depicted as a glamorous job, but there's nothing glamorous about it. For Alamo City News this is in the literal sense. It's completely unnecessary for us to have an annual sexual harassment seminar because there are no women here really worth taking a sexual harassment case for. There's no eye candy in the office, with the exception of our editorial assistant and a couple of employees in the advertising department, but they're married so they don't count. By looking at them it was obvious as to why they were unavailable.

I was one of the three staff reporters or writers, whatever you want to call us, in the culture section of our paper. We have hundreds of employees in a three-story building that's as big as a museum in the King William District downtown on South Alamo Street. Actually, I think it was a museum in the 1960s.

While working on finishing up a story that was due before lunch I received a call from the receptionist Nancy.

"This is Ruben," I said.

"Hey Ruben, there is a Pastor Randy Lowe here to see you," she replied.

"Does he look angry?"

"Yes sir."

"I'll be right there."

I hung up the phone and went to my fearless editor-in-chief's office. Her name was Elizabeth Fox, whom everyone called Liz. She was Mexican and married to a white man, the mother of two children who were never spanked. Liz and her husband were liberals that believed in letting their children decide how they should be disciplined. I can see them trying to negotiate what type of sentence they should receive after committing a crime. And people wonder what is happening with our youth today.

Back when I was growing up I couldn't negotiate myself out of a punishment. I learned my lesson when my parents swatted my butt with their belts. I was in so much trouble that they would alternate in spanking me. They might as well have done it in shifts because I was a rebellious child. Keyword is was. That's why I have a bubble butt, from so many spankings. I have the male version of a Jennifer Lopez backside.

The door to her office was closed. It meant she was having a conversation with her husband over the phone. The door was always closed whenever she was speaking, rather yelling, with her husband. It was pointless for her to close the door because we heard every word she shouted through the thin walls. They were arguing about who was going to pick up the clothes from the cleaners.

One of the things I like about this job is that there isn't a strict dress code. I like to dress up, but every once in a while, I like to dress down. On this particular day I was wearing some blue jeans with white Adidas and a yellow t-shirt with Bruce Lee in one of his famous karate stances with the word "Respect" printed beneath him. Ever since my dad had me watch Chinese Connection I've been a big Bruce Lee fan. Four years ago on Christmas my parents gave me a watch with Bruce Lee in his yellow suit from Game of Death with nun chucks swinging every second, minute, and hour.

While waiting outside Liz's door I put on my black polo shirt and black sports coat. I have to look somewhat professional when we have meetings and interviews. As I knocked on the door she invited me in while she hung up the phone.

"What's going on Ruben," she asked.

"Pastor Lowe is in the lobby," I replied. "I'm sure he wants to meet with me over that story we did on him. I will probably need you there with me."

"Alright let's get this over with."

We were walking to the lobby to meet with Pastor Randy Lowe. We ran a story on him in this past Sunday's religion issue where it was entitled "Renowned pastor on the down low."

Pastor Lowe had been getting involved with male prostitutes at a local park that is known for homosexual activity. For a month he was followed by one of our own private investigators who had seen him with a different prostitute every week and he was even spotted at a gay bar a couple of times. The last prostitute he had been with at the park turned out to be an undercover cop.

For the last three months Liz had assigned me the religion section, but mainly focusing on scandals in churches. Pastor Lowe was the third pastor I exposed not operating in integrity. It's a tough job, but it's what I have to do if I want to get the bills paid. Being a Christian it feels wrong to expose other Christians, but this is my job and it's not my fault they don't practice what they preach.

As Liz and I came near the lobby Pastor Lowe was pacing back and forth with the newspaper in his hand. His five o'clock shadow covered his face and his lips were pursed together perhaps preparing himself to give us a mouth full of his dissatisfaction.

As we got closer I couldn't help, but hope that the meeting wouldn't last too long because I needed to finish a story by noon and get started on a story about a minority owned business and also write a review on an independent film that was being released on DVD tomorrow. The story I need to finish by noon would be my third story. We had to turn in three stories every day. It's not too bad considering at other daily newspapers reporters may have to turn in four or five a day. Along with covering religion and culture I covered stories on minority owned businesses and I was also a film critic reviewing new movies on the big screen and on DVD. That's why I'm a film buff.

"Hello Mr. Lowe," Liz said reaching out to shake his hand. "I'm Eliza…"

"It's Pastor Lowe and where do you get off writing this filth about me," Pastor Lowe yelled not shaking Liz's hand. He walked up to me. "I should sue you for defamation of character." I wanted to push him off me because he was invading my personal space, but Liz stepped in.

"Sir, Mr. Wells didn't write a story just to write a story. There's video footage showing you frequently visiting the Ortega Basin Park as well as Reign Bo Bar."

Pastor Lowe turned his attention to Liz. "I was there witnessing to patrons of the park and bar."

"The prostitutes you had sexual activity with were interviewed and they confirmed you were one of their Johns. The arresting officer caught you ready to pay for sex."

"How could you do this to me? My wife is filing for a divorce and she's planning to take the kids with her. I'm going to lose my church." Tears started falling down his face. "My life is over. How do you people sleep at night?"

"I just consume a lot of Nyquil."

"Look Pastor Lowe we're sorry this happened and excuse me for being blunt, but this is something you brought on yourself," I said, as his head was hanging down. "I don't know how or if this is something you have been doing longer than a month, but you were caught doing this when you could have stopped anytime. Things may be horrible right now, but you can turn things around. Pastor Lowe it will probably be hard, but you can start over. Doesn't it say in Proverbs 3 verse 11 that you should not despise the Lord's discipline or resent his rebuke because the Lord disciplines those he loves. I know I'm probably the last person you would want to hear that from, but in this trying time you should seek God's love."

"I will be leaving now," Pastor Lowe said looking at me. "I'm sorry...I'm sorry." He walked out of the office.

"This is the part of my job I hate most," Liz said folding her arms.

"What's that," I asked.

"Making people we write stories on feel like idiots for trying to make it seem like we're incompetent."

"Liz you need Jesus."

"Keep praying for me."

* * * * *

It was near noon and all that could be heard throughout the editorial side of the office was the pounding of keys and paper being printed as we were all rushing to beat our deadlines.

"Hey Ruben," said Cory Delk, another reporter who covered the real estate beat. "What was that movie with Jack Nicholson where he's investigating an adulterous affair that ends up involving something bigger in some kind of water scandal?"

"That's Chinatown," I replied.

"Thanks."

My top five favorite movies of all time are Heat, Good Will Hunting, Braveheart, The Godfather, and Glory. Of course honorable mention goes to Ray. It was a great movie, but my top five have been out longer. It's a part of my top ten list along with The Quiet Man, Scent of a Woman, Forrest Gump, and The Lion King. Yes, I said the Lion King. Even though they're not in my top ten lists, I did enjoy The Star Wars Trilogy, Indiana Jones trilogy, The Matrix trilogy, and The Lord of the Rings trilogy.

I also did some freelance work for SA Prevalent, a weekly newspaper that focuses strictly on culture, entertainment, and art. I had a column called "Choose This Day", that appeared in the paper every week. I got paid $200 per column. With permission from Liz I was allowed to do it.

My column appeared in their paper for the last three months. I went to them for the idea and it got some positive responses in the comment page of their web site. At first it was just going to appear every other week, but they saw how much readers loved it so they decided to have me write it every week. In it I wrote about life and the different issues we come across in life and how we choose to address what life throws at us.

The Editorial and Advertising departments were rivals and couldn't stand each other like the Bloods hating the Crips or dogs not being able to stand the sight of cats. We got along well with the creative/production department, as they're like the mediators in our quarrel. They were the holy ground or neutral territory where peace was bestowed.

We also got along well with Circulation, as they were just pleasant people to be around.

I don't know what started this rivalry, but it's gone on for years. I think in any publication the Editorial and Advertising departments can never get along.

The people in our advertising department feel they're better than everyone else is and there wouldn't be a paper without them. I can somewhat agree with the latter, but there would be no point in having a newspaper if you didn't have stories. Besides we have thousands and thousands of readers for 17 years.

I was thinking about dropping this profession and getting involved with real estate. In February, I completed a total of 150 hours of real estate courses. Now all I had to do was take the national and state exams and pass them to qualify for my salesperson license. I scheduled to take it next month. I've heard that only about 30 percent pass it the first time. I was hoping to be in that percentage.

Getting in real estate might not be the best thing to do as the economy is not in the best shape, but a lot of people want to sell their houses at any price someone can afford. It would probably be best to start off part-time in real estate just to see how things progress.

I was finishing up a story I did on this advertising/public relations firm, Rabbit's Foot, created by three Latinos who were all 26. They had been in business for two years and in the midst of the economy collapsing their company was already making $3.2 million in revenue, but I had to report to this meeting that my publisher just called.

He wanted to speak to everyone in attendance, as he stood in the middle of the newsroom.

Our publisher's name was Keith Kimball. With his silver hair and thin frame, he was always clean cut wearing a tie with buttoned long sleeve shirts and slacks creased with shoes that were always shining. He resembled Clint Eastwood.

Once everybody from all the departments gathered around he spoke.

"I'm sorry to have you all step away from your work," he said. "But, I have received some news that I feel should be shared in person and not by email." He dropped his head and bit his bottom lip. He picked his head back up and was going to speak, but he remained silent. His hands were rested on his hips, as he dropped his head again. This must have been some very disappointing news that he was sharing with us. He picked his head up. "As you know times are tough in our economy. It's affecting every industry and the journalism industry isn't immune. The Express News has been the leading newspaper of San Antonio, but we have still put out a great product. I just want to say that you have all done excellent work. And it is with great sadness that I must tell you that Alamo City News will be closed for business two weeks from today. I know this comes as a shock, but if there's any questions you have please see me in my office."

Some people were in an uproar while others were silent, as Mr. Kimball walked to his office. Tears were falling down Liz's face. It bothered me, but I hated working for a newspaper. I thought when I left here it would be on my own terms, not someone telling me I had to leave. In a way I was getting my wish. It's time to update my resume and start looking for a new job. I hate Mondays.

It's choice – not chance – that determines your destiny

~Jean Nidetch~

8

Don't Stop Til You Get Enough

After hearing a couple of days ago that I would be unemployed in less than two weeks I needed to get out and take my mind off of the disappointing news.

Unemployment isn't the worst thing in the world compared to getting your container ship hijacked. Saw on the news that some Somali pirates boarded a container ship called Maersk Alabama that was in route to Mombasa, Kenya. The captain of the ship was being held hostage by the pirates. My prayers are with the captain and the crew of that ship. If this ends on a positive note there could probably be a film made about it.

Every other Wednesday night I played with The Foundation. Unfortunately, this Wednesday Alejandro got sick so we had Torres fill in on bass. Along with writing, he could also play bass. Is there anything this man couldn't do?

It was a packed house, which means the Spurs weren't playing. And Raquel was the lead vocalist tonight. As she was singing a song that had me thinking our band was led by Alicia Keys I was multi-tasking playing the ebony and ivory keys and checking out Bianca who cracked a smile while she sat alone in a dark booth.

After the song was over we took a break and would be back to perform in twenty minutes. In that given short amount of time I was going to make the most of it with Bianca.

Walking over to her I kept my hands in my pockets, as if she was dangerous to touch. She got up and gave me a hug along with a moist kiss on the cheek.

"You look nice," she said. I was wearing my thick frame glasses with a navy blue beanie covering my head along with a sky blue suit, white button shirt, and some white Giorgio Brutini shoes that were as white as rice. My teeth were holding my empty pipe.

"Let me get a look at you," I said. Instead of curls her long hair was straight. She was dressed casual with a black blouse and tight turquoise jeans that cut off at the knees along with black open toe heels. "You are looking really good in those jeans. If only you were single."

"What would you do if I was?"

"Stop it, I'm trying to behave."

"I'd love to see how you are when you're misbehaving."

"Don't get me started." She smiled. We sat down in the booth. I could feel her hips, as well as the phone in her pocket. I took off my glasses and rubbed my eyes. Paranoia was in the air, as I looked around the nightclub for any suspicious characters that were watching us.

Bianca put her hand on my leg that was shaking. That nervous energy had to be released somehow. "Hey you need to relax," she said sensing what I was thinking. "My husband is far from us and there's nobody here that can report back to him. Besides, my husband

and all his friends enjoy country music. He also enjoys a little hip-hop, but trust me nobody knows that I am here, okay."

"Okay."

"Besides, what do you have to feel guilty about?"

"Well…"

"I came out here to see my friend who's in a band play and I'm just out here enjoying myself having a friendly conversation with a good friend."

"Yeah you're right." Due to staying cautious my fingers were still shivering, as if they were freezing.

"So what's with the pipe?"

"I just like pipes. I feel sophisticated when I'm seen with one." She laughed. "I don't fill it with tobacco and I know it looks strange to walk around with an empty pipe, but it's peculiar and I don't mind being peculiar. Plus I'm a big Sherlock Holmes fan."

"Kind of makes you look like a douche doesn't it."

"Maybe, but what do I care. After all I'm a douche."

"It's kind of cute," she smiled. "You're brilliant on that piano."

"Thank you."

"I wonder what else you can do with those fingers of yours." She leaned in a little closer to where she was invading my space. I looked at her and smiled not sliding away from her.

"You are too much. So what would you say is your favorite movie?"

"That's what you want to talk about?"

"Yeah, what's the problem?"

"I'm in my stripper heels, some tight jeans that show how well rounded my butt is, and a blouse that is showing a significant amount of cleavage and you just want to talk about my favorite movie?"

"Yes, I'm trying to avoid talking dirty after dark…so let's talk about movies."

"Okay, well I have to say my favorite movie is Gladiator."

"Really," I said leaning back.

"Yeah, why does that surprise you?"

"I'm impressed because most women would say some chick flick like Stepmom, Fried Green Tomatoes or The Joy Luck Club."

"I'm different from most women."

"Yes you are," I said scanning her body.

"What's your favorite movie?"

"My favorite movie of all time is Heat directed by Michael Mann and starred two of my favorite actors Al Pacino and Robert DeNiro," I said looking in her eyes.

"It's a great movie. So why is that your favorite one because most men I know say either Braveheart or The Godfather?"

"Well those are on my top ten list, but I love Heat not only because it has my favorite celebrities in it, but the story line was great. It dealt with the personal lives of a detective and a thief and you don't see that in a lot of movies like that. It's a classic cops and robbers flick. Normally they just focus on one side, mainly the cop because the cop is always the hero. I like that they show the human side of these individuals because it shows they both pursue excellence in their careers and they have their flaws and besides being on different sides of the law they're not that much different. It kind of makes you think that if they were both on the same side, who knows they probably could have been the best of friends." She looked amused, as she rested her chin on her hands with a smile. "The best scene of the movie was that only scene that Al and Bobby were in together, in the cafe. Remember that."

"Yeah I do remember that."

"It was cinematic history because it was the first time these two legendary actors appeared together in the same scene."

"It's not the first time they've done a movie together however, Godfather Part 2."

"You know your movies, intriguing. That café scene was filmed on location at Kate Mantilini, on Welshire Blvd. in Hollywood. A couple of years ago a friend and I visited that café and sat at the table they sat at in the movie. Matter of fact there's a long picture from that scene hanging over the entrance to the restaurant. Excuse me if I sound like a geek, but I'm a bit of a movie buff because it's part of my job to talk about movies as a film critic."

"That's alright. I hear some people talk about movies saying they were cool or they sucked. When you ask them why they can't give you a good enough reason, so I don't mind you being vivid."

"Correction, talking about movies was part of my job."

"I'm sorry to hear about that. How are you doing with the news?"

"It is what it is and what it is, sucks at the moment. But in a way I'm getting what I wanted because I always said I wouldn't be a reporter forever. I'm getting a way out. Just need to figure out what I'm going to do full-time to make some good money. Just doing freelance work or performing in clubs can only take me so far."

"Who is your favorite jazz musician?"

"My favorite jazz artist of all-time is Thelonious Monk."

"Who's Thelonious Monk?"

"Who's Thelo…" I grabbed my chest faking a heart attack. "You don't know about the monk."

"No."

"Well I'll have to give you a history lesson." I put my glasses on like I was a scholar. "Thelonious Sphere Monk was one of the most inventive pianists of any musical genre. He had an innovative style that some of his devoted followers couldn't imitate. He had an improvisational style and he made many contributions to the standard jazz repertoire. Many would say that he was ahead of his time, but still deeply rooted in tradition. Along with Duke Ellington he was considered to be one of the century's greatest American composers. He was an interesting cat because while he was the most talked about, he was also the least understood artist in the history of jazz. I think what drew me to him was the mystery of the man."

"You like to think of yourself as a man of mystery."

My right leg was shaking and I was tapping on the table like I was playing an imaginary piano. "Sometimes I think people can't figure me out and I guess that makes me a conundrum."

"So why is that?"

I loosen my shoulders up a little bit. "Well I guess it's because…well from what my ex-girlfriends have told me is that I shield myself from the world. Now I have a few people I let in, but not everybody."

"So are you going to let me see the real Ruben Wells?"

"Maybe, if it was under different circumstances."

"That's fair."

"Do you go out a lot even when your husband is in town?"

"Yes I do."

"Why is that?"

"Because he doesn't care about what I do."

"Do you give him a reason to care?" She looked at me like I slapped her in the face. I just realized I said something that should have just stayed in my mouth. "I'm sorry I didn't mean it like that…"

"No, no it's okay. I try to get him to go out with me, but he never wants to go out with me. He would rather stay home with a beer in his hand while watching television. When he takes a shower I try to join him, but he won't let me come in. I'll even wear sexy lingerie for him and he goes to sleep."

"Wow, he really doesn't care. If I was married to you I would either go out with you or do all sorts of things with you if we stayed home."

"I don't know if you would say that after 12 years of marriage."

"I guess you'll never know."

"Oh you're smooth," she smiled while taking a sip of her apple martini. "You smell good."

"Thank you."

"Why is a handsome, intelligent, articulate, tempting, simply irresistible man like you still single?"

"You really meant all that stuff," I laughed. She nodded her head. "The real reason is because I don't have time to deal with drama." She looked at me confused. "I like doing what I want when I want without having to think about someone else's feelings. I like not having that feeling that I have to be responsible for someone else."

"So it's because you're selfish and you wouldn't know what it means to give your whole heart to someone."

"That sums it up."

"At least you're honest." She took another sip of her drink. "So you wouldn't want someone missing you, thinking about you or loving you."

"Oh of course, but for that to happen it has to be the right person. I would love to have someone to love, but I won't be with just anyone. A relationship just isn't a high priority for me at the moment, but maybe it will when I meet that special female."

"You sound like you're very particular."

"Well if we're talking about the rest of my life I feel that's necessary."

"Do you think I'm a catch?"

"So far from what I know about you I would say that you're a catch."

"So if I wasn't married would you pursue me?"

"Would you want me to pursue you?"

"Yes."

"You're not just saying that."

"I really mean it."

"If we met each other 14 years ago who knows what would have happened. Of course I would have still been in junior high while you were in high school." We both laughed. "What was the first thing you noticed about me besides my face?"

"After looking at your face I paid attention to your shoes."

"Really that's what you paid attention to?"

"Yeah that's what I was focused on."

"Well were they pleasing to the sight?"

"They were shiny and clean, which means you know how to take care of yourself. I think it also shows that you'll take care of a woman you share a relationship with. And with the different pair of shoes you have on right now it shows that you can be open to change." I smirked. "What?"

"No it's just kind of funny you say that I would be open to change because sometimes I feel like I have a little bit of a bad case of OCD."

"That is ironic."

"Why's that?"

"Well you're in journalism, which sometimes in that industry you never know what to expect, right?"

"Right you are."

"And you also play jazz music, which if you want to be really good you have to be open to improvisation right."

"Correct."

"It's just funny you would say that because a lot of great musicians were great because they were flexible and could adapt to changes."

"When it comes to music, I know how to let myself go and just cut off my boundaries."

In all the laughter and the conversation, we held I didn't realize that I had wrapped my arm around her. She didn't look disturbed at all by it, as she would sometimes rub my leg. We sat in the club in silence listening to the dj play Dave Koz. As we looked at each other she moistened her lips and her eyes narrowed in on me while she was biting her bottom lip causing me to reminisce on our first kiss. Thinking about it made me want to kiss her again. I continued looking at her, but I couldn't help, but crack a nervous smile.

"You look nervous, why," she asked softly, while grabbing my hand.

"You need to stop looking at me like that."

"Like what."

"You're looking at me with those hungry eyes of yours." She laughed. "You've got that look like you want some Ruben Wells." She patted my leg while she laughed. Dang, why did she have to be married? "Thelonious Monk is my favorite jazz musician, but my favorite musician of all time is Michael Jackson." She cocked her head to the side, as if I said something weird. "I know I may have spoiled a moment, but I ain't misbehaving so I'm just changing the subject."

"Really, why is he your favorite?"

"Why, I say why not?" She looked at me like I was crazy. "Now I know he seems bonkers and maybe he really did do something to those kids or maybe he didn't, but the only ones who really know are him and the kids. And set aside the change in his skin tone and all the nose jobs he had and forget about him no longer looking like a human being, but what he's contributed to music, it will be a long time before anyone can surpass all that he has accomplished thus far."

"You've got a point there."

"Watching him perform at a very young age is what inspired me to get into music. Who would you say is your favorite musician?"

She thought about it for a moment. "Ooh, I've got to go with Sade, she's the greatest."

"You have some great taste in music. Sade is definitely in my top ten lists." Speaking of Sade, the club was playing her song "No Ordinary Love." "Oh they need to turn that off. Her music is baby making music."

"I know that's true because I got pregnant from listening to No Ordinary Love." We both laughed.

"Sade's Lovers' Live is a great album."

"That's probably my favorite one."

"I would have never thought Sade was a forty something woman. She is alluring.

"So have you ever made love to a woman while playing Sade?"

"Well, no."

"Who have you played while making love to a woman?"

"Well…I'm not sure how to answer that."

"What do you mean?"

"You won't believe me if I told you."

"Told me what?"

I was hesitant to speak the words that would come out of my mouth. I knew what route this conversation would take if I answered her question. It could possibly lead to her coming to my place tonight or immediately leave me alone. Either way I didn't want to take that chance, but she needed to know.

"Hey Ruben we need to get ready for the next set," Roland said. That was perfect timing; saved by the bandleader.

"Alright thanks." I looked at Bianca. "Well I need to get ready. You'll be here."

"Yeah, I'll be here all night," she said.

"To be continued."

"Who was the pretty young thing you were talking to," Roland asked as we walked back to the stage.

"She is a woman that is going to probably be the death of me."

* * * * *

We played until one o'clock in the morning and Bianca was there until the end. It was a little breezy outside while I was walking her to her car. I took off my coat and wrapped it around her shoulders.

We leaned against her car talking a lot about our professions and what's involved with them. Then our conversation segued into music and how it seems almost anybody can get a record deal. Somewhere in the conversation she interjected that her son and daughter were staying overnight with her mother.

I had to ask myself if I was really that endearing because she would look at me in adoration like I was from another planet. I felt a bond was being established that could never be broken between us. It felt wrong that I was emotionally intimate with her.

"You were great on that piano," she said. "Your band sounds really good."

"Thank you love," I said.

"It's almost like you're at home when you're on that stage."

"I get pumped on the nights I'll be playing like athletes before a game. Music is just something I'm passionate about. Music is something where creativity is endless. The thing that caught my interest about jazz music is that in America, the first generation that came out of slavery created jazz music. You know why?" Bianca shook her head. "Jazz music is a free-form expression. It comes from the soul, thus making it more real. Listen to me I'm just babbling on and on. I'm probably boring you. What would you like to talk about?"

"No, no you're not boring me. It's actually intriguing what you have to say. Not only are you passionate about jazz, but you're familiar with it, which probably makes it so easy for you to adapt to it." We both smiled.

"I could speak for days about jazz music and the influence it has on one's life. It's just something I love. It comes after God and my family of course."

"Of course," she smiled. "Maybe that's what you should pursue full-time."

"What, music?"

"Yeah, that's what you should pursue."

"I would probably need to live in Austin or Dallas, because San Antonio is more about Tejano music. Have you lived in San Antonio your whole life?"

"Yeah I have."

"Do you ever think about leaving?"

"Honestly, no, but I don't mind traveling. But I was born in San Antonio and I'll be buried here because this is home for me. What about you?"

"I like San Antonio, but I'm open to moving away from the city."

"Why would you want to leave?"

"San Antonio is one of the largest cities, but there are a lot of people here with that small town mentality where they're not open to change, but want to stick with tradition. I need to be at a place that's about thinking big."

"And you think you have OCD." I laughed. "Where would you want to go?"

"I'm looking into either Austin or Dallas. Austin is a great place for people who have musical aspirations and Dallas because it's all about handling business and living on the fast track. Of course I need a job first in either one of these cities to move there." There was a crowd of people walking out of Tucker Magee's.

"What time is it?"

"It's almost two. I was so caught up in the conversation that I forgot about the time."

"Yeah, we did get caught up."

"Well once again we must separate. Who knows when we'll see each other again?" There was a silence between us, as the wind blew. I could hear the siren of an ambulance on San Pedro Avenue. I could also see in the sky a plane descending as it was arriving at the airport. As Bianca's hair blew in her face I brushed it back behind her ear. She smiled, as I ran my fingers through her hair.

"Oh I do have a question for you?"

"What?"

"So what kind of music have you played while making love to a woman?"

I laughed. "Oh you weren't going to let that one go."

"You thought I forgot didn't you."

"I did." I bit my bottom lip contemplating what to say.

"Come on it can't be that bad."

"Well I've never made love to a woman. I'm not gay, but I'm just saying that I've never made love to a woman."

"Wait, are you telling me that you're still a virgin?"

"That… is… correct."

"Really, you're a virgin?"

"Yes."

"And you've been in a few relationships right."

"Yeah, I have."

"And you never had sex with any of them, not even oral sex."

"I never had sex of any kind with any of them. With the women I dated we just made out and there were times I may have felt a couple breasts and we may have had some grinding with clothes on moments, but that was the closest I came to having intercourse."

"Wow, that's impressive, that you've never had sex. So why are you still a virgin?"

"Honestly, sometimes I don't know. I do want to wait until marriage, but I don't know if I will ever get married. Sometimes I wonder what the point is in waiting. But you never know who will come into your life. I'm saving myself because it's a precious gift that can't be wasted. There are times though that it is frustrating to wait. There are times I just want to give it up, but in the end I feel that if I give in to premarital sex, I'll hate myself after having doing it. Pardon the pun." Or maybe I'll feel liberated relieving all the tension.

"That's understandable." We were quiet for a moment. We stood in silence like two sixth graders at a dance afraid to ask each other for a dance. "Would you like for me to give you a ride to your car?"

"Sure." I knew I should have just walked on to my car by myself, but I didn't know when I would see her again, so I wanted to make my time with her last as long as I could. We drove up in front of my car that was parked in the back of the nightclub. I told her to just go on ahead and park next to it so we wouldn't hold up traffic. She put the car in park turned the ignition off, but music was still playing on her stereo, as she had Sade's Greatest Hits playing. She unbuckled her seatbelt and rotated her whole body facing me.

As she did Roland was leaving with Torres. They took off in Roland's orange Mustang. Two other cars remained. The other car belonged to the owner and the 2005 black Explorer was mine. Tucker Magee, the owner of the club, came out and got in his car. When he pulled out he waved to us and we waved back. Now it was just the two of us in the parking lot.

Besides Sade being played it was quiet in the car. Bianca started rubbing her left leg. "So you mentioned you touched some girls' breasts," she said.

"Yes I have."

"So there are some things that you are open to."

"I'm a virgin, but I'm not exactly pure."

"Are you open to oral sex?"

"Honestly, even if I was married, I don't know if I would be so willing to have my wife go down south on me so early in the marriage. For some guys it's the greatest feeling in the world, but I wouldn't be so quick to get into it. It's just something I haven't been curious about. Plus, it would feel kind of weird kissing a woman knowing where her mouth has been. You know what I'm saying." She laughed while nodding her head.

"Has a girl ever copped a feel, like showing you she can do some handy work?"

"No."

"Is it something that you're curious about?"

"I'm not going to lie to you, but I am curious about that. So tell me, does me being a virgin arouse you?" She laughed. "The fact that I'm inexperienced in the sheets gets you all riled up doesn't it." After she laughed it was quiet again, as Sade's "Is It A Crime" began playing in the car. "It's funny that this song is playing now."

"Yeah," she laughed. "This is funny."

"I feel like I'm committing a crime sitting in a car alone with a married woman."

"It's cute how guilty you feel."

"Come on Bianca."

"No for real it's sweet." She touched my face. "You're a gentleman. Don't meet a lot of men like you. Most of the boys I meet claim to be men, but you're a man and you don't have to prove it. Trust me you're one of the good guys."

I took off my WWJD bracelet placing it in my pocket. She looked at me again with those hungry eyes of hers as her hand never left my face.

"I feel like being a bad boy."

With the back of my left hand I delicately rubbed her face. She kissed the palm of my hand, as it ran down her face.

"This ankle bracelet is really provocative on you," my voice got a little deeper, as if it wasn't deep enough.

"Thank you." Her voice softened up.

I saw the way she was looking at me with come-hither look. "I wish you would not look at me that way. It makes it harder for me to resist you."

"Sometimes I like things hard."

I paused for a moment seeing that she was using some innuendo. I was so tempted to jest and say "That's what she said," but I let that punch line pass.

"Would it be a crime for me to be touching your face right now?"

"No." She pulled my hand away from her face and placed it on one of her covered breast. "It would be a crime to my husband if he caught you touching my breast right now, especially if you rubbed it." As she let me rub her breast her head tilted back, as she was biting her bottom lip and a soft moan sneaked out of her mouth.

Dropping our barriers, I pulled her near me and our lips met once again. She wrapped her arms around me and began to lean back pulling me with her. The kiss didn't seem to last for an eternity, but it was long enough. I really wanted to whisper something sexy in Spanish in her ear, but she couldn't understand Spanish. Her tongue slid in my mouth and my tongue met hers.

The kiss was longer and sweeter than the first time we kissed and I felt more guilt. She pulled my hand away from her breast. I could feel her leading it to her jeans. As I touched one of her legs our eyes were locked on each other and I shook my head. We slowly backed away from each other.

"As much as I want to, I can't keep doing this Bianca," I said. "We can't talk to each other or see each other. First it starts with a conversation, then there's kissing, and next thing you know we'll be on a deeper level that only married people should be on. We can't do this any longer."

"I know," she said looking down.

"So let's just end this by kissing and saying goodbye."

"Okay."

We kissed one last time. I put all my effort into it wanting to give her something memorable since our lips would never be able to meet again.

After we kissed I got out of her car and walked to my vehicle.

I looked at her, as she rowed down the window.

"Goodbye Ruben Wells," she said.

"Goodbye Bianca Jones." As she pulled out of the parking lot she waved to me with a smile on her face. I waved back.

As she drove off I stood there watching her leave thinking that I would never see her again. The few hours we spent together I would forever remember as a time of pleasure and pain.

I was with the woman of my dreams, but she was married and I compromised myself. Felt vulnerable like a secret agent blowing his cover. Since she was the woman of my dreams part of me felt that it was all a dream and nothing ever happened.

But the harsh reality is that she was real and she belonged to another. This should have never happened, but I couldn't resist the tempting opportunity that was before me.

This is what happens when people start sightseeing what temptation has to offer. It seems a person will always do the opposite of what they would normally do when they get caught up in the moment. As the thunder rolled I ran into my Explorer not taking that chance that the lightening would strike me.

* * * * *

It was still early in the morning, but it felt like it was noon. Good thing Thursdays are kind of a slow day at work because I was falling asleep at my desk. I saw online that there was a standoff in that Maersk Alabama ship situation. The captain was held hostage by the pirates on their lifeboat. This is getting intense.

To wake up I was listening to a CD that my mother gave me. For the last twenty minutes I had been enticed in the message that I was hearing. It was a message on singleness from her pastor, Raymond Carl. He was a middle-aged clean cut white man with a deep southern drawl as he was from a small town in Texas that I don't even think was on the map.

"Don't get me wrong being single is not a bad thing," he preached. "Some people have the misconception that almost makes it sound like they're codependent on a figment of their imagination." I could hear laughter in the congregation, while I saw some people in the office loading up some boxes or taking down pictures from their cubicle. "Even in your time of singleness you never feel like you're a half person still trying to find your other half to make you whole. I have never heard of someone's life drastically changing because they got a boyfriend or girlfriend. I remember before I got married while I was dating my wife I still had to get up and put my pants on the same way. I also had to learn how to still be a decent human being. That doesn't change when you're in a relationship…it shouldn't. Even though I was single I was still whole. Even in marriage I am a whole human. Some of you in your 20's or 30's are too old to be caught up in all the propaganda that comes with marriage. In singleness or marriage, life will still have its difficulties, but also its good times. People that are still single you need to make a choice to just live your life. Don't wait for your life to be perfect because it never will be. It's tough to hear that, but it's the truth."

I stopped listening to the message, as I decided to make a call.

"Hello," the woman said.

"Hey Deanna, it's me Ruben Wells," I said.

"Well, hello stranger. Glad to see that you actually called."

"It seemed fair seeing as how you accepted my friend request on Facebook."

"How have you been," she laughed.

"I've been doing well. I know its short notice, but would you like to join me for lunch today?"

When you have to make a choice and don't make it, that in itself is a choice

~William James~

9

Man in the Mirror

It was hitting over 100 degrees almost every day during June.

Deanna and I stayed in contact ever since we met for lunch a couple of months ago.

I didn't want to wake up one day seeing that I will have to keep my head shaved because of a receding hairline so I grew my hair out to show off my natural curls. I'll enjoy my hair while I can and hopefully that will be a very long time.

It was a late Wednesday night and after performing at Tucker Magee's I was at Deanna's place browsing the Internet while she was packing her suitcase. She wasn't leaving for good, but she was flying out to Chicago the next day for a job interview with a public relations agency that she would have on Friday morning.

Deanna should be a top prospect for any job because she graduated with honors, had military experience where she did some work in their public affairs department and community relations, and she was pleasant to be around. Plus, it was undeniable how attractive she was, which can make a prospective employee a major asset in public relations or advertising.

She had done a lot of other interviews since the middle of April in San Antonio, Austin, Houston, Dallas, Miami, New York and Atlanta, but Chicago was the one she really wanted.

Part of me hoped she would get the job, if this is what she truly desired, but there was another part of me that didn't want her to get it because I didn't want to see her go. The thought of her leaving was saddening, but this would be an opportunity I wouldn't want her to regret passing up. Especially for me!

God forbid, but what if it didn't work out between us. There were some things about her that bothered me, and vice versa, but it was things we could probably look passed.

She enjoyed listening to Frank Sinatra and Elvis Presley and had a turtle for a pet, but I still enjoyed her company. She liked basketball and football, but she mostly enjoyed watching baseball, which was completely boring.

I don't know if I was totally committed and submitted to her, but it looked promising. We hadn't officially called ourselves a couple, but we were acting like a couple kissing each other a lot and spending every spare minute we had with each other.

"So what does the company do again," I asked.

"They provide creative online and off-line branding expertise," she replied. "They specialize in digital design, marketing, and of course public relations.

"And what position are they interviewing you for?"

"It will be general manager. And who knows if I get hired and prove myself to be a major asset to the company they could possibly name me a partner."

"That's impressive. I also like the name of their company, Red Cloud. It's just unique."

"Eso es muy cierto." Deanna spoke about Chicago like the slaves spoke about the North, as if it were a promise land. She spoke highly about Red Cloud. It was as if they were the Disney Land of the workforce, the greatest job in the world. I couldn't help, but be excited for her.

While she was packing I was doing some research on Texas real estate laws, preparing for my real estate state exam that I would be taking on Friday afternoon.

I took the exam for the first time last month and failed the state portion of the exam by one question. I barely passed the national portion of the exam. So luckily I didn't have to take both again, just the state part. There was only another four more months left for me to pass it, but I wanted to get it out of the way. In the given time frame that was allotted to me if I didn't pass than I had to register all over again and take both exams again. It cost a lot of money to take the exams and I wasn't trying to be broke for some exams.

I gained an interest of real estate when I spoke with Torres' father who was a realtor. He talked about the money he was making and how much he enjoyed his profession. The sky is the limit as to how much you make because it's commission. When he spoke about real estate he was talking like a kid who got a basketball player's autograph. I wanted to be in a better financial situation and staying unemployed wasn't going to do that for me, so I decided to look into real estate where the amount of money accrued could be limitless. It required taking some initiative, having people skills, and being able to close a sale. I knew there was more to it than that, but I had all three of these qualities.

I also took an interest in it because I couldn't find a full-time job. The economy was affecting every industry making it tough to find a job anywhere. I wish Deanna luck because I couldn't find work myself even in public relations. Maybe I didn't have the credentials they were looking for. I could have left the private sector I had been in my whole professional career and go into the public sector working for the government, but they were strict with policies and procedures like the military. In a way, I wanted to be my own boss so I decided to pursue real estate. While receiving unemployment compensation I was still a columnist for SA Prevalent and I would also do some freelance writing for small Christian newspapers or magazines. They only paid $100 to $150 a story written. It wasn't much, but I had money for gas and groceries. I would also still perform in the nightclubs whenever a gig became available.

I never failed an exam until I took the real estate exam. It's vexing that the exams in the classes were so easy, but the material in the national and state exams was like taking a foreign language exam. I think I can pass the exam now that I've studied it a little more and just actually apply it to life.

"Ruben baby, come to bed," Deanna said sounding exhausted. I logged off the Internet and turned off her computer as well as the lamp in her living room. Her bedroom was pitch black.

"You all packed and ready to go," I asked as I took off my Dallas Cowboys t-shirt and fell under the soft sheets with her. I kept my gray muscle shirt on as well as my jeans.

"Yes I am." I was the blanket covering her body, as she wrapped my arm around her. I ran my other hand down one of her legs as she was wearing some blue shorts that could almost pass for underwear along with a white sleeveless t-shirt. I always loved touching her legs that were smooth and firm like marble.

I know that if people from my church knew that I was sleeping over at Deanna's place they would all look identical with frowns on their faces. In the singles ministry at my church they would teach that an unmarried couple shouldn't have sleepovers even if they don't have sex because it's still like shacking up and that wasn't right in God's sight. I heard what they would say, but personally I don't see anything wrong with having a sleepover. As long as there's no sexual intercourse, it shouldn't be a problem.

If Deanna moved to the windy city, maybe I would consider moving out there, after all Chicago needs some realtors. And there were plenty of publications I could do work for out there as well. Jazz music was popular out there. Maybe Common or Kanye West would want me to do some stuff for them if they heard me play any instrument. Plus Chicago had a professional basketball and American football team. They had two professional baseball teams, but I was never into baseball like Deanna. The snow and furious winds of Chi-town were something I would have to grow accustomed to. There's a reason it's called the windy city.

Deanna's possible move to another city inspired me. I was thinking that I could start off small moving out to Austin. Live there for a couple of years and hope my musical career takes off. Austin is the place to live in Texas if you want to build a career in music or even the film industry. It's also one of the top ten places for people in their 20s to live because it's lively.

But then again there's Dallas, which is a much bigger city than Austin. It was my kind of city where there's people on the move living life in the fast lane and another hot spot for musicians. San Antonio was home sweet home for now.

"So you tired baby," I asked kissing her shoulder.

"Yeah," she replied while rubbing her bare feet against mine.

"Why, you haven't done anything," I chuckled.

"Shut up," she laughed while slapping me on the arm.

"What time is your flight?" I could hear the wind blow hard, as if the trees were going to take flight, while thunder could be heard as if Thor was coming down with his mighty hammer.

"It's at 9:45 in the morning, which means we have to leave here before eight because you know the traffic on 410 will be ridiculous. I won't arrive in Chicago until close to four because I have that layover in Houston." She rubbed my hand. "Thank you again for agreeing to take me to the airport."

"De nada."

"You're too good to me," she said interlocking our fingers.

"Lo facilita demasiado."

Even though we were seeing each other almost every night we were stable enough to give each other some breathing room. I liked that she wasn't needy or clingy wanting to know my every thought or watch every move I make.

My reservations were the reason we hadn't officially called ourselves a couple. I hadn't dated any other women since we started talking, so some people would call that a commitment, but the moment we become official I felt like I had to be responsible for her. There would be no more room for surprises or nothing more to pursue once I decided to settle down. Yes it's selfish, but I had gone through too many relationships to know what to expect. I didn't want to find myself no longer wanting to be with Deanna. She is a one in a million. Even though we haven't said we're dating exclusively, we still acted like it, but I felt that if we said it, than like B.B. King said, "The thrill is gone baby."

And maybe I was afraid to move forward because I knew what a serious relationship required...letting go.

Normally a woman's face was something I could never forget. Bianca might as well have been one of those blurred faces they would have on the show COPS because no matter how hard I tried, I couldn't visualize her face when trying to remember her. And I couldn't find her on Facebook. God was definitely at work making sure I couldn't process her in my memory.

There were many times my fingers were itching to speed dial her to find out if she and her husband had gotten a divorce, but I didn't call and neither did she. I thought about her wondering if she was now happily married or still just married.

There were times I thought I could feel her near me. If I saw a short woman with curly hair I thought it was Bianca, but it was just my imagination. She would show up in my dreams and even in my dreams I couldn't have her. I used to heavily anticipate seeing her. I was hoping that I would see her walk through the door of the clubs I performed at. And if we couldn't talk to each other, I would have been content with just staring at her. That sounded creepy.

I was seeking her out like pirates searching for treasure. I should have been searching for God that way. I hadn't read my bible for awhile. Nor did I read any devotionals or attend any bible studies. I would have been content just to hear one word from Bianca, the same way God would have been happy to hear me call his name, which I hadn't done for a couple months. Not even to bless my meal.

I won't be surprised if I decide to exclusively date Deanna that the next time I see Bianca she'll probably be single and available to date me. I know my head is as big as a beach ball, but I really felt that if she did leave her husband she would give me a call to experience a new beginning.

Deanna was wonderful. At the moment I was content in having a relationship without any obligations. Things were flowing well with the current system we were under.

She met my parents at a Memorial Day barbecue and they loved her. They asked me why I hadn't asked her to marry me immediately. They loved the way she looked, the words that came out of her mouth when she spoke, the way she carried herself, and the way she made me feel…happy. Wow, I hadn't said that about a woman in a long time…since…since Monique. Deanna, a flame on the outside, who was really a gazelle on the inside, was probably meant to be my lioness.

A lioness is like the President's First Lady. A lioness is the woman who will walk by your side because you're both equal. A lioness will always have her lion's back. A lioness is your better half.

There were so many nights we stayed up late just talking and I found myself not ever wanting to leave her presence, but she respected me enough to not compromise my virginity in any way. There were some times that we had some close calls, but we never had sex.

She loved that I treated her like a lady and not a whore. She didn't find that in a lot of men she surrounded herself with. That's because none of them were a fine gentleman like me.

"Take your pants off," Deanna said as she was rubbing her legs against mine.

"What," I asked.

"Just so you can feel more comfortable."

"No I'm fine."

"You're not hot in those jeans?"

"I'm fine D, it's not a problem." I was sweating a little.

As we lay I felt aroused as I had my hand wrapped tighter around her stomach. Outside rain was pouring down. My jeans felt tight, as I was erect.

"Someone's getting a little excited," Deanna said sounding a little more alert and erotic than she did five minutes ago.

"Don't flatter yourself…just a little bit."

"That feels like more than a little bit." She began to slowly rub her butt into my crotch area. "You're as hard and long as a Louisville Slugger."

"Well…," I was losing my train of thought, as I slowly began to rub up against her.

I began kissing her neck. She turned around and we began to French kiss. As we kissed I got on top of her and we both kissed each other more aggressively, as if we were competing to be the best kisser.

The harder we kissed the more I was grinding. Along with the thunder came some lightening. As I would rub up against her she would moan. The more she moaned the more excited I got, because it was arousing hearing a woman moan.

"Oh baby, please take your pants off," she sounded almost as if she was begging. With that kind of tone I couldn't help, but oblige. Plus she asked politely. I took off my jeans and was stripped down to my blue shorts. I actually felt more comfortable.

My fingers were tugging on her shirt fighting the urge to slip it off and see her breasts. She wrapped her hands around my waist pushing me even closer to her as she wrapped her legs around mine. Her hands were tugging on my shorts fighting the urge to rip them off so that I could be inside of her.

Before I knew it she flipped on top looking down on me with some hungry eyes as she was straddling my thighs. Her body was moving on top of me like a snake being charmed out of a basket.

"Pueda lo toco," she asked.

How could I say no? "Toquelo," I replied.

Deanna pulled down my shorts and licked her right hand. With the same hand she grabbed my...well let's just say she grabbed a microphone. Her mouth looked like it was ready to speak into it. For the moment she was manually pleasuring me.

This never happened to me. I was speechless, as it was more relaxing than a back massage. She was firm, but gentle as her fingers were wrapped around my member and moving her fist up and down in a slow, steady motion.

Thunder was even louder, as more rain came down. The more I moaned, wait women moan...the more I grunted, yes grunted, she sped up her motion a little more. She had my toes curling as she put both hands on scaling down the shaft.

"You can do to me whatever you want," she whispered, as one of my hands felt her breasts. "Hazme el amor."

I wanted to throw away my ATM card, my abstinence 'til marriage card, and let us invade each other's privacy. I wanted to make love to her so bad. In a way we were already opening a door so why not walk through it. As we were both fighting the urge to go all the way she was stroking me faster, as if Tito Puente was playing the bangos at a rapid pace. I felt myself ready to erupt, but before I could I pushed Deanna off and ran into the bathroom.

It may not be true and maybe it's a way to scare kids into not having any kind of sexual contact, but I heard it was possible to get a girl pregnant even through outercourse. Pardon the ignorance, but I never got to view the sexual education video most kids watch when they're in the fifth grade. My parents didn't want me seeing any nudity. DARN THEM!

I let myself calm down while I stood in the bathroom. As I looked at myself in the mirror my libido was diminishing. I felt I didn't know this person I was looking at in the mirror. I felt like Lot, a Christian that wanted to be accepted by others even if that meant he had to compromise himself. Deanna was a great woman, she was a Christian, but even Christians can be unequally yoked.

Sometimes fire can be a man's greatest ally when he needs a hot meal or just needs to stay warm, but it can also be his greatest enemy when it destroys his home or even his life. Growing up in the church I would always hear that saying "do not be unequally yoked, light and darkness can't co-exist with each other." Most people associate that with Christians not being yoked with non-Christians, but sometimes there are some Christians you can't tie yourself too.

Deanna and I did everything together, but go to church. She stopped going to church for about a year because she felt she could still be closer to God without having to go to church. Even though I was regularly attending church, she probably was closer with God than I was.

But she didn't tithe feeling it was a waste of money. This was some of the stuff my parents didn't know that they would frown on. She would only go to church on Easter or for Christmas. Whenever I would talk about spiritual related topics it ended with us majority of time debating and agreeing to disagree.

Once I calmed down feeling my heart beat at a normal pace again I walked out of the bathroom.

* * * * *

Ruben came out of the bathroom and jumped back into bed with me. It was my first time touching him like that and it felt so good. I wanted to feel him like that more and more, but only if he saw me as his girlfriend and not just someone he could hook up with. We would go out in public where he would take me out to eat or go see a movie. Heck he even went shopping with me, even if it meant all he was doing was carrying my bags. There just had to be something more between us than being make out buddies. He introduced me to his family. That tells me he wants a relationship.

And since he is a virgin, letting me touch his...well I don't know how else to be tactful about it...his penis...that has to mean something. After what just happened I can't let him act as if it wasn't a big deal. I would be remiss if I didn't ask him where we stand.

"Ruben, can I ask you something," I asked facing his back.

"No, don't say that," he said burying his head under the pillow possibly thinking it would make him invisible. "Please don't say that!"

"What?"

"Whenever a woman says that it's always something serious they want to ask and the question ends up leading to an argument that jeopardizes the relationship." He sat up with his back against the wall. "Plus it's late, I'm tired, and why couldn't you ask me what was on your mind earlier when I was alert and active. You know that a man's testosterone level is low in the late afternoon. Why couldn't you have asked whatever you wanted to ask me around that time?"

"It's just a simple question that requires a simple answer," I replied looking up at him while resting my head on the pillow.

"Whenever a woman needs to ask me something it never ends well for me."

"Ruben!"

"Okay, what is it?"

"Where are we going with this…connection…relationship?"

"Oh," he replied getting up from the bed like he had a cramp in his leg. I turned the lamp on. "Come on Dee, it's too late for this. Why can't we just let things be the way they are?"

"What does that mean?"

"We like spending time with each other. Can't we just leave it at that?"

"We've been spending every available minute we have with each other for awhile now." He was walking back and forth while I stayed in bed with my arms folded. "Come on papi, we connect well with each other. What we just did I don't do with just any guy. And I know that you don't do that with just any girl. I know we didn't go all the way, but it meant something to me. We haven't dated anyone else, yet we don't want to be identified as exclusive, so what direction are we trying to lead to?" He stopped pacing and just stared at me. I could only think two things were going to happen. Either way he was going to be a coward by grabbing a pillow and try to suffocate me or put on his clothes and just walk out the door avoiding this conversation. "Do you still want to keep your options open? Do you want something serious or do you still just want to be, to a certain degree, friends with benefits?"

"Things are convenient the way they are. Why do you have to ask me this now? Where is this coming from?"

"Can you blame me for asking? You've introduced me to people important to you. If we're not together we talk on a regular basis. I feel like in the last month and a half we have grown closer with each other. I'm ready to be exclusive, I want us to be a couple, but I know you have your reservations. I don't know for sure we're meant to last forever, but I'm willing to take a chance and find out." He turned around and looked out the window. I got out of the bed and walked over to him placing my hands around his waist. Maybe I'm being too intrusive. Maybe it's hard for him to commit to someone because he's still not over her. Perhaps he's having a hard time letting go, even though it ended a while back. Maybe he never really took the time to get over her because he never thought anyone could take her place. "Sometimes I feel like you close yourself off from me. Sometimes I feel like you're waiting for someone else to come along. I feel as if you expect me to be like her. Sometimes I feel you're waiting on her to come back or you expect me to be like her. I can only be me." He was still quiet, while my head leaned up against his broad shoulders.

"You have never mentioned her until now."

"I respect what you had with her, but I just want to know if you see me as an appetizer or am I the main course you've been waiting for?" He laughed. "Hey don't laugh."

"I'm sorry, but that sounded corny."

"I don't know how else to put it, but you know what I mean. Am I an option or a priority?" I smoothly ran my hands up and down his stomach like I was petting a dog.

"Dee…"

"You don't have to give me an answer right now. It's just something for you to think about." I kissed the back of his neck. "Come on let's go to sleep."

* * * * *

As I was joining her in bed she turned the lamp off. As she rested her head on my chest about to fall in a deep and peaceful rest my eyes were staring out the window wondering if this relationship was the last thing I needed. I came to the unfortunate and unpleasant realization that no matter how great a woman Deanna was, she was an appetizer that couldn't fill my hunger.

My heart wasn't with her. In marketing you have to find a need and fill it. Deanna was filling my need to no longer feel lonely, not to feel loved.

"You okay baby?" she asked.

"I'm fine," I said kissing her on the lips knowing that I wasn't fine.

After five minutes of lying down with each other she fell asleep.

She had a CD player on her nightstand. I put an old message from Pastor Harper in the disc player and covered my ears with some headphones. It was the second part of his series on sexual sin.

"We're told from society and the media, especially in movies, that we couldn't possibly live without sex," Pastor Harper said. "We're told that if we indulge ourselves into sexual activity that our life will have a copious amount of joy. But yet, they can't tell you the truth, which is that a relationship with God can meet such a claim. Don't get me wrong, sex is beautiful and it's pleasurable, but it's temporary. Having spiritual oneness with God is much more important because it's much more valuable." There was applause in the church. When there was no more applauding Pastor Harper brought up another point. "Another deception that the devil likes to bring to you is that you don't have to be "in the know" as to whether or not the person you are with is the one you are meant to marry unless you experience sexual intimacy with him or her. Church pay attention to me, single people especially I want you to hear me. Compatibility isn't defined by good sex. Compatibility is defined by how you can serve that other person. People fail to realize that God isn't against sex. It's premarital sex that he doesn't favor. God wants married couples to cultivate their sexuality within the sanctity of marriage. I think that if you step outside that boundary, couples that are engaging in premarital sex or even extramarital affairs don't really have the opportunity of feeling free to be themselves because they are going to worry if they're fulfilling someone else's expectations. They can't enjoy themselves because they're too worried about being accepted."

After hearing that I fell asleep holding Deanna, as we were all together separate.

It is about choices we make. And how the direction of our lives comes down to the choices we choose – Catherine Pulsifer

Chapter 10 - Preparation

Torres and Shiloh both had the day off from work on the first Friday of June so we met up at the Regal Fitness gym for a workout session. Later this afternoon I was taking my real estate exam. Hitting the weights was helping me relax as well as relieving the tension I was feeling from my conversation with Deanna a couple of nights ago.

None of us looked like bodybuilders, but we were all hitting the weights hard like we were in a weightlifting competition. They were spotting me, as I finished barely pushing up 265 pounds on the bench press.

"What's going on fellas," Buster asked walking up to us in a red polo shirt and black shorts with an issue of SA Prevalent in his hand.

"Hey what's up Buster," I said.

"Ruben, are you trying to piss God off?"

"What are you talking about Buster," Torres asked.

"I'm talking about the latest story our boy did on another pastor caught in a scandal."

"Hey I just present the facts, there are no opinions," I replied. "The man of God was stealing funds from the church that was supposed to go to a building fund and that building fund ended up being a time share in Miami as well as a condo for his mistress. His church members needed to know what their offerings were actually contributing to."

"Yeah well I guess what's done in the dark will be found in the light right," Shiloh replied.

Buster moved away from me with a wide step towards Torres.

"What's up with you," I asked looking at him like he was crazy.

"I didn't want to be near you just in case God poured down his wrath on you," Buster said.

"Whatever Buster," I replied waving him off while everyone else laughed.

"How has your first week at work been Bust," Torres asked. Buster had been working part time as a personal trainer at Regal Fitness Gym for a week. He was always running through different jobs like he did women.

"Not too bad. This is definitely a great way to meet the ladies." Women was all Buster ever thought about. "Well I'll see you gentlemen around." He had his eyes on a blonde with a tan and some huge breasts. "It looks like there's a member that needs my assistance," he said walking off.

"He seems to have a new girl every other day or every other week."

"With all those women he's been with he needs to seriously get himself checked out at the clinic," Shiloh said.

"Torres do you think you can avoid having sex until marriage," I asked.

"Yeah, I do," Torres replied.

"So when are you going to get married?"

"I'll get married as soon as I get a woman that wants to marry me." I laughed. "Someone once said the cure for love is marriage, and the cure for marriage is to love again. Well that's all good for the married folk, but what's the cure to singleness. I've been single a very long time and it seems everywhere I go I see nothing, but couples. It's as if I'm surrounded by nothing, but people who are in relationships. I even see dogs or cats that are together, as if we're back in the days of Noah getting prepared for a flood. One day I hope to have that." He focused his attention on an elderly couple with matching sky blue jogging suits that walked around the indoor track at the same pace.

They looked feeble as if they didn't eat a meal in days, but completeness was written over their faces. They were so strong that no one could loosen the grip of their wrinkled hands because they had walked side by side for many decades. While the joggers around them ran like they were in a 400-meter dash they continued to walk, peacefully maintaining their pace.

"When you see them you see that they have been through their seasons of give and take," Torres said. "They have learned to be strong for each other. They have discovered that intimacy extends outside the bedroom and it doesn't always have to be in between the sheets. In their union they have arrived at different seasons that most couples can only dream of. Um, single people for that matter."

"My whole thing on that matter is that a relationship will happen when it's meant to happen," Shiloh said. "And Torres what did I tell you about being corny?"

"Shut up Shi."

"Please Shi, you can have any woman you want," I replied. "Compared to all the women Buster has had, he's probably still trailing you." Torres and Shiloh looked at each other laughing. "What's so funny?"

"He doesn't know," he asked Torres.

"I thought maybe you told him," Torres said.

"I don't know what," I asked.

"Hey Wells, I'm still a virgin too man," Shiloh said confidently.

"What, shut up."

"No it's true. Now I'm not as pure as young Torres here. I've made out with quite a few women, I've given some massages, and I may have even felt a breast or two, but I never actually did the deed. My zipper has stayed zipped up."

"No offense, but I find that hard to believe."

"I could say the same thing about you."

"Well I mean you look like you could have any woman any time of the day and you mean to tell me that you have never had sex."

"Never have man."

"How do you control yourself?"

"I've been in some situations that were difficult to walk away from and have been given tempting offers that I wanted to consider indulging myself in and I have even been confronted with a naked woman, but in the end I guess I thought about the consequences. I could say that I want to please God and honor him in all my ways, but if you want to be practical I'll say that I would be too concerned about getting a girl, that I'm not in love with, pregnant or catching a disease. I know I could wear a condom, but are they 100 percent reliable? Plus I hear they take away some of the enjoyment."

"Do you carry a condom?"

"I'm not going to lie, but I have been carrying one. I've been carrying it for so long that it probably won't do the job it's supposed to do." We all laughed.

"Do you guys ever worry that the person you marry may cheat on you or divorce you? And then you're left wondering why did I save myself for someone that ended up betraying me?"

"Sometimes I do think about that, but if I'm with the person God had originally planned for me to be with than I don't have to worry about that," Torres responded. "In order for it to work we both have to agree to not cheat on each other when times get rough or not make divorce an option and just stay strong and work hard when things get tough. We have to have an old school mentality. Like that elderly couple on the track if we were to ask them what their secret was to a lasting marriage they would probably say that when things got hard we didn't run away from each other, but worked hard together to make it last forever. It says in Jeremiah 29:11, God's plans are not meant to harm me, but to give me a hope and a future. That's something I have to trust in. Why do you ask Ruben?"

"I wonder if it's really worth the wait."

"Do you carry a condom?"

"Yeah, I do."

"Why," Shiloh asked.

"Just in case that moment comes I want to be prepared. I always live in preparation. I can say that I'll wait until marriage, but what if I get myself in a situation that I don't want to turn back from, at least I'll be ready for it. I know you carry one Shiloh, but do you carry one Torres?"

"No," Torres answered.

"Why don't you carry one," Shiloh asked. "Are you sure that's smart. To me it's not very wise to leave home and be without it."

"This may sound preachy, but I want to honor God in such a way that I wouldn't put myself in a situation where I would be tempted to give into my desires at an inconvenient time." Dang that was preachy. Poetic, but preachy. "It's almost like me saying I'm going to go out on a freeway and learn how to dodge the cars instead of just choosing to stay off the freeway. If I see a burning building I'm not going to run in there and see if I can walk out without being burned. The best thing for me to do is to just avoid it and let the firefighters do what I'm not qualified to do. I'm not trying to come off as self-righteous, but you know me. You know that when I say I'm going to do something I'm going to do it. The way I see it is if I say I'm maintaining abstinence until marriage than that's what I'm going to do. I want to honor my relationship with God. By doing that I'm honoring the woman God has in store for me saving myself for her and no one else."

"So you love God more, than you do pussy." Shiloh replied keeping a straight face, making Torres and I laugh. When he saw us laugh he cracked a smile. As soon as Torres stopped laughing he continued on with his point.

"If you want to put it that way, yes I love God more. So there's no point for me to carry a condom because I know I'm not going to put myself into a situation where I know I can't resist the temptation. And sometimes condoms don't protect you." Torres didn't talk much, but when he spoke he was thought provoking.

"You're stronger than me." We all laughed, as we began clearing the weights off the bar.

"I don't advise you to give in, but we're all grown men and we're going to make our own decisions. And I'm well aware that when the moment comes, it's difficult to pass it up, but one of the things I heard about premarital sex is that it can do two things to a relationship."

"What's that?"

"Sometimes it will either end a good relationship or it can prolong a bad relationship. If you end up getting with someone make sure it's with someone you really love or care about and make sure they love and care about you as well, otherwise, this sexual intimacy that is supposed to be beautiful will end up turning ugly."

"My man, when are you going to come out with a novel?"

"You need to stop playing around and get something on the bookshelves," I added.

"You never know, but maybe I'll do it when Shiloh is in a big budget film or makes an appearance on a tv show that is not reality-based or maybe when you come out with a CD," Torres replied.

"True that."

Strangely enough beautiful women were at the gym. I thought they would all still be asleep getting their beauty rest or at work. Torres noticed a petite, beautiful light skin black woman with features similar to Jada Pinkett Smith lifting some 15-pound dumbbells.

I encouraged him to go talk to her. As he hesitantly walked to her, Shiloh and I heard him muttering the name Veronica Mencia. I imagine the first step he took towards the Jada Pinkett Smith lookalike his heart pounded.

"Who's Veronica Mencia," Shiloh asked.

"Veronica Mencia was the first girl that ever rejected Torres when he was in the sixth grade," I replied. "He accidentally let it slip out to one of his friends that he liked her and soon word spread throughout the halls of Coke Stevenson Middle School that Torres liked Veronica and wanted to marry her. When the news came to Veronica she emasculated him by laughing hysterically in front of his face. He told me her laugh hurt so much that it cut like a blade."

"It looks like the more steps he takes the more rejections he is remembering." Torres got close to the Jada Pinkett Smith lookalike. "Hasn't even said a word to her and he already looks wounded."

"Hi, how are you," Torres said hesitantly, as she was wiping sweat from her forehead.

"Hello," she said looking preoccupied. She looked at him strange because while he spoke to her he was looking down on the ground and his body was wobbling back and forth like he had to use the restroom.

"I uh, I uh, don't mean to interrupt uh you in the middle of your workout. I was just uh, uh wondering what your uh name was." Torres wasn't as skillful with socializing as he was with writing.

"Are you okay because you look like you need a bathroom break," she asked with a concerned look on her face.

"Huh." It looked as if he was going to burst. His head was sweating profusely and it wasn't from a workout. "Oh this was a bad idea, I'm sorry I interrupted you."

Torres quickly walked away before he could further embarrass himself.

"What the heck was that," I asked.

"I told you I wasn't ready for that," he replied. He saw the Jada Pinkett Smith lookalike leaving. "Man she thought I needed to use the restroom."

"Well can you blame her for thinking that," Shiloh quipped. "It's a miracle you didn't go at that moment."

"I can't come back to this gym anymore because every time she sees me she's going to laugh."

"You know who that was right?"

"She was another woman that I struck out with."

"Not only that, but that was Miss Jazz from Jammin' 94.1 FM radio."

"What?" He looked back as she was wiping her neck. "No, that can't be her."

"Yes, that was her."

"Dang it, now she's going to have a funny story to tell on the radio for all of San Antonio and probably Texas to hear. Dang it Ruben this is your fault."

"Be quiet," I replied. "You'll be fine. You just need to practice more on this. You also need to relax when you talk to a woman. Women love to be approached and they fear rejection just as much as we do. You just need to remember to play it cool and not make it seem like you're approaching a celebrity or Wonder Woman."

"Miss Jazz is a local celebrity."

"HOOK...LINE...and SINKER," Buster said as he was walking back to the office. "Hey Torres I think you better go catch her because she walks off with your dignity."

"Oh shut up Buster before I give you a busted lip." Buster kept on walking as he was laughing loud like a hyena. "Man let's work out."

"Yeah you need to loosen up and work off that tension," Shiloh replied. While we were lifting dumbbells Shiloh was trying to give Torres a pep talk. "Torres my boy, when it comes to women you need help."

"Oh gee thanks," he sarcastically replied.

"You desire to be in a relationship with a woman, but are afraid to take a risk with any woman. You need to learn how to talk to a woman with confidence."

"And you're the man that's going to teach me how…my own Hitch."

"Don't be like that man. I'm just looking out for you." I have to agree with Shiloh. I think that's what Torres was lacking in his life…confidence that he was better than he thought he was.

"Torres you've always been good looking; you just aren't aware of it," I chimed in. "I'm secure in my sexuality to say that another man is good looking. That's just a part of my confidence." Torres would tell me stories of when he was in college and girls called him "Peanut Butter Passion" because of his light skin complexion. He didn't have a relationship in college because he was too focused on his academics and sports. The girls' nickname for him meant he had their attention. "Tell me Torres what do you want in a woman?"

"Ethnicity doesn't matter, but I want a woman who is a Christian, not just in title, but in lifestyle," Torres said. "There's got to be some kind of a physical attraction. I can't just be looking at their butts and breast all the time, eventually I have to look up at them. I want a woman that's attractive, you know that natural beauty. When I say natural beauty, I mean a woman that doesn't have to wear too much or no makeup to look beautiful. I need a woman who is strong, not just physically, but mentally and spiritually. I need a praying woman. A woman that seems like she walked right out of Proverbs 31. Now she doesn't exactly have to be everything written down in that passage, but I don't know maybe pursue to be that. I need a proverbial woman…a pro."

"You want a prostitute," Shiloh asked.

"No, I'm not talking about a prostitute fool. For me "pro" is short for a Proverbs 31 woman."

"Well I think Jesus would agree with me when I say that you picky," Shiloh responded making us all laugh.

"I know what I want and need what about you Shi?"

"Well you got me there."

Torres' father was black and his mother was Puerto Rican. A lot of people thought he looked more Puerto Rican than black because of his features, especially when he shaved his head. His head was so clean that it was like looking in a mirror. He would shave it during the summer, but grow it out in the winter.

It was a mystery as to why Torres was afraid to look a woman in the eye. He had hazel eyes that Frank Sinatra could only dream of having. He had the full mustache along with a goatee that could be his trademark like Tom Selleck's mustache.

Torres was so humble that he was the first to admit he wasn't the finest guy around, but proud enough to say that he wasn't the ugliest guy in the world either.

Torres may have come off as picky, but he kept an open mind. Not only did he want an attractive woman, but she also had to be intelligent.

Torres needed to be with a woman who was strong in character. He needed her to be so strong that she challenged him to be a better man every day of his life. The man I'm sure he knows he can be.

I admired Torres because he knew what he wanted and that he didn't have to settle for less. I wish I could have thought the same way.

I'll be happy for him when that day finally comes when he finally has a novel published and finally meets his pro. As for myself I felt I had met my pro and no one could take her place.

If you limit your choices only to what seems possible or reasonable, you disconnect yourself from what you truly want, and all that is left is a compromise

~Robert Fritz~

11

Lady in my Life

I'm free! I was only one answer away from failing my real estate state exam again, but I passed…HALLELUJAH! I didn't ace it, but I passed, which is all that matters.

Now that I passed both exams I could look for a real estate firm to join. I was thinking about looking into possibly applying at the firm Torres' father was a part of. I'll see what his firm has to offer.

"I cannot believe how terrible I'm bowling," my father said looking up at the screen that had our scores. It was a little after two and my father and I were celebrating my success at the Universal Bowl trying to bowl as many strikes and spares as we could, but we were both coming up short. "I have a hundred on the ninth frame. Normally I have 150 on the ninth frame."

"How do you think I feel, I have 85 on the ninth frame when I usually have over a hundred," I said. "But then again we haven't bowled for almost half a year. This is just a warm-up."

"Yeah, but this is still a terrible game even for a warm-up. But you know what that doesn't matter because you passed your real estate exam."

"What a relief."

"Congratulations, I am really proud of you. So what do you plan on doing?"

"Since I don't have a job I'll do it full-time. Of course I have to get with an agency. Hopefully I'll make $200,000 in my first year. But with it being my first year, I'll settle for half of that."

"Sounds like a plan." My father took a sip of his Sierra Mist. He offered me a sip, but I didn't drink sodas. "So how are you and Deanna doing?"

"Things between us are . . . fine."

"Things are just fine?"

"Things are good and I like being with her, but I don't know if I can say that I'm totally committed to her."

"Why is that?"

"It seems like we're both going in different directions with our lives that don't meet up with each other. I know that neither one of us needs to put our goals nor dreams on hold for the other, but I'm wondering if we really are meant to be together in the long haul. Maybe there's a part of me that just wonders if I want to be with her for the convenience."

"Son, can you honestly say that you have ever committed to anyone?"

I was going to respond yes, but I held my tongue for a second. "I was willing to marry Monique."

"Yeah, that's true, but since she left who have you committed to?" I remained silent. "You may have committed to sticking with the same routine, but I think it's going to be hard for you to commit to anyone because since you graduated from college you haven't had to commit to anything." After I took a sip of my water I looked at him with curiosity. "When you were in high school whether it was basketball season or soccer season you were up early in the morning working on your jump shot or your kicking technique and conditioning. Because of your commitment you made all-district and all-state in both sports. In college your main goal was to graduate with honors within four years. Well you did what was required of you to do that studying as much as you needed to and you committed to doing what had to be done.

"Now that you're out of college you've just worked to pay the bills and have a meal and a place to live. You've committed to avoid being homeless. But is that how you really want to live? Just live to get by. That's no way to live. I know you love playing your music, but there has to be more to it than just playing at clubs or parties. What is your ultimate goal? Just how you have to figure out what you want with your music you need to figure out what it is you want or need in a woman. Shoot, just like figuring out what you want out of life. Are you going to take what's given to you or go after what you want?" He took a sip of his drink. "I think when you have everything figured out, as far as what you want for yourself that's when you look at life differently and don't just take what life throws at you. You begin to realize that you don't have to settle for less. You're not meant to settle." My father looked up at the bowling screen with our horrible scores. "I'm not meant to settle for this low score," he said getting up to bowl leaving me with something to ponder.

Monique was the only woman I was ever totally and completely committed too. When I chose to be with her I knew that I wasn't settling. I wish I still had that certainty about everything else.
* * * * *

Rain was falling so hard one night that it looked as if a monsoon was on the horizon. It was almost midnight when Monique was at my place and we had just finished watching The Notebook. She was wiping her face, from all the tears that ran down her face. It was my first time watching it and I'm not going to lie, but a tear fell down my face at the end. Only one tear, not tears.

"I always cry every time I see this movie," Monique said blowing her nose.

"You've seen the movie how many times now," I asked.

"I've only seen it 15 times."

"And you still cry."

"You're such a guy."

"And I'm proud of it." She playfully slapped me on the chest.

"I should get going before it gets worse out there."

"Spend the night here." She looked at me like I confessed to being a serial killer. "We both don't have to work tomorrow so we can sleep in."

"I don't know…you sure you're ready for that."

"Woman please, I have self-control. I don't know if I can say the same about you because I could be irresistible," I laughed.

"You're so full of it," she said cuddling up next to me.

"I can take the futon in the studio and you can take my bed."

"Sounds like a plan." She turned the television off, as more rain was coming down.

"You don't want to watch another movie?"

"No, besides haven't you ever just sat in silence and listened to the rain drop."

"No I haven't."

"You should try it."

"Okay." It seemed pointless to sit in the living room in silence and do nothing, but there we were listening to the rain fall. As the rain fell at a furious pace the thunder roared. As I heard lightning strike I thought the power in my place went off because the room was pitch black. But Monique turned off the lamp. "What are you doing?"

"Relax; I'm not going to do anything to you. Just relax," she said pushing me back on the couch with her finger, as she lay with me with her head resting on my chest. We heard the thunder roar even louder. It was almost as if the paparazzi was at work, as there were a couple flashes of lightening.

"Woman it's so quiet in here..."

"I can hear your heartbeat."

"Yeah."

I thought it only happened in films or television shows, but Monique and I had a habit of finishing each other's sentences. At first it appeared meaningless, but I realized that silence could be a beautiful sound. Even the simple things like listening to the rain fall on concrete, trees being blown by the wind, and lying down with the one you value most can be simply irresistible.

"You're right this is peaceful," I conceded.

"I told you."

"We should do this more often."

"You should listen to me more often."

"Ha ha, very funny."

"I find that sometimes when you're sitting alone in silence that's the time for you to hear God speaking to you."

"You're such a Jesus Freak."

"It takes one to know one."

"Well you got me there." She pinched my nose.

"Everything feels peaceful when I'm with you. Being around you makes my day. Even if it were five minutes I spoke with you or if you made a cameo appearance that makes my day. You always bring a smile to my face. Even at times when you've pissed me off, you still manage to find some way to make me smile."

"When have I pissed you off?"

"That time you were late for our third date."

"I told you rehearsal ran longer than I thought it would."

"But you didn't call ahead of time."

"And I apologized."

"Yeah you did, but you weren't considerate."

"Hey, I've gotten better about that."

"Yes you have," she chuckled. While we listened to the thunder roar and the rain plummet she was rubbing my chest, while I rubbed her neck with my hand that was free. Her head stayed on my chest. "Your heart is beating faster than normal."

"That's what you do to me."

"Well calm down before you go into cardiac arrest," she laughed making me laugh as well. "Even though we've been together a little over five months I feel so close to you. I feel like...I just feel...are you going to let me do all the talking here, I mean say something Ruben."

"I love you." When I said three words almost everyone longs to hear from the one they treasure most her eyes shined on mine. I nodded my head. "Monique Olivia Valdez, I, Ruben Alexander Wells love you. You're the first woman I have told that too. Well besides my mum and my sister." She smiled as a tear fell down her cheek. "And I'm not saying that because we just watched The Notebook, but I think about you constantly. I love being able to have that feeling I can tell you anything. I love that you feel secure with sharing delicate matters with me. I love the way you feel when I hug you. So much so that I don't want to let you go. I love how cold your hand feels when I'm holding it because I can warm it up. I love that you pinch my nose because you're the only one I will ever let do that to me. I love that every spare minute you have you make available to me. I love that even if we're not around each other I can trust you. I love that you are a part of my world and have accepted me into your world." I touched her face. "I love you Monique." I wiped the tear that raced across her cheek.

"Wow Ruben Alexander Wells, you know how to make me shut up don't you." I ran my fingers through her hair. "I love you too." Her face moved in closer towards me at the pace of a tortoise. As she moved in closer all I could think is "This is happening, it's really happening." As I touched her face she grabbed the back of my head. For the first time our lips met. The kiss was slow, gentle, and long overdue.

Monique was old-fashioned and took her time with everything. She didn't believe in kissing on her first dates. She wasn't the kind of girl who would kiss just anyone and if she did kiss someone it had to be with someone she's seriously considering being with and not just someone who was a fly by night kind of guy. In a way, I felt honored that she was kissing me. It was worth the wait.

Kissing her was as relaxing as yoga. Just like herself, her lips were sweet and delicate. It was the first time I had ever told a woman I love her and it felt liberating. I felt I was moving forward in my life taking another bold step. As we lay on my couch I grabbed the remote and turned my stereo on playing Miles Davis. As Miles played we snuggled up not wanting to let go of each other. Even though Miles was playing, I could hear Michael Jackson singing "Lady in My Life." It felt appropriate seeing as how I was with the woman whom I could call my first lady. Monique Olivia Valdez was the love of my life.

It will save you from the unfaithful wife who tries to lead you into adultery with pleasing words. She leaves the husband she married when she was young. She ignores the promise she made before God. Her house is on the way to death; those who took that path are now all dead. No one who goes to her comes back or walks the path of life again. But wisdom will help you be good and do what is right

~Proverbs 2:16-20~

12

Can You Feel It

Alejandro and I were downtown at Roberto's eating a taco salad while listening to some awful three-man group attempting to perform some music from the 70's. They were doing an injustice of songs I once loved to hear.

We were partially suited up for a night out on the town as I was wearing a camel brown sports coat with a burnt orange shirt, blue jeans, and brown Stacy Adams. Alejandro was covering his head with a tan fedora along with a tan sports coat, golden as honey tight fitted muscle shirt, blue jeans, and brown Steve Madden dress shoes that matched his shirt.

My phone rang. I looked at my caller screen and ignored the call when I saw that it was India. For the last couple of months, I had been ignoring her calls. She didn't need glasses to see that I wasn't interested.

"Okay so who would you want to spend a day with if you had a choice, Rosario Dawson or Zoe Saldana," Alejandro asked.

"Whoa, now that is a tough one," I responded. We had been playing this game since we were in high school. If we could date or marry a celebrity who would it be? "Let's see they both got that natural beauty. They both also have some rhythm. Those enticing faces and child bearing hips make them look angelic. Rosario was looking rather tempting in Sin City when she was strutting in that S&M gear." Alejandro nodded his head. "But if I had to make a choice, I'd have to go with Zoe Saldana."

"Really, you wouldn't want the alluring Miss Dawson?"

"Yeah, but Zoe is naturally sexy in just about every movie she's been in. I guess my only problem is that she's always hooking up with white guys in her movies. I wonder if it's just because she has a thing for white guys or producers think it looks better for white men to be with someone light skin instead of dark skin."

"If that's the case give Rosario Dawson more leading roles in romantic comedies."

"This group is the reason hardly anybody ever comes here anymore. People only come for the food, not the music. And honestly this food is not worth the prices they charge."

"You're right about that," Alejandro said shoving a nacho covered with beef and cheese in his mouth. "When does Deanna get back?"

"She gets back on Sunday." Ever since we sat down in Roberto's I couldn't stop talking about Deanna, like a father bragging about his son who graduated high school with honors or geeks having an endless debate on whether Star Wars or The Lord of the Rings is "The Trilogy." "She's the first woman in a long time that I enjoy being around. If she gets a job in Chicago or anywhere it would suck to see her go."

"Well if she goes you can move out to wherever she is."

"I don't know if I can do that."

"Why is that?"

"San Antonio is my home."

"You don't have a job."

"But my family is here, my friends are out here, and I know this city well. I'm getting by just fine here and to give all that up I don't know if it's worth it. Plus, as far as the economy goes, San Antonio is a safe place to be with the low cost of living we have compared to other major cities."

"True, but one of these days you have to be willin' to move on man. Can you be honest and say that you're where you want to be. Are you doin' what you love?"

"Sometimes Mo would ask me those questions?"

"Maybe there's a reason it keeps on comin' up."

"I did send some resumes to some magazines and newspapers as well as pr firms or ad agencies in Austin and Dallas. I'm taking a chance. I've got a few friends from ORU who are living in Austin and Dallas waiting for me to come out to where they are."

"They're both great places for musicians to live in Texas. Austin is the music capital of Texas. Dallas is all about taking care of business and it's like the Atlanta of Texas. There are definitely a lot of great job opportunities for black men. I'll still be your boy if you were to move there or anywhere. We'll just have a long distance friendship." I laughed. "Plus if things don't work out for you in another city you can always come back. San Antonio ain't goin' anywhere. You definitely got more talent than those three guys playing on the stage right now."

We both laughed.

After Alejandro and I left Roberto's, he went to the Rivercenter Comedy Club to meet with Kat. They had been dating each other for the last two weeks. I was going to Miel by myself.

It wasn't a long walk from Roberto's. There was a long line of people outside Miel waiting to get in. Roberto's was once the place to go to get your salsa on, but even though it was smaller more people congregated at Miel after the musical format changed at Roberto's.

Officer Logan had been working security at Miel for the last couple of weeks because a lot of fights had occurred. If there was anybody I wanted to be cool with in a club it's the man carrying the gun or tazor. Officer Logan was a white man in his late forties and 200 plus pounds with glasses. His nickname was Popeye because he had a tattoo of Popeye on his right wrist.

He shook my hand telling me to have a good time, as I walked in. He also told me there were plenty of lovely lady's present.

Miel was a great place, but it was as big as a one-bedroom apartment that left very little room to move, let alone breathe with all the people who attended.

A nine-piece band filled out the stage. The group, Puerto Rico's Finest, played every Friday night. They had just finished playing a song. One of the trombone players I knew shook my hand. As I stood near them waiting to hear the next song I felt someone touch my arm. The touch was familiar to me.

My knees were feeling feeble and my heart was rapidly beating when I saw Bianca with her flawless skin and impeccable smile.

"Hello," I said.

"I thought I recognized you," she said. "You look different with hair. I really like your curls." The band started playing the famous Elvis Crespo song, "Suavemente."

"Thank you."

"Are you here by yourself?"

"Yes I am. What about you?"

"No, I came with Monica and her friend, who I think is her ex-boyfriend. Oh they're on the dance floor right now."

I felt guilty for talking to Bianca. I even felt guilty for standing next to her. I noticed that her left ring finger was naked. Since we were at the club without significant others I embraced the moment. "Come on, let's dance." I grabbed her hand and took her to the small dance floor.

As we danced she was looking at me again with her hungry eyes. It felt like it was only yesterday that we parted ways. She had dyed her curly hair, as it was now dirty blonde. She looked exquisite and ravishing in her sleeveless and strapless violet skirt that ended a few inches above the knees. I spun her around in her violet open toe heels that matched her dress. Her bronze legs were glistening and they looked like they were as smooth as a baby's behind. Pardon the cliché. Her aroma was like a Hawaiian breeze that the fruity scent of a tropical island. I could feel her mountain of curls that were soft like velvet.

How could her husband leave her alone? He was either very stupid or gullible enough to believe that she would never leave him. My lips were yearning to touch her lips again, that were the sweet nectar of forbidden fruit.

I couldn't help, but wonder if this was a part of God's plan for us to run into each other again or was it by my own doing. Was I really meant to be at this place at this moment?

The more crowded the dance floor got, the more congested it felt, and the more Bianca and I closed in on each other.

After the song was over she held my hand and walked me over to Monica and her friend. Monica remembered me and gave me a hug. Her friend's name was Mario Flores. We stepped outside as Bianca was fanning herself.

Bianca and I sat at a table outside and talked as if it had only been a day since we had last seen each other.

"So what's been new with you Mr. Wells," she asked.

"I passed my real estate exam today," I replied. "I'm going to try to get into the real estate industry."

"Really, that's great."

"Yeah, maybe start off doing it in the residential market and if things go really well end up doing it in residential and commercial."

"Do you know which firm you want to be with?"

"I was thinking about looking at 22nd Worldwide, Bakersfield, and possibly Phil Browning."

"You're really smart; you should be fine in that industry."

"We'll see how smart I am when it comes time to close a deal. I've been hitting the books hard for the last month, but I'm glad to be done with it and just..."

"Clear your mind."

"Yeah." I took another sip of my water. "What's been going on with you lately?"

"I finished school, so I'm glad to have that out of the way."

"Congratulations."

"Thank you. I'll be going to San Francisco in a few days, so that's why I'm out right now. I'm going to visit an old friend. My husband and son are out of town this weekend on a fishing trip. They come back Sunday night. My mother is watching our daughter overnight so I could have my ladies' night out."

"How are you and the husband doing?"

"We're fine," she said nervously tapping the table. She couldn't look me in the eye when she said that. "You know we have our moments, but what marriage doesn't have their moments. Overall we're doing fine."

"That's good to hear." I still wanted to know why she wasn't wearing her wedding ring, but I wasn't going to bring it up.

"I still think about the time we spent together. It felt like...I really love kissing you, but I wanted to do so much more to you." I just sat there looking at her wondering how far my jaw fell and if she really did say that or I was just imagining she said it. "Did I say something wrong?"

"No I think about that night, a lot as a matter of fact."

"I just liked being close to you even if it was for one night."

"Hey girl, its getting way too crowded here," Monica said with Mario standing behind her. "Let's go to Club Reno. Ruben you should come with us."

"Yeah why don't you come with us," her voice was ecstatic, as her eyes lit up.

"What kind of club is it," I asked.

"It has four clubs in one. They usually play a lot of hip-hop."

"How much does it cost to get in?"

"It's only five bucks."

I knew I should have said no and let us go our separate ways again, but I wanted to savor the moment of being around Bianca. "Sure I'll go."

"We can just go there in my car," Mario said.

* * * * *

As we walked in Club Reno there was a table filled with tequila shots that were a dollar each. Mario threw down four one dollar bills. Monica grabbed two as Mario grabbed two and was going to hand one of them to me.

"Don't bother Mario, Ruben doesn't drink," Bianca said.

"You only get to live once," I said, as I grabbed tequila shot. "This is a night of first for me." Alcohol was something I was never curious about. I don't know why I decided to have my first drink ever because it's not like I was pressured to drink. Maybe I just wanted Bianca to see that I can let loose and make some compromises. I looked at this small glass the tequila had flooded. Its aroma was stronger than coffee.

"Salud," Monica said before her and Bianca quickly drank their tequila like it was an antidote to the toxin in their system. I was hesitant to taste it like a child timid to eat broccoli. I finally stopped wondering what it tastes like.

"Cheers," I replied chugging it down, as if it would quench my thirst.

To my surprise it left a burning sensation. It was so hot that my throat was flexing like it was getting a workout. I coughed after drinking my tequila.

"You got that pure system that's not used to this kind of medicine," Mario laughed.

"You have to take it easy on that babe," Bianca said rubbing my back. "Are you okay?"

"Oh yeah," I said. "Nobody light a match because that stuff burns." She laughed. "Let me get one more."

"Are you sure?"

"Yeah." She threw down two one dollar bills. She grabbed one for herself and handed me one. We clang our glasses and drank up. I felt the same burning sensation, but this time I felt a little looser. "Oh my, that's some good medicine."

"Come on," she laughed grabbing my hand.

We didn't stay to listen to the alternative rock band playing in the main room with a lead singer who looked like Christ Martin from Coldplay, but sounded like Adam Levine of Maroon 5.

We followed Monica and Mario into a different room that had crimson curtains for doors. On the wall was written "Heat" in red lights. As we walked in the first thing I noticed was two women, one in a red two-piece bikini and another in a pink two-piece bikini both of them wearing knee-high white kinky boots dancing on their own pole like strippers. Some guys were putting dollar bills in their g-strings. The bartender blew fire in the air.

"What do you think," Bianca asked with a smile.

"Did I just walk into hell," I replied making her laugh. I was beginning to feel a little lightheaded. Those tequila shots I consumed were small, but they packed a very powerful punch.

The dj was playing some old school music, as he had just played Wild Cherry's "Play That Funky Music." I was surprised to see people around my age actually dancing to it. After the song was over he scratched into Bell Biv Devoe's "Poison."

When the song came on Monica and Mario were on the dance floor. Bianca went to the dance floor. I stayed behind watching her dance, as I was trying to get myself together. I was feeling a little woozy. She was swaying her hips and brushing her hair back. As she was dancing she looked at me and motioned with her finger to come to her.

"That girl is poison," is what Bell Biv Devoe was singing. I felt they were standing next to me trying to advise me to take precaution.

I walked up to her on the dance floor and still watched her while I was bobbing my head back and forth. It was impossible to stay immobile to the beat of the song. As I danced by myself she was smiling at me. She pulled me in when the dj segued into Sean Paul's "Temperature." The alcohol must have been kicking in because I was laying aside my inhibitions with her. Our bodies were rubbing against each other. As we danced I pulled her in even closer and she was running her hands down my stomach. One of my hands was slowly falling down to touch her buttocks. As I did she gave me a devilish grin.

* * * * *

After a few songs in Heat we went upstairs to Blue Sky where it was less crowded and filled with neon blue lights. They were playing hip-hop music. We all got some more drinks. I requested some water, but I also asked for gin since I was curious about it. Bianca handed me my drinks as we sat down and watched some people dance to 50 Cent's "P.I.M.P." As soon as they finished their drinks Mario and Monica were on the dance floor.

"I would have thought they were still together with how close they are tonight," I said.

"Yeah I know," Bianca said.

"Was I slurring in my speech."

"No, but you do look a little buzzed."

"Oh man, I don't think I'll be driving home tonight," I said taking a sip of gin. "I may just have to hail myself a cab." She laughed. I loved to see her laugh. Her husband probably didn't make her laugh enough or even bring a smile to her face. "It might be the alcohol talking, but I have really missed you Bianca."

"I've missed you also Ruben." I took a sip of my water, as we sat there looking at each other in silence.

"I know you want me," is what the Pussycat Dolls were singing. As the song was playing I took Bianca with me to the dance floor. People must have felt the real party was upstairs because a lot of people I saw in Heat were now in Blue Sky crowding the dance floor.

I missed the feel of Bianca's hips. As I squeezed a tight grip on her hips she wrapped her arms around me and we were close enough to kiss each other, but we kept our distance. She then turned around and was rubbing her posterior into my crotch area. As she did she wrapped one of her arms around my head and brought my face closer to hers. I softly kissed her on the neck, as she held me tighter.

The temperature was rising so much that I felt like easily flipping her skirt up.

We were close together like that until one in the morning when she had to leave because Monica had to get up early to go to work.

* * * * *

Mario dropped us off, as our cars were in the same parking lot near Roberto's. Monica quickly took off in her Red Dodge Neon leaving Bianca and I alone in front of her Audi.

We stood across from each other in silence smiling. She came up to me and squeezed me. I felt like a giant as her head rested on my chest. Our hug lingered, as if this would be the last time we would see each other.

"It was really good to see you again Ruben," she said keeping a tight grip. "I really hope to see you again some time."

After only two shots of tequila and a glass of gin I felt that I wasn't in the best condition to drive. I couldn't believe what I was going to ask Bianca. But it would prolong our goodbye.

"Look I don't really feel I can drive tonight, but would you mind driving me home," I asked. She backed up and looked at me with suspicion. "I can just have a friend bring me back here tomorrow to pick up my ride. I know it's an odd request, but I would like to live to see another day."

"Sure, I'll drive you home."

* * * * *

While Bianca was driving me to my apartment, I couldn't help, but wonder if the reason Bianca wasn't wearing her ring was because she and her husband were separated. Maybe that's what made her even more attractive.

It was close to 1:30 when she arrived at my apartment. She parked her car and turned off the headlights.

"Thank you for the ride," I said. "I believe I owe you for gas money."

"No, that isn't necessary," she replied. "Maybe you can pay me back some other way."

"Would you like to come inside my place?" What am I doing? What is wrong with you Ruben, what the heck is wrong with you? Are you out of your freaking mind asking a married woman to come into your apartment during the booty call time of the evening?

"Why should I go into your place when you don't plan on having sex before marriage and I am a married woman?"

"Get your head out of the gutter I didn't have sex on my mind." Even I don't believe that. "You have never seen Hitch, right."

"That's right."

"I thought maybe we could watch the movie since I have it. I could just heat up some popcorn and get out some cold drinks. We could just chill and share some laughs. Just because I want you to come up, doesn't mean it has to be sexual. Besides if I didn't know you, I would have thought you were single because you're not wearing a wedding ring."

"My finger got swollen from a bug bite."

"Oh, right."

"But I would love to see your place and watch Hitch."

She pulled the keys out of the ignition and turned on the car alarm, as we walked upstairs to my place. Ash was outside my door. When we walked into my apartment I turned one of my lamps on. I grabbed my little bowl and filled it with milk. I placed the bowl outside my door where Ash didn't let the milk go to waste. I turned the lock on my door three times as usual to be sure it was secured.

"Welcome to my humble abode," I said as I noticed she was sitting on the couch with her heels on.

"This is beautiful," she said. "It's very clean in here." Her purse was on my coffee table along with her silver butterfly earrings on top of my bible that I hadn't read in a few days. I hung up my sports coat. My attention was still on Bianca wearing her shoes. Normally I tell people to take their shoes off, but there was something sexy about her in heels. I didn't mind her keeping them on as long as she wanted. I turned on my CD player and had D'Angelo asking, "How Does It Feel." "It's just so big for one person." Was she already getting into foreplay?

"Excuse me."

"Your apartment, it seems so big for one person."

"Oh, well I like to have my space." I sat next to her, but the alcohol must have worn off because I had been fidgeting and uneasy since she walked in my apartment. My heart was beating at a rapid pace and my forehead and armpits were sweating. It was the first time I had ever been alone with a married woman in my place. I was rubbing my knees like I was scrubbing a stain.

"Are you okay?"

"No I'm fine…I just -." She ran her hand up my thigh.

"Am I the first woman you've had here?"

"Besides my mum or my sister uh…" She laughed.

"Just relax Ruben, I'm kidding. We don't have to do anything you're not comfortable with." I would be comfortable just lying down with her. I was really comfortable with the thought of her curling up next to me like I was a blanket keeping her warm.

"I just uh-"

"Look it's getting late maybe I should head home," she interrupted.

"Don't be silly," I said waving my hands. "There are probably too many drunk drivers out right now and if something happened to you I would feel guilty. You can just sleep here." Why was I so desperate to keep her around?

"Are you sure?"

"Yeah, you can take my bed and there's a futon in my other room that I can sleep in."

"Okay. I can't believe I'm still wide awake right now."

"You must have gotten a lot of sleep over the week or taken a nap a lot earlier today. I know I'm tired," I yawned. We sat in silence listening to D'Angelo hit a high note. She turned the lights off. We were sitting so close together that she could have sat on my lap if she so desired.

She still had her shoes on, but she curled up next to me resting her back on my chest, as my arm was around her. "I know I shouldn't say this, but I wish I could have more nights like this with you."

"There's nothing wrong with you saying that." She leaned in a little closer to me and whispered in my ear. "Is it wrong for me to say that I really want you right now?" She was running her fingers through my hair and delicately kissing my neck as if she was massaging it with her lips. When she kissed my neck it tickled a little bit. It was also arousing. "I see how you look at me and I love how you look at me. I know you want me." Her nose slowly traced down the side of my face. "It's okay because I want you. We can give that movie a rain check because tonight I'm yours. If you want I can be your first."

"You know I don't have any experience in sexual education," I whispered.

"That's okay baby, I can teach you some things. You can learn so much from me."

"Don't stop kissing my neck."

With that being said I lifted up her legs and gently ran both my hands across her curvy legs. "You have such long fingers."

"The things I would do to you with these long fingers." I knew the route I was taking with this conversation and I no longer cared about keeping integrity. I knew what route I wanted my hands to go.

"I know something I want to do with them."

"What's that?" She grabbed my left hand and stuck my index finger in her mouth licking it like a Blow Pop. When she released my finger I moved my hand up her thigh and we both moved in on each other like two trains colliding. Our lips met. Their meeting was longer than before. At first I kissed her gently, as if our lips were caressing each other, but then as Maxwell crooned Til the Cops Come Knocking I kissed her aggressively, as if I would never feel her lips again. We were like teenagers making out in the movie theater. She slipped her tongue into my mouth.

God was looking down on us and I didn't care. I knew it was wrong to kiss her, but I couldn't stop kissing her. As far as I was concerned she wasn't doing anything wrong because her husband was out of town.

"Your mustache is so soft," she replied kissing me softly.

"You feel so good," I replied not letting her get too far away from me.

After whispering some dirty words into my ear she licked it and I licked her neck.

Instead of keeping her at a distance I grabbed her and let her straddle me. Her knees pressed into the seat and her hands were up against the wall as she faced me leaving very little room to escape. *As if I really wanted to leave.* My hands were sliding up her thigh elevating her skirt.

While kissing my neck she unbuttoned my shirt and took it off. She rolled up my shirt I wore underneath and felt my abs.

"You work out a lot," she said while rubbing his stomach.

"It's all natural, girl," I joked making her laugh. "I have to put in some work."

She proceeded to kiss my chest.

As she kissed my chest and nimbled on it, with one of my free hands I grasped a handful of her breast. She moaned as I rubbed them. I wasn't satisfied with feeling cloth, so I slipped my hand under her bra and felt her naked breast and firm nipple. As I felt it she proceeded to moan a little louder. I than kissed her neck and ran my other hand up her thigh.

I wondered if what was happening was a hallucination.

While we kissed I held her tight and got on top of her, as we fell to the floor. My jeans were still on and I was slowly grinding her. As I was on top of her I wondered when I would wake up from this wonderful dream.

"That's it baby, get me warmed up," she said in a provocative tone. She raised her legs, as I got in between them. As I continued moving, she moved with me and pretty soon we were moving fast. "You feel so good." She got a tight grip on my pants and was pushing me into her even more. I could hear her exhale, as I was perspiring. Thank God this isn't a dream.

As we were kissing she rolled on top of me and began to feel my crotch through my jeans.

"Mmm, aye papi" she said. It was exhilarating hearing her call me papi. I was so excited I wanted to break out into a salsa dance. "Baby you feel so hard." When she said that she sounded more like a prostitute than a housewife, but I didn't care. It aroused me even more thus making my jeans feel even tighter. "Let's feel how hard you really are." She then unbuckled my belt, but she was having trouble unbuttoning my jeans that were the cage keeping my private property on lock down. "Oh this freaking button."

At this point I should have stopped, thrown her out the door, and taken a cold shower. Instead I unbuttoned and unzipped my jeans for her. As I did that I felt like I was letting a bird out of its cage at the same time making it vulnerable to creatures that would want to harm it. After my jeans were unzipped she felt my red shorts that I wore underneath. "Are those basketball shorts?"

"Yeah I like to wear them underneath just in case I play a game on a spur of the moment."

"What about gym shoes?"

"Oh I keep a pair in the trunk. In case it's soccer I also leave some cleats and shin guards in the trunk as well."

"You're always prepared." She kissed me again, as she was feeling my shorts. I felt Bianca was teasing me, not feeling the real deal. Even though I knew it was wrong I really wanted her to touch me. After knowing how it felt I was greatly anticipating it once again. Sensing my anticipation, she then proceeded to slide her hand under my shorts and she grasped my penis. "It's so long and firm. Oh...yes...yes. You like that papi." As she rubbed me, profanity is all that was running through my mind. John Legend's So High was playing and I was feeling elated. I could feel my toes curling up and I felt like going into falsetto like a soprano.

I was euphoric. We weren't having intercourse, but as she continued to rub me I felt I was ascending into another dimension. My mouth was just left wide open as she continued to rub my penis. "Don't stop," I whispered. I didn't care that a married woman was touching me. I was feeling more of an adrenaline rush than I was apprehension, as my eyes were shooting towards the ceiling.

"Oh I want to put my mouth on it so bad," she begged. "You gonna let me put my mouth on it."

"No," I replied closing my eyes. Chances are her mouth has been on her husband's whole body and no telling if he may have something that I don't want.

"Why can't I taste it? Come on baby please it looks so good." This conversation felt corny like a porn film, but the way she was talking was making me extremely horny.

"I'm afraid you're going to bite me," I replied.

"Trust me it won't hurt. Open your eyes baby." I opened up my eyes. "Come on baby let me taste you." Who says that, 'taste you.'

"I feel like I'm disrespecting you by having you do that."

"You're too adorable, but I am volunteering to do this. It looks so delicious. You will enjoy how my mouth feels on it."

I was hesitant, but I obliged her grabbing the back of her head and slowly pulled her down.

The moment I felt her mouth wrap around my member I was in awe. It was almost as if she was licking chocolate ice cream on a cone, a very big cone. I could feel her tongue going like a merry-go-round. She lightly gripped me with both hands, as she bobbed up and down, massaging me with her tongue. Every sense, but touch was out the window. This was the first time this had ever happened and I felt as if I was going into warp speed like the Starship Enterprise.

She must have done it for about five minutes before she sat up and slid one of my hands up her thigh a little higher. "Touch me baby." She was sliding her black thong down and she slid my hand up toward her vaginal area. "Don't be afraid of it papi." She was pulling my hand towards her vagina.

"Bianca I…" I almost pulled away.

"Come on baby I want you to touch me." As she continued to whisper in my ear she pulled my hand towards her vagina and I didn't fight her anymore. "Just touch me right here." She closed her eyes and moaned as I was touching her while she grabbed my penis. "Oh yeah…that's it…that feels so good."

This was my first time to ever invade a woman's privacy, if you know what I mean. I slid my long index finger along the top of her private parts until I felt an area that was rougher than the rest of her vaginal wall. I did a lot of research on the internet on the female anatomy. Just to prepare myself for that day I would lose my virginity. It appears to be happening a little earlier than I originally planned on. There must have been an abundant amount of arousal in Bianca because I easily felt this rough area that was the size of a quarter. As I touched what I felt might be the G-spot Bianca moaned with pleasure. The more I touched her the louder she got.

So there we were on my living room floor touching each other's private parts. This is definitely going to need a cleaning. I suddenly stopped touching her and pulled her hand away from my penis.

"What are you doing," she meekly asked, as Floetry was singing "Say Yes."

I got on top of her, as I was pulling my jeans off and sliding her thong completely off. "The anticipation is killing me. Let's just do it."

She didn't even put up an argument, as she pulled my wife beater off. She kicked her shoes off. I pulled out the condom I had been armed with for far too long to where it was beginning to feel like I was carrying a family heirloom.

"That's not necessary," she said. "I'm on the pill."

"Still you can never be too careful."

"You'll like how it feels without one."

"I want to play this safe."

"You trust me don't you? Nothing bad will happen. You just have to trust me. You trust me don't you?"

"Yeah I do."

"Then put the rubber away."

I obliged her suggestion throwing the condom to the side. I took off Bianca's dress and she took her bra off.

There we were, finished with the foreplay and now naked and unashamed. When she saw me completely naked she smiled. "You're so freaking sexy you know that," she said. Only she didn't say "freaking." She said the other "f" word whose second letter is a "u."

She was rubbing my stomach with her right foot. I thought watching a sunset was beautiful, but it holds no comparison to a sexy woman in the nude. Bianca could have been a portrait with her firm breasts and lovely nipples staring at me.

"Come here," she said pulling me in.

She grabbed my face and buried it in her breasts. When I kissed them she shook a little. I was about to ask if she was okay, but she kept my face buried in her full breasts. As she kept me near them I cupped her breasts and licked her nipples. As I continued to lick them she called out my name. "Oh Ruben."

She squeezed my posterior and opened her legs a little wider giving me access to her throne. The clock read 2:13. As I entered she wrapped her legs around my thighs. I gently moved in an inch and then slid back out a bit without leaving completely. I slid in a bit farther and back out a bit. I did this a couple more times until I was all in. While I slowly moved in I could hear her moaning and the sound of her moans was liberating. "Oh you feel so good Ruby," she moaned. Felt like paradise was between her legs. It was the closest thing to having heaven on earth. I was trying my best to take my time because I wanted to savor my first sexual encounter, but I was so anxious.

As I delicately moved inside her sensitive spot she leaned her head back.

"OH BABY," she yelled. "AYE PAPI." That's the most Spanish I had heard her speak.

"DAAAAAANNNNNNNGGG," I yelled. Fantasy was becoming reality. I felt like Captain James T. Kirk going where no man had gone before.

The animal in me was exposed, as I was breathing heavily like I did a P90X workout.

For the last 27 years I had been missing out on what most men my age experienced on prom night or homecoming. I never thought my first sexual intimacy moment would be with a married woman on the carpet, but here we were embracing the moment putting aside our inhibitions. While I was having sex with Bianca the song that ran through my mind was, "Me and Mrs. Jones have a thing going on."

We were blending, like sponges absorbing each other. She had broken a promise to her husband and was making a new covenant with me.

I was more connected with her than I was with any other woman.

The more she moaned the harder I pushed and the more I grunted. With every thrust her tone would get higher and higher. The more she moaned the more excited I got and the faster I moved inside of her. I tried to slow down, but I couldn't control myself.

We finally exhaled when we reached our climax. When I was lying on her catching my breath she kissed me on the cheek and asked me to take her to my bedroom. I was a little disappointed to see that the clock read 2:16. Well at least I lasted longer than a minute for my first time. No woman is going to make time for a one-minute man.

I carried her to my room like a groom carrying his bride over the threshold. I placed her on my bed. She slipped under the covers. I turned my fan on and slid under the covers with her.

As soon as I got in the bed she immediately embraced me like she had just been spooked.

I didn't know what to think. Not just of her and everything that happened, but also of myself. What had I become? In my mind I could hear gospel singer, Tonex, singing "Why?" *Why did I make my savior cry? Why did I let him out my life? Oh Lord I know it's no one's fault but mine...Why do I make the same mistakes...Taking advantage of your grace. I know I slapped you in your face, by putting my wants in your place...*

I had become immoral...carnal. I didn't feel like I was a Christian anymore. I no longer felt spiritual, but instead I felt like a natural man.

I certainly wasn't a virgin anymore. With everything that happened tonight I felt as if I had cheated on God with what I had done. I desired affection from a woman so much, that I went as far as finding it with a married woman. I felt as if I was the one who committed adultery.

After everything happened we looked at each other exhausted. With sweat running down our bodies we laughed. As she curled up next to me her body trembled. As she rested her head on my chest I was running my hand down her back while she traced my stomach with her index finger.

As Floetry had finished serenading us the CD changed to Angie Stone and "Brown Skin" was being played. Bianca lied on top of me. It felt so good when she kissed my head. With the tip of my tongue I licked her chest that was exposed.

"You are so bad," she whispered. By her tone I knew she was smiling.

"So are you." I looked at her. "We're both going to hell. You know that right." I smiled at her wrapping my arms around her and pulled her in.

"We might as well go out with a bang."

"You're crazy."

"Ruben do you think if we were married we would both be faithful to each other."

"Yeah I do."

"You're not just saying that."

I looked at her, as she rested her head on her hand that was balanced by her elbow. "When I see you I see my future. I'm not big on love at first sight, but I definitely wanted to know you the first time I saw you. When I first saw you I was thinking what life would be like with you in the long-run. I imagined white picket fences and sunny days. I imagined actually being happy majority of the time. I was thinking this is a woman I would want to have deep conversations with or even have a few arguments. Of course I would be right all the time." She laughed while playfully slapping me on the chest. "I imagined that if we had a daughter she would have more of my complexion and your eyes and curly hair."

"Why would you want a girl first?"

"I don't know, but if I was to have a child, there's a part of me that would want to have a girl first. That's just what I would prefer. Maybe it's the whole daddy's little girl."

"What would you want to name her?"

"I would have to give her a name that is different. I would probably call her Unique."

"That is rare and also unique. Why that name?"

"Well because she would be unique. After all, everybody is different."

"True."

I was in pain realizing that this dream of being with Bianca in a house with white picket fences, colorful garden, and a lovely daughter could never happen. She was married. It bothered me thinking of not being able to see her again after tonight.

"What are you thinking," she asked. I was hesitant to speak. Even though it was dark she could see the sadness in my eyes. "What is it baby" she asked leaning in closer.

"You know we can't see each other again, not after tonight."

"Let's just enjoy the time we have left with each other."

"Okay."

"It's hard to believe that you've been a virgin all this time." I laughed. "So what did you think of your first time Ruben?"

"It was better than I imagined. It was incredible."

"You did alright for a rookie."

"Oh for a rookie, come here I'll show you."

As the music was playing we were not thinking about tomorrow, but savoring the present. When we weren't doing that we cuddled and talked. And if we weren't cuddling or talking we were lying in silence listening to the music being played.

It wasn't until 4:30 in the morning that we finally fell asleep.

Our character…is an omen of our destiny, and the more integrity we have and keep, the simpler and nobler that destiny is likely to be

~George Santayana~

13

Don't Stop Til You Get Enough

It was close to nine in the morning when I woke up. Bianca looked peaceful while she slept, as if she was having pleasant dreams. It felt strange waking up with someone. My bed felt warmer lying next to her. I had grown accustomed to sleeping alone. I could get used to having company; especially when that company has as lovely a birthday suit as Bianca's suit.

I turned off my CD player and went into my studio room.

While checking my cell phone I saw that I missed a call from Alejandro last night. It was probably while I was at Club Reno.

As I sat in the studio looking at my trumpet Monique ran through my mind.

The trumpet was her favorite instrument. Whenever she came to my place we would listen to Miles Davis or Chris Botti.

As I thought about Monique I was playing my trumpet trying to mimic one of Miles Davis' songs off the Kind of Blue CD. As I played my eyes were closed thinking about the times I would sometimes go early in the morning to Monique's place. Sometimes I would play the trumpet outside her window wake her up with a smooth melody. It brought a smile to her face seeing me play the trumpet. Maybe it was just seeing me that brought a smile to her face.

As the thought of Monique faded, I imagined myself playing in a jazz concert in New York in front of millions.

As I played I imagined the women in the audience screaming my name. I imagined some of them not being able to compose themselves and just getting up out of their seat shouting like they were in church hearing a good word being spoken. But then again I would be a jazz musician, not a hip-hop artist, so the women would most likely be more conservative and maybe just toss me a key to their hotel room.

I always loved playing the piano, but I enjoyed playing the trumpet because there wasn't just something sexy about it, but it was soothing to listen to as well. That's if it was played right. When most people hear the word trumpet they automatically associate it with Miles. He had a way of playing the trumpet the way no one else could.

While I was playing I opened my eyes and I saw Bianca standing in the doorway wearing nothing, but my red Bruce Lee t-shirt that fit her like a dress and holding the lid of a mouthwash bottle. I put my trumpet down.

"You're wearing my favorite shirt," I said. "I'm going to need you to take it off."

"If you mean it, believe me I have no problem with that," she said.

"I didn't wake you did I."

"You did, but that's okay. You're really good on that trumpet Mr. Wells," she said with a smile. "You have a gift with those lips." She winked, as she drank some mouthwash like a tequila shot.

"Thank you."

She walked around the room. She picked up a book from my desk. "You are actually reading A Walk to Remember?"

"I'm a Nicholas Sparks fan."

"It seems in a lot of his stories the two lovers don't end up happily ever after."

"I guess I like that because in real life hardly anyone ever ends up happily ever after. Sometimes his endings are tragic, but they're poetic and realistic."

"You're weird." She smiled while brushing her hair back. "But maybe I'm a little weird for liking that about you." I saw my digital camera that was sitting on a nightstand. I grabbed it and took the lens cap off.

"I want to take some pictures of you." I was looking through the viewfinder and adjusted my focus.

"No I'm a mess."

"No you're not. Without the makeup you're showing your natural beauty. Besides you have no idea how sexy it is to see a woman wearing a Bruce Lee t-shirt. Now strike a pose for me dang it." She showed off her sparkling white teeth. I didn't have to give her any instructions; she just did what naturally came to her. She would strike some poses like she was taking photos for the front cover of Maxim or Cosmopolitan. After taking a few photos she came over to me and sat on my lap. I placed the camera in front of us and took a few shots of us together. The photos looked perfect.

"We look good together," she said, as I put the camera down.

"Please don't make this difficult."

While sitting on my lap, she slipped her hand under my shirt and was feeling my stomach. "Take off your shirt." I didn't hesitate to take it off. Whenever I played basketball or football I always made sure to be on the team that would keep their shirts on because I wasn't very fond of exposing myself. I know I have a nice body, but I'm not big on showing off what I have. She pointed to my chest. "Are you a Leo?"

She was referring to the tattoo of a lion that I had over my heart. "Yes, but that's not why I got this tattoo."

"Why did you get it?"

"Well I'm fascinated with lions. That's why I have so many pictures of them in my apartment. Lions are the kings of the jungle that are the most feared and respected animal. They stay low key and it seems they only attack when they are threatened or their loved ones are threatened or just when they need to eat." She laughed. "Maybe that's why I enjoy the Lion King so much." She smiled. "But I believe they signify valor and that's why I like them so much. The reason I have this tattoo over my heart is because I like to think I have the heart of a lion."

"You're so sexy." Bianca began to lick on my nipples and it tickled a little bit. She then licked my chest upward toward my neck. "Mmm." I looked at her and kissed her again.

She straddled me while we were making out in the chair. I was getting uncomfortable so while we were making out I got up from the seat with her legs wrapped around me and fell on her on the futon.

When we fell into the futon she giggled. For a few seconds we were silent as we looked at each other while I was on top of her.

"Where have you been hiding all of this time," she said.

Lying with her I didn't feel guilt, but I felt pleasure. I felt passion like I couldn't live without her. I felt she was filling an area of my heart that was vacant. I never thought a married woman could do that to me.

One of my hands slipped under my Bruce Lee shirt she was wearing. While rubbing her stomach I felt an erection.

She rolled on top of me and unzipped my pants making me feel elated as she touched me.

With our eyes locked on each other she took her shirt off and began straddling me with her hands rested on my chest. With a lot of exhaling and perspiring Bianca was grinding me.

As she moistened her lips I sat up with her and she wrapped her legs around my back. She grabbed my neck and closed her eyes, as she pulled my mouth towards hers. As we kissed she held my face, while I held her hips. I pulled her in even closer to me and entered her throne once again. Once I entered her she leaned her head back and I kissed her neck.

I felt like I was the lowest of the low because a man's wife is the jewel of his heart. Whoever he was, I was robbing Bianca's husband of that. I never wanted to be that guy who sleeps with another man's woman, but I became that guy. It kind of feels good to be that guy right now.

* * * * *

I haven't felt this good in a while. Of course I couldn't help, but wonder if Ruben was with me because he knew that in being with a married woman there are no strings attached. Most men get involved with married women because they know they can have a relationship that is only physical and expect nothing more. I hope Ruben isn't that kind of guy. Oh I love the way he feels inside of me.

* * * * *

Maybe she was faking, but I didn't care that she was screaming my name as if it were a song. The more aggressive we kissed the harder and faster we were grinding each other. It was so nasty that I felt like I was in a pornographic film. I was expressing enough passion, but I couldn't express the guilt that was stuck inside of me.

I knew I was wrecking a family, but I wanted to feel fulfilled by any means necessary. To know what it felt like to be one with another. I knew that as a Christian this wasn't a very effective witnessing tool. I knew that I was hindering my potential relationship with Deanna, but this was Bianca. A woman like Bianca was rare to come across. She was blowing my mind while we were making love on my futon.

I felt like a jerk the viewers hate in movies. I felt like I was no longer the underdog a person would root for.

There was a first time for everything.

* * * * *

Normally I didn't work out during the weekend, but this Saturday morning I was getting a workout. Bianca and I were insatiable sexual beasts.

After having sex with her on my futon, while I was cooking us both some bacon and eggs she sat on the countertop naked requesting we go another round. Of course after finishing scrambling the eggs I granted her request and we did it on my kitchen countertop. So I need to wash the sheets on my futon as well as clean the kitchen countertop. After eating our breakfast, we proceeded to have sex on my dining room table. Need to polish that. It wasn't even noon yet and we were having sex in the shower while the water covered our bodies.

After doing a full tour of my apartment we finally got around to watching Hitch. After watching the movie, we took a nap in my bed and didn't wake up until a little after two.

The more sex we had the less guilty I was feeling about jeopardizing her marriage. I loved every minute of the connection we were making.

When she woke up she decided it was time to leave.

* * * * *

Bianca gave me a ride downtown to pick up my car. The skies were royal blue and there was plenty of sunshine, but I felt like there was a dark cloud hovering over us. We didn't have much to say, as we were going downtown listening to some sad love songs by Mint Condition.

Hopefully my car wasn't towed or vandalized. When we pulled up near it I saw that it was in one piece. We both sat in silence listening to Stokely sing "What Kind of Man Would I Be." I was scratching my goatee thinking about how much I didn't want our association to end.

I was choking up inside wondering what kind of man I had become. Not only did I persuade a woman to be unfaithful to her husband; I was disloyal to my potential girlfriend. I was selfish by getting what I wanted instead of being selfless and making myself available to God and what he desired for me to have.

It's a little too late to be receiving a spiritual revelation.

We both looked at each other a couple times like two shy kids noticing each other at a dance afraid to approach each other. Bianca's cell phone rang, but she ignored it.

"You look cute when you give that nervous smile spread across your face," she said.

"Nervous smile," I replied.

"Yeah, you give me that smile sometimes." She took off her seatbelt and leaned a little closer to me grabbing my left hand. "That's kind of the way you looked at me when you first saw me."

"Well I am nervous," I said squeezing her hand. "I know that once I step out of this car and we both drive away to wherever it is we need to go that I will never…"

"Shhh," she said placing a finger on my lips. "Don't say it, please let's not do it like this." She looked at me with tears running down her face.

"Okay, well…I guess that's that right," I said wiping the tears off her face.

"Yeah," she said kissing my hand.

"I have to let you go," I said opening the car door.

"Yeah," she said letting go of my hand. When I got out of the car I winked at her and closed the door. I walked around her car and unlocked my driver side door. Before stepping into my car I looked back at her and she rolled down her window.

I walked up to her and ran my hand down her face. As I did, she closed her eyes and moved her head towards my lips. I kissed her lips one last time knowing that we had passed the point of no return.

"I'll see you around Bianca Jones," I said rubbing my backhand against her smooth face for the last time.

"See you later Ruben Wells," she said kissing my hand.

I smiled and got in the car putting the key in the ignition. Bianca pulled out, as I sat there in the parking lot alone. Once again seeing her leave once more had tears running down my face.

I held my face not only thinking that I would never see her again, but what bothered me more is that I gave up my virginity. I gave it to someone who was lawfully unavailable. What if I had waited just a little longer? Twenty-seven years deprived of sexual intercourse was long enough in my eyes. What if God needed me to wait just one more year to hold onto my virginity? I'll never know because I gave it away and it's something that can never be returned.

It made me sick to my stomach that I was disloyal to Deanna. Even though we weren't officially a couple I felt like I was doing her an injustice in not giving all of myself to her. At this moment, I made Deanna more of an option and less of a priority.

Some would probably say that I was the luckiest man on earth having my own place, my own car, a successful career, if you ignore the layoff, and about to venture into a new industry, a loving family, and great musical talents. For everything I had done early this morning, I felt ashamed to be Ruben Wells.

I looked in my rearview mirror and saw myself. The corners of my eyes were watering up.

"Sometimes I hate you," I said to myself.

What consequence would I have to live with after this simultaneous pleasurable and painful moment? My head fell back against the headrest while the air conditioning was pushing up against my face. I thought of how naked and unashamed Bianca and I were to be with each other. The thought that she was going back to her husband had me pounding on the dashboard, as if it were trying to attack me. If Bianca wasn't the one for me, then who was? Is there such a thing as the one? Waiting for the potential Mrs. Ruben Wells was frustrating?

My head fell on the steering wheel while I was catching my breath and trying to regain my composure. My cell phone rang. I looked at the call screen and saw that it was Deanna. I wiped my tears and kept my eyes closed while I spoke to Deanna. It was time to get back to reality.

You don't have to buy from anyone. You don't have to work at any particular job. You don't have to participate in any given relationship. You can choose

~Harry Browne~

14

Second Time Around

Deanna told me her job interview was fantastic and would tell me more about Chicago when I picked her up from the airport tomorrow. They had to interview some other candidates, but she was confident they would offer her a position. I tried to share her enthusiasm, but it was difficult because I was mourning the loss of my virginity, as if a relative passed away.

Prior to cleaning my place up, I had spent more time in the shower than usual thoroughly washing myself as if I had been exposed to a deadly chemical. I would apply extra amounts of soap when I was washing below my waist.

Every square inch of my apartment reminded me of Bianca and all that had transpired between us. No matter how hard I scrubbed throughout my apartment to wash the filth away, I couldn't relinquish the guilt that was boiling inside of me. It was annoying me like a kid being loud in a movie theater.

Oh dang, what if I got her pregnant? I'm not ready for fatherhood. She said she was on the pill, but what if she was lying just so I would sleep with her?

While cleaning up my bathroom I couldn't look myself in the mirror. I poured some Cool Mint Listerine in the lid of the bottle filling it all the way to the top. Didn't bother swishing it around for 30 seconds or spitting it out, but sunk it down like a tequila shot. Just like Bianca did earlier.

After pouring myself another and swallowing it down I finished cleaning my bathroom.

My desire for Bianca's affection infected me with eternal pain that outweighed temporary pleasure.

I wanted something meaningful and all I received was sex. I gave Bianca my virginity and in return she gave me her body, but her heart was still with another.

There was a knock at my door. I looked through the peephole and saw that it was Alejandro. I forgot that we were going to see the movie Terminator: Salvation. Seeing Alejandro was making me nervous as if the cops were stopping by to make a drug bust. He had this annoying habit of being able to read me, as if he knew me better than I knew myself.

When I opened the door he was taking his shoes off before stepping into my apartment.

"What's happening playboy," Alejandro said falling into my couch in the same spot Bianca sat. I turned the lock on the door three times just for security purposes.

"Nothing much, just doing some spring cleaning," I said avoiding eye contact while I was polishing my dining room table.

"You mind if I get a glass of water," he said getting up walking towards the kitchen.

"Go ahead. Just grab a straw." Whenever people drank from my glasses I always had them use a straw. I know after washing glasses they drink from I am free of germs, but I'd also play it safe by having them use a straw. I have no idea where other people's mouths have been.

"You okay man, you sound a little sick," he asked pouring a glass of water from the jug I kept in the refrigerator. Now the interrogation begins.

"No I'm just a little exhausted, that's all." I was cleaning the place, as if I was trying to not leave any evidence behind at the scene of a crime. "How was the comedy show last night?"

"It was alright," he said sitting back down on the couch drinking his water through the straw. "There were a couple of comedians that were on fire and others that just needed to pass the mic or exit stage left. After being there Kat and I along with a couple of her friends went to Suave. They had a good crowd there last night." Alejandro took a sip. "You should have met up with us there because I ran into Torres and Roland out there. I also got to meet Raquel's boyfriend Saul Russell. He's the ball player that's Torres' cousin. He's like that guy next door. The kind of guy that if I were holdin' a barbecue at my place he would probably ask if he could come. Definitely doesn't have his nose stuck up in the air. They were celebratin' Buster's birthday. I'm pretty sure Buster will be throwin' another party tonight and tomorrow." Alejandro placed his glass on a coaster and rested it on the table end. "You know Buster knows how to have a celebration. He's like a one-man fiesta parade," he laughed. "I called you last night, what happened?"

"Yeah I saw that you called, but by the time I checked it was early this morning."

"I guess you were having too good a time at Miel."

"Yeah," I said walking with my head down eyes locked on the carpet at the very spot I gave Bianca my virginity. I got down on my knees and started furiously scrubbing the spot. "I've vacuumed this living room three times today and it still looks dirty."

"Ruben, your carpet looks clean," Alejandro said leaning forward with his hands rested on his knees. I was scrubbing so hard that my forehead was sweating. "You need to chill. With the way you're scrubbin' I would think you were trying to remove blood."

As I scrubbed all I could hear was Bianca moaning and all I could see was me inside of her losing my virginity. "It seems no matter how hard I try it just won't leave." I scrubbed even harder when I remembered reaching my climax with her.

"It's not the end of the world Ruben." He took another sip of his drink. "Besides you can just call some carpet cleaners to take care of your carpet if you can't do it yourself."

I couldn't contain myself anymore. "Ahhhhhhhhhh," I roared. I grabbed the glass from Alejandro's hand and threw it against the wall. The glass shattered into pieces as it collided with the wall. "Oh God, what have I done," I cried resting on my knees. "I can't take it back." The straw was on Alejandro's lips. While he looked at me like I was crazy, I was wiping the tears off my face.

He walked close to the shattered pieces of glass. He looked back at me with his hands on his hips. "That's just some more cleanin' you'll have to do man."

* * * * *

I told Alejandro everything that happened last night. He didn't have to ask me any questions, but I was openly confessing to him as if he were my priest. I felt like we were in a therapy session because I was lying down on my couch.

"Was it everything you thought it would be," Alejandro asked while sitting in my loveseat.

"I've heard so many people talk about their first time and how great it was," I replied. "And I'm not going to lie I enjoyed it, but I am ashamed that it happened so soon. I guess if waiting until marriage isn't a big deal to you and you have premarital sex it may not matter. But there was a time that mattered to me. I think I may have realized that a little too late."

"You're not goin' to kill yourself are you?"

"No, no, but I can't look at myself in the mirror right now."

"I remember after my first time I didn't feel the guilt you are feelin' right now. I didn't feel the guilt until the girl I was with at that time that I gave up my virginity to she decided that she wanted to see other people. She had also given me her virginity, but she soon found herself curious about other men. I sometimes wish I had valued my virginity more. I was 20 at the time and in love. That's why I want to do right by Kat. Even though there are times it's difficult…"

"Please spare me the details." Alejandro laughed.

"Look Ruben, I still have much respect for you. You're human and sometimes you'll make mistakes. I know that you're probably disappointed in yourself right now, but you need to decide what you'll do from this point on. Are you gonna try to be abstinent or are you gonna have even more sex. Were you plannin' on tellin' Deanna what happened?"

"I don't feel there's any need to because we're not officially a couple."

"Are you sure you want to do that?"

"Yes I am." I sat up in the couch. "We're almost getting sentimental like a Hallmark film. You want to go see this high octane, testosterone filled movie."

"Yeah, let's roll out."

* * * * *

Christian Bale offered a somewhat pleasurable viewing experience as a grown up version of John Connor, but I couldn't take my mind off of Bianca and what we had done.

I was supposed to be at choir rehearsal tonight for church tomorrow, but I called in sick. Lying is starting to feel natural for me.

I visited a Macy's store at North Star Mall to get myself some new clothes. Maybe some retail therapy would make me feel better. I was trying on a navy blue fitted pin stripe suit and black Kenneth Cole dress shoes. As I was buttoning the four buttons on the single breasted suit I heard a woman complimenting me. Looking in the mirror I saw that it was Mari.

"Hey there handsome," she said with a smile that brightened up my day. "That suit looks really good on you. Blue is definitely your color."

"Thank you," I replied as I gave her a hug. "I don't have a blue pin stripe suit. I've been meaning to get one." I turned around to face her. "What are you doing up here?"

"I'm just browsing. The hubby is watching the girls at home so this is how I spend my free time."

"Ah, living the dream."

"Yeah, you know it. So are you going to buy that suit?"

"Yes, I believe I am. I like how it fits and I also look good in it." She smiled. "Yeah, I'm going to buy it. I want to get a shirt and tie with it, but I just don't know what to get that would be perfectly coordinated with it."

"Hold on I think I saw something that might go with that. You like fitted shirts right?"

"Yes I do."

"And your shirt size is what a 16, 32/33?"

"Dang, it's as if you have known me my whole life."

"Okay, give me a minute," she smiled. "I'll be right back."

"I'll be right here."

As I was looking back in the mirror I saw Mari walking towards the shirts section and I couldn't help, but notice that she had a very nice looking rear end that was shaped like an apple. She looked really good in her tight black jeans that she was wearing with her knee high black boots that made her five inches taller. Okay stop! I do not need to make a habit of getting involved with married women.

The guilt of sleeping with Bianca was hovering over me and no matter how hard I tried to shake it off it was still attached to me like steel to a magnet. How could I face Deanna when she's done nothing, but been a good woman to me? Was Bianca feeling the same guilt or was she acting like nothing ever happened? Journalists are taught to ask who, what, where, when, why, and how so they can get an idea as to the direction they want to take their story. I should have applied this to my dating life.

I should have been asking myself who I really need to be involved with for a relationship. Who and what does my potential mate believe in? Where does my potential mate want to go with her life? When will I know I'm ready for a serious relationship? Why do I feel I need to be with this woman? Last, but not least how can we both benefit each other's lives and make the relationship work? Too bad I'm not a journalist at heart.

It's a little late to be asking myself those questions. That's stuff one should already know before they get involved with someone.

"Okay I found something that I think will be the perfect combination," Mari said. She had a long-sleeve white shirt with blue pin stripes and a silk blue tie to match the fitted shirt.

"Wow, you have a great eye for this stuff." I took off the jacket as I was walking back to the dressing room. "That goes with it perfectly. You should shop with me more often."

"I wish my husband felt that way," she replied as I was taking the pants I tried on off behind the curtain that served as a door.

"He doesn't like to get your opinion on what he's going to wear?"

"When we first started dating he would have me tag along and point out what worked and what didn't work. After a while I guess he got tired of it. Maybe he felt I was being bossy by letting him know what he looked good in. I just enjoyed being able to do something with him. You know spend time with him."

"I'm not married, but I understand what you mean." I came out of the dressing room going to the register with a whole new wardrobe still speaking with Mari.

"You understand what I mean?"

"Yeah, that's part of the reason nobody wants to be alone forever. You want to have different experiences with someone, even if they're small ones."

"Yes exactly."

After purchasing some new clothes Mari and I were in the food court drinking some smoothies still having an informative conversation. In a way I was learning from her what women want in a man.

"My husband has never been the possessive type, which is one of the things that I love about him," she said. "And he was never passive either. He was assertive, but lately for the last few months it just seems he's nonchalant."

"What do you mean," I asked.

"It just feels like he is not trying to fight for our relationship. I've always loved the freedom he has given me. He never put any demands on me and that had me love him so much more. Jealousy is something I have never cared for, but there is a part of me that wishes he could show a sign of jealousy, just so I know that he still cares."

"You know it says in the bible that jealousy is as cruel as the grave."

"I know I know it destroys a relationship. I just want to feel a sense of passion from him."

"Sometimes I wonder if passion is overrated."

Mari was silent as she folded her hands. "So who is the woman that got away from you?"

"What makes you say that?"

"There's pain in your eyes. Your eyes say your heart has been broken and you're afraid to let someone else in." I was hesitant to speak up, but I opened up.

"Um…her name was Monique. I would sometimes call her Mo or Mo V, since her last name was Valdez. Her middle name began with an O, so it worked. I thought we would be together forever. There are some relationships you get into and your outlook on it is if it's meant to be it will work out, if not then there's someone better out there for the both of us. My outlook with Mo was that I want to spend the remainder of my life with her. I don't want to speak out of line and stop me if I do, but sometimes when I see you I see her."

"Really," she replied combing her hair back over her ear. "How do I remind you of her?" I must have gained her curiosity because she leaned in a little closer.

"Mo was funny, strong, honest and real. You almost have the same build and look as her. I liked how tall I looked standing next to her. Standing next to her I felt like her bodyguard or even her superhero. But I loved that she was shorter than me because every time I hugged her it would last longer than your average hug. What I loved most about our hugs is that she could feel how my heart would beat for her."

"Oh, that's sweet."

"I remember at the church Memorial Day picnic you were wearing a Flash t-shirt. I thought that was hot because it's not every day you see a woman as attractive as you are wearing something that would be considered geek related."

"I've always been a fan of the DC comics," she laughed.

"Mo was refined and just on first impression I would have never thought she was a fan of Marvel comics or comics in general. Her favorite was Captain America and she looked beautiful in her t-shirt that had the Captain America logo. We went to one of those comic book conventions one time and I was wearing a Captain America costume and carrying the shield. She was dressed like that as well only as a female, wearing a bra with the logo and little red, white, and blue dress and a mask to match it along with the knee-high red boots that looked kinky. And of course she had the shield too. I still have that picture of us. That was one of the things I loved about her, was her confidence and her creativity. She was a big fan of Star Wars, which caught me completely off guard. She would dress conservative most of the time, but I remember when we went to a Halloween party I was dressed as Lando Calrissian. She was dressed as Princess Leia in the slave outfit she wore in Return of the Jedi. She was strutting in some gold high heel sandals and we both ended up winning the costume contest...mainly because of her. I never thought it was possible to be seductive, revealing, and classy all at once, but she pulled it off. She was so beautiful. It's a picture I definitely have in my photo album." Mari smiled. "Your smiles are similar in that they have a calming effect. Every time I would enter a room she would smile at me. Sometimes her thing was to pinch my nose. It was just a thing that only she did. I remember after we confessed our love to each other sometimes when we were in a crowded room we would look at each other and scratch our noses with our left ring finger. It was our signal for saying "I love you."

"That's so corny," she said wiping a tear that ran down her cheek. "It's corny, but sweet."

"I know right." She laughed. "We never had sex." Mari's eyes light up. "I know it's shocking especially when she was wearing the Princess Leia slave costume you would have thought that would have been the night to do it. The relationship wasn't about sex, but she was the queen of touch. She could hug you and almost make you forget what made you angry in the first place. Just holding her hand or getting a massage from her felt right. Talking with her was always warm. Even when we disagreed or had an argument it felt like a conversation. Amazingly she never raised her voice to me, but her tone was still stern when necessary. There were times I raised my voice, but she had a way of calming me down. Like I said before she had that calming effect. She was someone I respected. Mo was pure and so was my love for her. I was in awe of her. I was in love with her."

"I don't understand."

"What is it you don't understand?"

"If you were in awe of her and loved her how come you're still single?"

"It wasn't meant for us to be together forever."

"I just don't get how that could happen."

"I don't understand how it could happen either. There's that saying you want to make God laugh tell him your plans. I guess I gave him a really great laugh when it came to Mo and me."

It felt strange, but Mari squeezed my hand and never let go. Naturally I squeezed back.

It was close to closing time at the mall as I was walking Mari to her car, which was a 2001 black Camry.

"I enjoyed talking with you," she said. "I definitely learned a lot about you."

"Hopefully I didn't freak you out."

"Oh no, of course you didn't freak me out. I'll see you tomorrow at church."

"Yeah I will be there." As she went in for a hug I wrapped both my arms around her as if I was protecting her. I was hugging her the way I hugged Monique. Mari's arms were wrapped around my waist and her head was next to my heart that was rapidly beating. I was holding her a lot longer than I should have been and yet she wasn't letting me go. She whispered something that caught my attention. "Oh that feels so good."

After she said that our eyes locked on each other. I wanted to kiss her so bad, but she was married. I had already slept with another married woman, so why stop now. She bit her bottom lip, as her eyes were looking like they were giving me an invitation to kiss her. I kissed her on the forehead and slowly backed away from her. We both looked at each other.

"You know I want to give you more than that, but I can't do it," I said.

"I know and you're a good man Ruben," she replied.

"Sometimes I don't want to be good."

She walked up to me and touched my face. "You're so adorable."

I grabbed her hand and kissed it. "You better go before I do something that is not adorable."

"Yeah." She stood still.

"Mari I am serious. You have five seconds to walk away."

"And if I don't walk away."

"If you're still standing where you are right now I am going to grab you by the hand, be like a boa constrictor and hold on to you tight, and kiss you as if it's the last thing I will ever live to do."

Mari stood straight and immobile as a lamppost with a smile on her face saying "How can you expect me to walk away after hearing that."

"Five." She bit her bottom lip. "Four." Even though I moved in a little closer she remained still. "Three." She was looking into my eyes with an invitation to cut my count short and kiss her. But I'm a man of my word. If she is still standing in front of me by the time I reach the number one, it is on. Man I hope she doesn't walk away. "Two." After I said a tear fell down her face and she slowly backed up. I didn't bother counting to one, as she walked away and got into her car and drove off.

Even though I didn't want her to, Mari made the right decision.

Is there something in the air? It just seems like I'm attracting women who could be classified as an OAT. Women who are older, attractive, and already taken...OAT.

* * * * *

As I began driving on 281 my cell phone was ringing.

There was a part of me hoping it was Mari, but I never gave her my number so who could it be. I was then hoping it was Bianca, but hopes sank quickly when I saw India's name appear on my caller screen. I finally decided to answer her call after ignoring her for months.

"Hello India," I said lethargically.

"Hey you," she replied. "It's so great to hear your voice. I was beginning to think that you disappeared off the face of the planet."

"No I'm still here. You're definitely persistent. Most people stop calling if they haven't heard from someone after a few days, but not you."

"I miss you and I just wanted to talk to you. I haven't heard from you in a while is everything alright?"

"Yeah I'm doing okay. How are you doing?"

"I could complain, but I think there are other people out there who have more to complain about than I do."

"I get ya." As I was driving down 281, I realized that I was close to India's townhome, as she lived off on Bitters. "So what are you doing right now?"

"Nothing, I'm just sitting at home about to watch some movies I rented. Would you like to come over and watch some movies with me?"

"Sure I wouldn't mind."

"Don't play with me."

"No I'm serious. I wouldn't mind watching some movies with you."

"How long will it take you to get here?"

"Probably less than ten minutes."

"Where are you at?"

"I was just leaving North Star Mall and I was just driving around on 281."

"Well I guess it's fortuitous that I called you."

"I guess so. I'll see you in a little bit."

"Okay." We both hung up.

Maybe I was visiting India out of pity. She was 43-years-old and single. I know that it's unorthodox for a much older person to date a much younger person, but at the time that I met India I really thought she was in her late twenties. Her family has some great genes, as they age very well like fine wine. She got married when she was 19 because she got pregnant, but she suffered a miscarriage. Her marriage endured for 15 years. It reached its conclusion because she left her husband. She had enough of being abused verbally and physically too many times and all the other women he was seeing behind her back.

I met her on a Saturday night at a Barnes and Noble bookstore. We were both sitting in the café section of the bookstore and I noticed that we were both reading Five People You Meet in Heaven by Mitch

Albom. I broke the ice by approaching her and asking her how far she had gotten into the book. We both discussed what we liked about the book and then we talked about other books that were good reads.

My top five favorite books were The Alchemist by Paulo Coelho, Tuesdays with Morrie by Mitch Albom, The Millionaire Next Door by Thomas J. Stanley and William D. Danko, Maximize the Moment by T.D. Jakes, and Wild at Heart by John Eldredge.

But I digress.

When she told me her age it did bother me at first that I was old enough to be her son, but I put those thoughts aside when I felt she looked young for her age...very young. Plus, I'd always been curious about dating a cougar.

The relationship started off as lustful. We never had sex because she knew that I was a Christian and that I wanted to wait until marriage...ha that's funny. Even though she wasn't a Christian and she wouldn't have mind educating me on the benefits of having sex, she respected me enough to wait.

Anyway the day after we met she invited me to her place and it was close to midnight. Of course I went and at first we cuddled while watching a movie, then we made out, and then I stayed the night in her bed with her wrapped in my arms and both of us fully clothed.

India was a lady in public, but in private she was a wild cougar. We never had sex, but we resorted to some alternatives that made me feel like I had sex. It was probably the closest thing to a sexual relationship I ever had...well prior to having sex with Bianca. My relationship with India was one I could say I may have still been a virgin, but I no longer felt pure.

If I had wanted to have sex with India, she would have agreed to have it with me.

We broke up because I felt she was putting her life on hold for me and I like a woman who is active, making moves with her life, and goal-oriented. India fell in love faster than I could spell the word "love." She was overwhelming me by making herself too available and too anxious for my attention, as if I filled the gaps in her life. Like any other man I enjoy attention and like feeling wanted, but having someone like me way too much is a turnoff. She was less intriguing the needier she became; to the point it was almost frightening.

A month after we broke up she had sex with another man even though she wanted to maintain abstinence. I guess it was a feeble attempt to make me jealous, but it didn't work. Part of me feels that I may have put those thoughts in her mind and one-day she decided to act on them. When we dated she had been deprived of something she enjoyed and when an opportunity came, she took advantage of it. I can't blame her now that I know how it feels.

I wonder what it would feel like to have sex with a woman that's almost twenty years my senior.

I pulled into the parking lot of India's place. She still had the olive green wooden sign hanging over her tan door that read "Place where everybody knows your name." I knocked on the door and I could hear her little brown Pomeranian, Brownie, barking.

I thought Gabrielle Union opened the door, but it was India with a new look. People used to joke around and call her Cleopatra because she had shiny long straight black hair, but it was now curly and dyed brown that blended in with her dark complexion. When we dated she was kind of chubby. She lost some obvious weight, as she now had the slim figure of a 30-year-old wearing a black wife beater that slightly revealed her flat stomach as well as chiseled arms with a tattoo of her name on her right arm. She must have been trying to make herself tempting, as she was wearing some very high tan shorts that were revealing her chiseled legs, very reminiscent of Tina Turner.

Her manicure toes were resting in some black high heel sandals, as she didn't like to walk around barefoot in her place. Last time I saw her eyes they were dark brown, but she was wearing contacts that made her eyes hazel.

I was reminded of how exquisite she looked and wondered why I ever broke up with her just because she wasn't age appropriate. After all age isn't anything, but a number.

"Look at you, I see you've been taking very good care of yourself," I said as I entered her apartment, as Brownie was jumping up and down near my leg still barking.

"I'm just trying to maintain the image that 43 is the new 23," she laughed while locking her door. When she turned around we hugged each other. As we hugged, we held each other as if we didn't want to let go. I was beginning to feel myself get aroused so I let go. "That was a nice hug. You look good Ruby."

"Well you know I do what I can."

She sniffed me, as she walked by. "Still smell good too. Grab a seat." I sat down on the left side of her black leather couch. I used to always sit there when we were dating so I could always wrap my right arm around her. Brownie jumped on my lap and stopped barking when I was petting him. "I have American Gangster and The Heartbreak Kid. Which would you prefer to watch first?"

"Would you mind watching American Gangster?" I had already seen both movies, but India wasn't into big blockbuster feature films like I was. She was more into independent films that were only viewed in film festivals or rarely seen.

"No we can watch that." After she put the movie on she kicked her shoes off, as she sat very close to me Indian style. Suddenly old habits were repeating themselves as I strangely found my arm wrapping around her. She obliged me by moving in a little closer to where her head was rested on my chest and running one of her hands under my shirt rubbing my stomach which was something I always enjoyed her doing. "Feels like you've been staying in shape."

"Do what I can."

"What else have you been up to these days?"

"I was laid off from the newspaper, but I recently passed my real estate exam so I'm going to be getting involved with the real estate industry."

"That's good. Are you still doing the musical thing?"

"Yeah, I'm still doing that."

"I was going to have something to drink," she said getting up. "I was going to have some Chardonnay. Would you like a glass of water?"

"Uh no, pour me a glass of Chardonnay please."

"Wow, really. You drink now. What other habits have you picked up? If you had sex that would probably end up being your favorite hobby."

Who knows how she would react if she knew the truth?

* * * * *

It was pointless to have the television on because while the movie was playing we were talking the whole time touching base as to what the other had been doing during our time of separation. For the last five years she had been the art director for the San Antonio Museum of Art. The lease of her townhome would end in six months and she was looking into moving herself into a new house by the time it was up. She also mentioned that she just completed her bachelor's degree this past May, as she graduated with honors in business with a concentration on accounting. She was looking into trying to get a job with some accounting firms. At the moment she was studying for her CPA exam that would be in a couple of months.

After we both drank three glasses of Chardonnay the buzz was kicking in, but India was still sober. I was wondering if I hadn't drunk those three glasses of wine, would I have been lying down on the couch with India.

"That's great that you're achieving so much," I complimented while my hand was wrapped around her stomach. Brownie was asleep in a red blanket that was in his little basket near the fireplace that had no logs burning.

"Yeah, but I just feel there's something missing," she said turning around. "I wish I was married and in the process of starting a family. You know." It kind of freaked me out that she looked deep into my eyes, as if she wanted to start a family with me on her couch. "I say that because this gentleman I dated broke up with me last week."

"Oh, I'm sorry to hear that. How long were you together?"

"We were together for a little over a year. He was Korean, 42-years-old, an architect, and he had a boy and a girl. His daughter's name is Deja and she's 15 and his son's name is Marcel and he's 7. I got along with both of them all that time we dated. His daughter liked going shopping with me and both of his kids would come to me for advice, as if I was their mother. I thought for sure when he told me he needed to tell me something he would be proposing, but he turned my world upside down when he told me he no longer wanted to be with me. It was like that Jagged Edge song, felt like Heaven ended when he walked out of my life." A tear fell down her face. "When I asked why he told me he didn't know, but he just knew that he didn't want to be with me anymore. He couldn't see us sharing a future together. I just don't understand why. I think there may have been someone else or he was getting back with his ex-wife. Before we started dating she would only call or see him to pick up or drop off the kids. When we started dating she was calling or visiting on a regular basis. They were divorced for five years. I just don't know why I bother hoping for a long lasting relationship." She grabbed some tissue paper. "I'm sorry." I nodded my head, as she wiped her tears. "I miss you Ruben. I miss your company. I miss talking with you. I miss us being close like this and me just feeling safe when I'm around you." She paused for a moment looking at me while I was taking in what she just said. "You know what I also miss about you," she said leaning in closer.

"What's that?"

"I also miss the massages you would give me. My neck is sore, would you mind rubbing me down."

"No, I don't mind," I smiled. I got up so she could lie on her stomach. I got down on my knees on the floor, as I began to rub her neck. As I was rubbing her I looked at her fingernails and forgot how meticulous she was about everything. I forgot how attractive her nails always looked when we were dating. They shined like a wax job done on a Mustang vehicle. Her feet looked the same way. I liked that they were never painted, but they looked clean, as if they were laminated.

"Ohhhh! That feels good Ruben," she crooned. Maybe it was the wine controlling my thoughts, but I imagined her saying that if we had sex. I imagined her feet kicking the ceiling and singing my name as I gave her a sexual voyage that she had never experienced before. After sleeping with one woman I was already acting like I was Casanova. As my imagination ran wild I began to feel myself getting an erection. I quickly thought about sheep, goats, an elderly nudist establishment to kill my expansion. It was working. I massaged India for another five minutes and she was satisfied. "That felt good Ruby."

"Thank you." I decided that I wanted to take advantage of India's vulnerability and have sex with her. "You know you owe me a massage."

"Oh do I?"

"Yeah, you know with me its quid pro quo."

"Just selfish," she laughed. "Let's go up to my bedroom because you're too tall for the couch." I gave her a suspicious look posing as if I didn't want to have sex, but curious if she was reading my mind. "I'm not trying to get down like that, come on." The carpet had might as well been broken glass because she always wore shoes around her house. After she slipped in her sandals I walked behind her as she grabbed my hands. As we were slowly walking to her room I was looking at her backside and immediately a bulge was rising like the sun. I was thinking impure thoughts as I wanted to seize the moment and be with India making her the first black woman I would ever sleep with.

As we continued to walk I wrapped my hands around her hips and pulled her in to me. As her head rested against my chest I kissed her shoulder. While I softly kissed her shoulder I could hear her breathing differently, as if she was in fear for her life.

"What are you doing to me?"

"What does it look like?"

"Be careful because I'm not wearing a bra or any panties." I held her even tighter and ran my hands down the inside of her thighs. "Don't stop," she moaned, as she wrapped her arms around my head while I began kissing her neck. I began to rub my body against hers just inches away from her room. I than pushed her up against the wall grinding her, as she was rubbing her posterior harder into my crotch region. "You like that daddy."

"Yeah I do."

"That's right, give me what I like." She turned around and our lips met. We kissed each other, as if that were the only thing that would keep us alive. She was like a dog very heavy in using her tongue wetting my face that I found both repulsive and arousing. She pulled me to her room. "Do you have protection?"

"Dang it, I don't."

"That's okay," she opened the nightstand drawer next to her bed revealing a pack of sealed Trojan condoms. "I have enough to help us make it through the whole night." She had more protection than any president of the United States ever had.

"What are you doing with a box of condoms?"

"I like to be prepared if the man isn't prepared." She came back to me and we kissed again. I leaned into her making her fall into the bed. As I was lying on top making out with India our weight shifted as she was on top kicking her shoes off, as I took my shirt off. Before we could do the deed, she still wanted to talk. "When we were dating my girlfriends had a nickname for you?"

"A good one I hope."

"Oh yeah, it was a good one."

"What was it?"

"They're nickname for you was Panty Dropper."

"Why did they call me that?"

"Because you are so sexy that just the sight of you makes ladies want to drop their panties." I laughed and grabbed her kissing her again.

There was no time to invest in foreplay, as we were both rushing to have sex like we wanted to be cured of lovesickness. My mouth was wide open when she took off her shirt exposing her bosoms. She unbuckled my belt while I cupped her chest. She took my jeans off. She unsealed the packet with her teeth wrapping the condom on me in a hurry.

I fitted my shaft into the condom feeling like I was wrapped inside a balloon. It felt funny because it was a little slimy. It's ironic that this small piece of rubber would keep me from getting a woman pregnant or catching an STD.

I took off India's shorts and there I was again naked and unashamed with another woman. Before being inside of her she inconveniently decided to start another conversation. I think that was another reason we broke up; she never knew when to shut up.

"Tell me you love me," India moaned.

"What," I replied shocked feeling like that was an alarm for me to retreat.

"Tell me you love me."

"I love you," I said knowing that if I did I would get what I want.

"I don't believe you, make me believe it."

"No I do love you, I've missed you. I love you India, I love you."

"Tell me again."

"I love you India, I love you."

"Oh Ruby I love you," she kissed me, as she pulled the condom off that I was wrapped in.

Unlike my sexual encounter with Bianca, there was no music with India. The only music that would be heard would be our own grunts, moans, and screams. As I looked at India she straddled me allowing me to enter the throne that rested between her legs.

She gave me a mischievous grin as I was cloaked in her warmth and moistness that felt like honey. I felt she was a little crazy asking me to tell her I loved her, but I really wanted to have sex. As I slowly entered her, she tilted her head back moving her body slowly like she was riding a bull for fun in a Cowboy bar. In a few seconds I was going to make her yell like she was on a roller coaster ride. She wouldn't remember her ex-boyfriend or ex-husband after I was done with her.

I clinched her cheeks as she was bouncing a little harder on me, as if she wanted to leave an imprint in my body. After almost 15 minutes she was probably surprised that I hadn't exploded yet because she assumed that I never had sex and would easily reach my climax within a minute, but I was still caught up in the motions.

"Ohhh you feel so good Ruby," she roared. "Mmmmmmmmmm."

As her hands were pushing down on my chest I reached up and grabbed the back of her head pulling her face to mine. My tongue was waltzing in her mouth and we changed positions, as I was now looking down on her rising to the top.

Her legs were rising like a flag, as I was finding myself in a rhythm sliding up and down inside of India. I was feeling a chill up my spine. Something happened that I couldn't explain, as I felt like I was lost in space not knowing where this journey would end.

My breathing was louder than her screams while she was pulling on the sheets. She was screaming so loud that I was afraid the cops would come busting through her place thinking she was being attacked. As my eyes were watering up I could feel my heart pulsating and my breathing was getting heavier. As we were going at it harder India was holding me tighter, as I could feel my muscles tense up and my veins ready to pop out. My hands were grasping the sheets like the bed was going to be flipped over, as I could hear India's bed squeaking louder. With one final thrust I felt myself erupt inside India's palace. Her body shook and trembled as she cried in a way that wasn't glorifying the one above, "Ohhhhhhh God."

As I lay motionless on her body catching my breath I didn't know what time it was, but I felt I achieved something sleeping with two women within 24 hours.

After half an hour of taking a breather we went back at it again and again and again until almost five in the morning when we were both drained and fell asleep. Her stamina was impressive for a woman her age.

Character is the sum and total of a person's choices

~Anonymous~

15

Ordinary Just Won't Do

Mari was staring at me. She was about to walk away, but I softly grabbed her face and slowly kissed her lips. She pulled me by my pants to where there was no air between us. Our kiss that started off as romantic turned strange when she started licking me all over my face.

I opened my eyes to see that for an alarm clock I had a dog's tongue licking my face. Brownie jumped off the bed and paced back and forth when I woke up. The shower was running and the ceiling fan was rapidly spinning cooling me off.

I jumped out of the bed as if I was running late for school and didn't want to miss the bus. I put my clothes on trying to set a world record for the fastest exit. I grabbed all my possessions making sure I didn't leave anything behind because I didn't want to have a reason to come back to India's home. I opened up her drawer where she kept the condoms. I don't know how many I grabbed, but I grabbed a handful of condoms. I know it's not right for me to say it, but at this rate I don't think I will stop having sex.

First I have premarital sex, then I sleep with two women, one of whom is married, and now I'm stealing…stealing condoms. Oh how the mighty have fallen.

Before walking out the door Brownie was standing next to me looking up at me with some sad eyes and raising one of his paws. I picked Brownie up and pet him one last time. "I'm sorry little buddy, but I have to leave. It's not you, it's me." I put Brownie down on the ground and walked out the door hearing him scratching the door after I closed it.

Deanna was returning and things had to be back to normal. I was denying that things were no longer normal. Bianca was forbidden fruit, but like Adam and Eve I indulged myself. India was fragile and I took advantage of her vulnerability. But I didn't give into making out with Mari, so nobody can say I was completely immoral.

If there's anything I learned in the last 48 hours it's that my virginity wasn't given away physically, but it began to vanish mentally when I entertained the thought of premarital sex. I entertained those thoughts for so long that it was only a matter of time that I would give up my virginity.

This whole time I could have set my thoughts on the things of God and invested my time in prayer.

I was going 80 on the highway trying to forget about everything that took place the last couple of nights.

When I saw India's name appear on my caller screen I knew that would be impossible like trying to pet an alligator. I acted as if nothing had changed between us, as I ignored her call, most likely to her chagrin.

Everything had to be back to normal.

* * * * *

Someone else filled in on the piano at church because I told the choir director I was not feeling too well to play. My body was seated in the Lord's house for almost two hours, but I wasn't mentally present. My mind couldn't escape everything that happened this weekend with Bianca and India.

I was so ashamed to sit in the pew that I sat in the café of the church and watched the message presented on the monitor. Plus, I wanted to make a quick exit when the service was over because I didn't feel like seeing or talking to anyone.

While sitting in the café I saw Mari organizing some products in the bookstore. She had smiled and waved at me. I waved back at her. I couldn't stop looking at her. I regretted not kissing her, even when she was so willing to do it. But as I was looking at her, I saw Monique.

I couldn't help, but wish I could have spent my life with Monique. It wasn't fair that she left. It wasn't fair that a woman like Mari was unavailable. I hate married women.

Hate is such a strong word, but married women aren't my favorite people to be around and I just wish they would not come near me. Like a cat near a mouse, I can't help myself when married women are around me.

While I was daydreaming about a life with Monique or Mari, India had shown up to the church looking upset. I forgot that I brought her here one time and she knew me well enough to know that I would be here.

She came in looking like she was ready to fight, as she bit her bottom lip and popped her knuckles. She looked ghetto fabulous in her black sweat pants with flip flops and a pink t-shirt with her hair tied up in a bun with no makeup on.

"So you just expected me to leave you alone after letting you get in my pants," yelled India.

"Woman lower your voice," I said getting up from my seat and pulling her by the arm. She yanked her arm back.

"Don't touch me."

"Get your tail outside woman." As we walked outside I saw a couple of people staring at us. I had to compose myself to keep from going off on India. "You need a sedative because your crazy right now."

"And with good reason," she went back to yelling.

"Calm down."

"Don't tell me what to do. I don't care who hears me. What you don't want me to make a scene?" In order to not make much of a scene I started walking away to at least get her away from the church and just make her follow me where we could get lost in between some cars in the parking lot. And of course it worked. She was multi-tasking walking, talking, and pushing me. The more she talked the more heated I got. There was fire in me that was ready to burst. I was afraid that once it erupted I wouldn't be able to control what happens. The last push India gave she put a lot more force in to where I almost tripped while walking. I finally turned around and faced her. "Oh so now you gonna face me like a man." My lips were pressed together and my eyes narrowed in on her. "What you getting mad now. Is that look on your face supposed to scare me? Boy please you ain't nothing, but a pussy." My hand rolled up into a fist. We were in between some cars to where no one would have seen me slap her. I kept my fist from making contact with her face because my parents raised me better than that. Plus, there were cops at our church who always directed traffic in the parking lot and the last thing I wanted was to get arrested. "You gonna punch me. Go ahead, punch me you little pussy. See if the cops won't arrest you. PUNCH ME!"

"You're not worth it," I said relaxing my hand.

She bit her bottom lip and raised her hand to slap me in the face. She swung her hand towards me. I grabbed her hand before it could collide with my face.

"Oh Ruby, please don't hurt me, please," she cried like a coward as I held her hand tight.

"What is your problem," I said as I let go of her hand.

"Why did you leave and why didn't you answer my calls," she cried with tears running down her face. She no longer sounded like a grown woman, but she sounded more like a naïve child. "All I want to do is love you." She was wiping the tears that were coming down her face. "When you say you love someone, like you said to me last night, you don't treat them bad. I thought what happened last night was something special. I thought we were reconnecting. I thought that…"

"You thought wrong," I interrupted feeling like a cold-hearted gangster getting up in her face with a deadpan stare like something I thought I would never be…a bully. I could just hear myself talking to her as if I didn't care about her. I almost felt like I was being condescending with her. "I'm only going to say this once. What happened last night was great, but it was a one-time thing. Don't expect to hear from me again and don't expect a visit from me. Don't ever call me again India because I don't want to be with you. Don't ever try to visit me or see me. I don't want to be with you. I am done with you. You have no place in my life. You mean nothing to me. Nothing, you understand?" Where was all of this coming from? Did I actually say all of that? I felt like I was having an out of body experience wanting to take back those words, but they were already gone. I backed away from her grabbing my sunglasses, as she was holding her arms. She was afraid to look me in the eye, as she stared at the ground looking helpless.

"Ruben what has gotten into you? You would never talk…"

"I believe I've made myself clear."

"But I was your first…"

"I'm with someone else." She was fighting to hold back the tears, but she could not hold them back.

"Someone else, why didn't you…you said that you loved me."

"From here on out we are no longer a part of each other's lives. Have a blessed life India." I looked at her as she was speechless with more tears racing down her face. All I could do was put on my sunglasses and walk away.

* * * * *

After I left church I didn't bother to change out of my navy blue pin stripe suit, but I had time to stop at a store and pick up a can of Red Bull. With tax included it cost me $2.69. I handed the cashier a five-dollar bill and in return she mistakenly gave me $3.31.

"Oh ma'am," I said. "You gave me an extra dollar."

"Oh did I," she asked looking at my receipt. "Yes I did." I smiled and gave her a dollar bill. "Thank you. I wish more people could be honest like you. Have a good day sir."

If she knew how dishonest I was she would feel differently about that.

I never thought I would be one of those guys that are seen on The Maury Povich Show who would be disloyal to his significant other, let alone persuade a married woman to be unfaithful to her husband. No matter how many prayers of forgiveness that I prayed to God I felt that my new residence would be hell regardless.

I didn't feel unique, as I blended in with every other typical male whose main concerns were food, money, and sex. Not that there's anything wrong with that, but ordinary just won't do.

I was chugging down the Red Bull like it was Kool-Aid. Deanna thought I looked sexy in a suit. While I was driving to the airport to pick her up I took off my silk sky blue tie that Mari had picked out for me. My shades covered the windows to my tormented soul that were filled with bags, as I didn't catch much sleep…the whole weekend.

India called me again. I think she suffered a worse case of OCD than I did. I ignored her call. I felt bad for basically taking advantage of her and then saying those harsh words to her. I wish I could take back everything that happened between us, but I can't take any of it back. Besides she is a grown woman and she'll get over it. It may take a little time, but somewhere down the road she will meet another man and realize that I'm not irresistible. Who am I kidding, I know I'm irresistible. But in all seriousness India will get over it.

Deanna text me to let me know she was walking out of baggage claim. Just in case India wouldn't stop calling I turned my phone off because Deanna would have been
suspicious if I was ignoring someone's call. When I pulled up she was standing by her luggage with a smile on her face.

It was the first time she came back from a trip that I was disappointed to see her, but I feigned excitement giving her a kiss on the lips hoping she wouldn't detect another woman's scent on me.

As she jumped in my ride I placed her luggage in the back. While I got in behind the wheel and took off I wondered if Deanna could detect any guilt on my face. For that matter I wondered if she could smell the scent of the two women I had been with. Wow, two women in one weekend.

I kept my eyes on the road so she wouldn't have a chance to investigate me.

The disappointment I was feeling in myself was eradicated because I couldn't get over how sexy Deanna was looking. She was casually dressed, but there was something alluring about the way she was carrying herself.

She was showing off her pedicure strutting in some brown open toe heels. Her firm hips were transparent as she was wearing some loose fitted white slacks that were cut off at the knees. She showed off her fairly structured arms, as she was sporting a red Derrick Rose basketball jersey. She always purchased sports apparel from the different cities she visited that had a professional basketball, football, or baseball team, particularly basketball. Her hair was curly and ran down passed her shoulders and bangs hovered over her eyes that were covered with brown-framed sunglasses that were enormous enough to cover her whole face.

All of a sudden it hit me. Deanna's hair was now dirty blonde.

"I love what you did with your hair," I complimented.

"Thank you sweetie," Deanna replied. "I had been meaning to go with a new look and I had some time on my hands yesterday so I just figured I'd get it done."

While she spoke I was strangely aroused just by her new hairstyle. I was aroused because seeing her with her new look reminded me of Bianca. All I could see was Bianca when I looked at her.

Oh dear, I am in real big trouble.

It was as if I had been under someone's spell because I found myself yearning to be with Deanna. Now that I was no longer a virgin why not have sex with Deanna. There was no guarantee we would be married to each other, so carpe diem. I could make her feel as if she's my first. She never had to know that I slept with two other women.

I still couldn't get over that in one weekend I slept with two women. I might as well make up for lost time.

I was going to give what Deanna had been wanting...all of me.

* * * * *

While walking upstairs to Deanna's apartment I carried her luggage and watched her posterior swivel, as if she was Jessica Rabbit.

As we walked in I placed her luggage in the dining room while she greeted her turtle that was swimming around in his little aquarium. She turned on her laptop wanting to check her email. While she waited for it to load her hands were resting on her hips.

I leaned against the wall with my legs crossed and hands resting in my pockets, as if I was posing for a Jet Magazine cover. As Deanna inhaled, her breast stood upright making me stand erect. She spun her neck around slowly like a ferris wheel.

"What," she asked with a smile on her face and a glow in her eyes.

"Nothing," I replied. "I just can't stop staring. You're so beautiful."

"You're too cute," she said grabbing a seat in front of her laptop. "You really wear that suit."

"Thank you." I took my coat off and hung it on the coat hanger. I stood behind her and placed my hands on her shoulders gently rubbing them.

"Oh, I like that," she said grabbing one of my hands and kissing them. "I really need that. You're always taking good care of me."

"I thought about what you said Deanna that night before you left. I don't mean to come off as distant or guarded. I guess I'm just a little too cautious or protective of myself. I'm sorry if I haven't made things easy for you." I turned her around and knelt down near her placing my hands on her legs. "I'm willing to see where things can go between us as a couple." My hands moved up rubbing her thighs. "Despite our differences you still treat me right and are always doing right by me." If only I could have done the same by her this weekend. "I want to be with you Deanna. I want us to be exclusive. I want to share a relationship with you. I want us to be a couple. So what do you say?"

"It's about time," she laughed. "How long were you going to keep me waiting?"

"Come here," I said pulling her in and kissing her. As we kissed she hummed, as if she had tasted the best chocolate chip cake in the world. Our kissing escalated to where I was picking her up like I was rescuing her and leading us to her bedroom.

When I carried her into the room I let go of her and she was standing looking at me erotically. "Do you really want to do this," she asked. I pulled out a condom that I had in my pocket and held it up like I was showing my identification. "I'll take that as a yes," she smiled. She pulled me in and our lips met again. "Wait I want to put on something I got just for you," she said with excitement running out of the room. She dug in her suitcase and tucked something underneath her jersey. She ran into the bathroom. "Just please be patient. Trust me it will be worth it," she said closing the door.

A few minutes later while my elbows were planted on my knees the door opened and my mouth was open unable to speak because I thought a model from a Victoria Secret catalog or Maxim magazine cover walked out of that bathroom. I had never seen Deanna dressed like this before. If this was a movie this is the part where parents need to kick their kids out of the room or cover their eyes.

She was wearing a leopard printed bustier that covered her breasts that weren't too big, but not too small standing upright. Down below she was covered with leopard printed lace thong.

There wasn't any fat on Deanna's healthy body that was as curvy as the number 8. It was obvious to her that I liked the way she looked because my mouth was still open, as if I needed a ventriloquist to speak for me.

She walked over to me in her brown heels.

"Dang Dee, you look breathtaking," I said.

"Shh," she said putting a finger to her lips. "You just sit back and enjoy. I'll do the work from here."

I grinned, as I leaned back on my elbows. I didn't break eye contact with her, as she knelt down and took off my shoes. She seductively looked at me while running her hands along the inside of my calves up to my knees. She then was running her hands up and down my thighs. Just when I thought she was going to touch me between my legs she stopped short. Her teasing me built my anticipation up even more.

While I'm lying flat on my back fully clothed my grin stretches a little longer like the Cheshire Cat, as she straddles me. With her finger she traces my lips, nose, and the outline of my eyes. She grabs my right hand and lets my index finger trace her lips. As my finger traces her lips she licks it and puts it in her mouth. I get even more excited as I feel her teeth and tongue. She let go of my hand and slowly leaned over me with her breasts coming in my viewpoint, as if she was letting me sneak a peek. Her face came to mine and she kissed me. I pulled her in and slowly flipped her over making the bed squeak.

While I was looking at her I thought this sexual encounter was much more romantic than the ones I had with Bianca and India. Can't believe I'm even thinking about that right now. I'm about to indulge myself in a third serving of physical intimacy in one weekend. DANG I'M GOOD!

I move my lips from hers and kiss her slim neck while one of my hands is lost in her hair and the other on one of her breast. I trace my hand along her breasts before I unfasten her bustier. I feel her back arch and her body slowly rising against mine, as she exhaled and runs her fingers through my hair, while I kissed her breasts.

She unbuttons my shirt and I help pull it off throwing it on the floor. No time to be neat and tidy. My chest was rubbing against her smooth breasts and while she touched my stomach it tickled a little because her hands were cold. As we push each other's pelvis into each other one of her hands dig underneath my pants and she touched me down below making me grow wider. "Oh papi," she says. "Oh my." As she continues to touch me and tells me the things I want to hear I slide her thong down and grab a condom. Deanna slid my pants off, grabbed the sex packet from my hand, and ripped it open. After she pulled off my boxers she wrapped me up in the rubber.

I move her legs wide apart, while she locked her feet around my ankles as I slide into the work of art that is her centerpiece. As I slowly pleasure her we are both looking into each other's eyes with sweat running down our faces. While we looked at each other I thought I was looking down on Bianca. I closed my eyes for a second and when I opened them I saw Deanna again. As she moaned telling me that I felt so good I saw India's face on Deanna's body. I closed my eyes again a little longer and when I opened them it was Deanna. As I saw Deanna I moved faster inside of her making her close her eyes and lock her jaw. "Oh you…sexy…that's my spot," she moaned. The faster I went the louder Deanna got, the more tears were squirting out of my eyes.

I was a male version of Jezebel becoming sexual in all my ways no longer wanting to be like Abel who would please God in everything he would do.

With one final thrust I exploded and Deanna screamed loud enough to break all the windows and make the neighbors want to file a complaint for disturbing the peace. Fatigued I lied down next to Deanna who kissed my shoulder and rested her head on my chest.

"Whoa, that was something," she said.

"Yeah...wow," I said surprised that I had enough stamina to have sex with three women three days straight.

"You're no longer a virgin Ruben, how do you feel?"

If only she knew the truth.

* * * * *

It was close to six o'clock when I went to my parents' house. My mother greeted me with a hug when she opened the door. I could hear Kat and my father in his office getting competitive over a game of Tekken Tag.

"So how have you been," Mom asked.

"I've been doing fine," I replied, as we were walking to the kitchen. "Deanna flew back in today from her interview in Chicago."

"How did it go?"

"She tells me that things look promising."

"Well that's good." I was looking down at the counter while she turned the stove off, as the spaghetti she had in the pot looked ready. She looked back at me noticing that I appeared depressed. "That's good...right?"

"Oh yeah, I guess."

"What do you mean, you guess?"

"Really it's great that she might be getting the job she always wanted, but where does that leave us?"

"You know you can't be selfish, Deanna has to do what's best for her right now. It would be different if you were married, but you're not."

"I know it's just that I don't know if I have the energy to have a long-term relationship that's going to keep us distant for who knows how long."

"So y'all are officially a couple."

"As of today we are."

"That's good."

"Who knows how long it will last though," I mumbled.

"Why are you so quick to judge son?"

"I just…I just…what are you saying, I'm judgmental?"

"Your relationships end so fast that they don't have a beginning. I don't need to break down every relationship you've had, but the reason you left those girls were foolish reasons son."

"What do you mean foolish?"

"Do you really want me to go there? You broke up with a girl because she didn't like Good Will Hunting. You left another girl because she couldn't dance well. That's just not healthy son. If you expect a woman to be perfect, then you're going to be alone your whole life. No woman is going to have everything you want, but spouses grow together and they cultivate each other. That's kind of the beauty of being in a relationship, helping each other improve themselves. You get to see the other person at their worse, only to see them at their best. You want to be with someone that you know is always going to be good to you and for you. Looks are great, but looks pass because nature takes its course, but having a good woman by your side who will go to hell and back for you…well now that's hard to find."

"Mom, what happened with Alton? I mean, when did he just start changing?"

She wiped her hands and rested them on the counter. "Alton became frustrated when I didn't seem to measure up to his so-called standards. He wanted me to be a dependent housewife, but I wanted to be a career woman that was a wife and a mother. When I started walking out of the boundaries he set for me that is when things turned for the worse. I got married right out of high school and didn't really know what I was doing." A big grin came across my mother's face. "You and your older sister were the greatest things he gave me. Some people would tell me that marrying Alton was the biggest mistake I ever made, but it's what led me to Sheldon, who you call dad. It's true that the Lord works in mysterious ways."

"Yeah, you said it."

"Dinner ready," my father said walking in with Kat behind him.

After having dinner with our parents I gave Kat a ride back to her place since her car was in the mechanical shop getting the starter replaced. Oddly enough she didn't say much to me while we had dinner and she was strangely giving me the silent treatment while I was driving her home.

"Cat got your tongue sis," I asked Kat while driving. She didn't reply or even look at me. "You have nothing to say to me little sis."

"So you're sleeping with married women now," she accused.

"Whoa, where do you get off throwing accusations like that at me?"

"You know Alejandro talks too much."

"I should have known better than to tell him."

"Don't be mad at him. So this is what you're doing now. You're sleeping with a married woman. What is wrong with you Ruby? You know better."

"Don't judge me. Don't talk to me like you're perfect."

"I know I'm not perfect, but you're the one that acts like he can do no wrong. How are you going to be reporting all the wrong these preachers do, when you're no better than all of them? You're just as flawed as the rest of us. If you ask me you're the one acting like you're in a position to judge. Maybe you should be exposed. And how are you going to treat Deanna this way. You're just wrong big brother on so many levels."

Kat looked back out the passenger window with her arms folded. All I could do was hold my tongue. There was absolutely nothing I could say to counter her argument. All I could do was just squeeze the steering wheel tighter, as I restrained myself from getting angry with my sister. I was just more so angry with myself. Needless to say we were both quiet the rest of the way to her home.

Love is like playing an instrument. With any instrument you have to learn to play by the rules. Anybody that plays music is creative and creativity means having no limits on your imagination, so you break the rules and play from the heart.

For some playing an instrument may come naturally, just how love comes easy for some people. There are others where it's a work in progress. It takes some time to find that perfect melody.

Take a guitar, for example, there may be only six strings, but some people play the guitar as if there's double that amount or as if they have more than two hands. Some people in relationships do more than what is required, like Jesus making a sacrifice that I don't think anyone else could make

~Choose This Day column by Ruben Wells of Alamo City News~

16

The Way You Make Me Feel

It was the last week of July. Deanna and I were growing closer in the last couple of months because we were doing sexual things I had heard about, but never encountered. We were getting into all types of positions that were probably forbidden for married couples.

As a Christian, I knew it was wrong to engage in premarital sex, but as a man I liked it…a lot…so much so that it seemed like we had sex every night; maybe every other night. The only problem is that it seemed like that's all we were doing when we would see each other.

Deanna was following my lead all along in our tango. If we weren't going to have sex all I had to do was say no and she supported that. In our sexual encounters I had been the student, while she taught me new things. Things I never thought I would do until I was married. Things felt great when we were doing what we shouldn't have been doing.

It was Thursday night and Jammin' 94.1 FM was going to be live at The Island nightclub playing the best jams from the 70's, 80's, and, 90's. They were going to be giving away free prizes that included movie passes, gift certificates to gyms or spas, and free t-shirts. Deanna felt like staying in, but she didn't mind that I went there by myself.

It was a little after ten o'clock and it was time for me to get ready to go, but I was strumming the strings of my guitar while my teeth were holding a pipe in my mouth. Time was passing by quickly as I ran my fingers up and down the strings.

As I played I closed my eyes imagining that if the world heard me play they would stop what they were doing.

I imagined that Monique was sitting across from me with a smile on her face, as she listened to the strings speak the love I had for her. She was the only woman I played the guitar for privately.

Monique was the first woman I broke the rules for in the game of love. She was my inspiration. She used to always smile watching or listening to me play. Sometimes I would play a song that she knew and she would sing. She didn't have a voice like Gladys Knight, but I still loved her. It was more fun teaching her how to play the guitar. It was her favorite instrument.

It would have been refreshing to hear Monique's voice, even if she was off key. There were so many things I wanted to tell her.

Instead of daydreaming I put my guitar down and got ready to go out to The Island.

As I was getting ready my phone rang. I didn't bother to check the number.

"Hello," I said.

"Hey Ruben, it's me Scott," he said.

"What is going on Scotty?"

"I'm just working hard as usual. Sorry to be calling you so late, but there will be a barbecue on Saturday at my house celebrating passing my real estate exam. I want you to come on by."

"Oh yeah I will definitely be there man. I appreciate the invite."

"I'll email you the directions to my place okay. How's everything going buddy?"

"I'm okay, no complaints on my end. I'm just getting ready to go out."

"Oh well hey, don't let me keep you. I'll see you Saturday."

"Alright see you then."

I'm looking forward to seeing what kind of house he has and how well the military life was treating him.

As I was getting ready my phone rang again. I checked my caller screen and saw that it was India. Sticking to status quo, I ignored her call.

* * * * *

I arrived at the club a few minutes before 11 and the whole parking lot was full. Even the street adjacent to the club was packed with cars. I pulled into a parking lot across the street where an insurance company resided. I looked at myself on my driver's side window making sure I was looking my best.

My hair was neat and curly, my dark brown sports coat was spotless covering my tight fitted lighter shade of brown shirt, my black Phat Farm jeans were baggy and wrinkle free and my black square toe Stacy Adams were gleaming.

There was a couple arguing three cars away from me. I thought I was hearing a conversation I may have shared with a few ex-girlfriends. The woman was telling her man that he doesn't step up enough and isn't there for her when she needs him.

I'm humble enough to admit that in a lot of the relationships I had I was only thinking of myself. I refused to relinquish an individual mindset for a couple's mentality, putting a so-called significant other before myself. With Monique that changed and I want to do right by Deanna with the mindset that this relationship isn't just about me, but it's about us. For some strange reason that is easier said than done.

When I was walking across the street I was a little pumped, as I could hear George Clinton's" Atomic Dog" being played. Men were walking into the club with stripe suits looking like corporate executives attending a business meeting. The ladies looked like they walked out of a Vogue magazine walking fast to the club like they were in a hurry to be first in line for a shopping spree. The entrance was surrounded with palm trees. On top of the building was a fake boat. When I walked inside the girl dressed like one of those aloha dancers in Hawaii was working the cash register telling me it was five dollars to get in.

"Okay," I said grabbing my wallet about to pick a five-dollar bill.

"Hold it Ruben, that won't be necessary," said Sonny Kim, the owner of the club. He looked like a bouncer with his shaved head and black suit that covered his defensive tackle frame. He belonged in an ultimate fighting championship octagon forcing an opponent to tap out. "Chelsea, his money's no good here. Come on in Ruben."

"Thanks," I said shaking his hand. "That wasn't necessary; you know I'm good for it."

"I know, but we're good friends." He wrapped his arm around me. "And you've hooked me up with more business after that story you did on my club. One of the studio engineers from 94.1 read the article and because of that they wanted to do business with us. All because of you, so I thought I'd return a favor. You don't ever have to worry about paying whenever you come here. From now on just call me when you're showing up and I'll get you on a VIP list."

"Thanks I appreciate it."

"Have a good time," he said patting me on the back on his way to walk up the wooden stairs that I was afraid wouldn't be able to hold his weight.

The dance floor was filled and all the tables outside the dance floor were occupied. Men were posted up against the wall with drinks in their hands watching beautiful women walk passed them acting as if they should have been approached. There was a mix of young and old people hearing the best in old school and r&b. At the moment Miss Jazz was the deejay on location making shout outs while Gloria Estefan's Shake Ya Body was hitting the airwaves.

"Yo Raw over here," Roland yelled who was dressed up in a gray suit sitting at a table with Torres and Buster.

"What's going on fellas," I said walking up to them. "Dang Buster, you weren't lying this place is jam packed."

"You know I wouldn't steer you wrong," Buster said dressed down in a John Stewart Green Lantern t-shirt and faded blue jeans with white sneakers that were tied up with green laces. He may have hardly ever dressed up, but he knew how to coordinate. Torres was looking around the club, as if someone were watching him. He kept on looking at his watch like he needed to be somewhere else.

"Torres, what's going on with you," I asked. "I see Miss Jazz is here. You want to go talk to her." While Roland was looking at different women, Buster and I laughed remembering Torres' debacle when he tried to talk to Miss Jazz at the gym.

"Oh shut up," Torres replied. "You don't think she's seen me at all the whole night do you?"

"I don't know and I don't care," Buster said. "All I know is I wouldn't mind having me some of all that jazz."

"You're a fool," I chuckled. "Torres you look like someone is out to get you. You're beginning to make me paranoid like something is about to go down."

"I'm sorry," Torres replied. "I just feel guilty being here."

"I'm sure Jazz won't think you're stalking her." Buster and I laughed.

"Oh he's been talking to this girl he met earlier this month at Suave," Buster said taking a sip of his drink. "And now he feels like he has to be Mr. Faithful because he got a number and they've been talking for a while, but haven't made anything official."

"I didn't tell her I was going out tonight and I feel like I'm already violating that trust," Torres replied. "Plus I feel like I'm making her a backup plan just by being here." A couple of women in bedazzled skirts walked passed us. "Here, the chances of temptation increase as the women obviously outnumber us. That is definitely a rarity in any nightclub in this city."

"Well if you want to be with her so bad than you should tell her that," I said.

"You're right Ruben." Torres grabbed his phone. "Gentlemen excuse me," he said walking to the bathroom dialing a number.

"Torres is going to be whipped if he hooks up with that girl," Buster said.

"I just hope she doesn't do him wrong," Roland replied. "The pain for him would be unbearable."

Two minutes later Torres left the club early, as he was going to meet up with his prospective girlfriend at a salsa club. After speaking with Roland and Buster for almost 15 minutes and a couple of other girls who joined us I got distracted.

I was no longer invested in our conversation, as I was looking around and my eyes were locked on probably the most attractive woman in the building. Knowing that she was the most attractive woman in the club I had to have her. Hundreds of brothers could try to win her over, but there could only be one. While Roland and Buster were making the girls laugh I walked away from the table not even bothering to excuse myself.

While I walked to the dance floor some women would look at me or touch me to get my attention, but my eyes were locked on what had originally caught my attention. As I got closer I noticed the woman was very provocative dancing to Tone Loc's "Wild Thing." As I saw this woman who stood a little over five feet swinging her hips from side to side I knew I wanted to rock with her. I stood on the dance floor close to her and watched her hoping that she would notice me looking at her.

She was resplendent wearing some open toe brown heels with straps laced around her ankles with a white mini-skirt that showed off her firm bronzed legs. She was wearing a brown spaghetti strapped blouse that fit her like a bra only covering her perky breasts. She had long curly dirty blonde hair that rested under a white derby slightly tilted to the right.

When she looked at me she smiled and motioned for me to come to her. As I walked to her I grabbed her hand and she gave me a hug.

"How are you doing sexy," Bianca asked.

"I'm doing a whole lot better now that I've seen you," I replied with a smile. "I like the hat."

"Thank you."

"You look good."

"I see you have a little more swagger in your walk since the last time I saw you. I wonder what brought that on." She winked, as I smiled.

As Miss Jazz was making more shout outs while the deejay changed from Wild Thing to Michael Jackson's "Billie Jean" Bianca turned around placing my hands on her hips pressing her butt against me and gyrating making me work hard to keep from getting an erection.

* * * * *

We must have danced for more than half an hour before we left the dance floor.

"So did you come up here with anyone," I asked.

"Surprisingly I didn't," Bianca replied wrapping her hand around my waist. Her breasts looked bigger than the last time I saw her, as if they had expanded. Of course I wasn't complaining. "What about you?"

"I met a few friends up here, but I don't think they would notice if I left because they're preoccupied right now." I pointed at Roland and Buster who had four girls sitting with them at their table. I noticed that Bianca was wearing her wedding ring unlike the last time I saw her. "How's your husband?"

"He's in Austin overnight and my kids are with their grandmother."

"Oh really is that so?"

"You want to get out of here and talk somewhere quiet?"

"Yeah I would love that."

* * * * *

Ten minutes later I was walking inside Ruben's place. After he locked his front door three times, the moment he turned around I pushed him against the door. My hands went around his neck pulling his mouth to mine. His hands conveniently rested around my waist. After rapidly breathing and kissing like teenagers only getting to first base I pulled off his coat and his shirt throwing them to the ground after he threw my hat to the ground and took off my blouse dropping it on the floor as well. I was the aggressor throwing him to the couch. I sat on his lap grinding him with intensity, as if I didn't want him to be able to stand up. As I took off my bra like it was burning me he took hold of my breasts with his warm hands making me throw my head back and moaning for him to not stop, as he squeezed them.

He took initiative lifting me up, as I wrapped my legs around his back. While we were kissing each other with our warm bodies pressed up against each other he was carrying me to his bedroom and we fell in his bed. He unbuckled my belt and slid my mini-skirt off leaving my heels on. I guess unlacing the straps would take too much time. I unbuckled his belt, unzipped his jeans, and slid them down to his ankles. I widened my legs while he slid my thong down getting inside of me once again filling a void.

* * * * *

After being inside Bianca, not once, but twice that night I finally found myself exhausted from sex. We were lying underneath the covers holding each other.

I couldn't believe that after deciding to be exclusive with Deanna I had officially cheated on her. What was wrong with me? The moment I lost my virginity my integrity left along with it.

* * * * *

While Ruben was lying on his back I was delicately kissing his chest. It had been so long since a man left me satisfied and that's what I felt with Ruben every time I was with him. I thought it would be a much longer time before I would see him again and be close with him.

He turned me on just walking towards me. When I saw him at the club tonight it was like seeing light in the darkness. And not because he's lighter than a lot of black men I've seen. Being with him warmed my soul that felt trapped in a blizzard. I hated that this feeling could only be temporary.

"So how have you been," Ruben asked. "Or rather how are you?"

"I guess I'm okay," I replied. "My husband and I seem to be content with just being roommates. I am so in love with my kids though. My son is so smart and he's taken an interest in football. My daughter, oh I just love my daughter. She's my angel. Every time I see her I can't help, but smile." Just thinking and talking about my children brought a smile to my face.

"What are the names of your children?"

"They are Logan and Angela."

We were silent for a moment until he slipped on his boxer briefs and got up from the bed. They were bright enough to not be red, but they were dark enough to not actually be pink. They might have been a faded red due to being washed too many times. Whether or not his boxer briefs were pink didn't matter to me because he looked good in them. His hands rested on his nightstand as he stared out his window looking into the darkness. "What's wrong baby," I asked sitting up pulling the sheets up to cover my breast.

"Bianca what are we doing," he asked lowering his head.

"We're just uh," I was scratching my head. "We're just having fun, enjoying each other's company."

"Everything we do together feels so good, but this is wrong." He turned around and leaned up against his dresser. "There's nothing right about this no matter how messed up your marriage is."

If only he knew how messed up it really was. "You know I just can't leave."

"If you're miserable why stay with him," he asked shrugging his shoulders. "If he doesn't make you happy why tolerate it?"

"I'm staying for the kids," I said brushing my hair back.

"You're not making things any better for them or for yourself."

"What do you want from me Ruben?"

"I want a divorce." I looked at him confused. "Not me, but I want to hear you say that you're getting divorced."

"You know that's not an option."

"So you'd rather be in a relationship and miserable than single and happy. That sounds real intelligent Bianca." He was beginning to raise his voice.

"When you get married talk to me, otherwise I don't have to explain myself to you. And besides how would you be able to support me? You don't have a full time job."

"You're going there?"

"Truth hurts, but you can't make a decent living off of musical gigs or freelance reporting."

"I got my real estate license. It's only a matter of time before I get with an agency."

"Spare me the lecture. Real estate is just a backup plan for you. Music is what you really want to do. Majority of the musicians I've seen end up broke and homeless and I refuse to be caught up in that. And you know what maybe I'm just an escape from reality for you. I'm just a fix to help you forget your problems."

"You need to stop."

"Even if I was single could you really see yourself with me? Let's not forget I would be the single mother of two children. Most men run the other direction at the mention of even one child. So you mean to tell me that you would still be with me?"

"Yes I would," he said walking back to the bed. He couldn't be serious. "I don't care about that; I just want you." He kept digging deeper into me. No matter how much I want him, I can't have him. "But I don't want to share you. I hate that the only time I see you is at nightclubs. I want to be able to go to the park with you and watch the sunset. I want to be able to hold your hand and not be worried if someone you know sees you with me. I would like to go out in public with you in the daytime and not feel we have to keep our relationship a secret."

"A relationship," I felt bad for laughing, "You call this a relationship. Ruby, baby, all we are doing is having sex."

"We don't have sex, we make love." He got up and just looked out the window.

"You're too cute," I giggled.

"Would you stop saying that?" He raised his voice a little higher slamming his hands on his dresser. "There is nothing cute about what I am doing with you." He turned around and faced me. "I'm having you go behind your husband's back. How is that cute Bianca? I'm the guy you're supposed to stay away from."

I had never heard Ruben raise his voice. It turned me on. I got up from the bed and wrapped my arms around him kissing his chest. "Just because two people have sex doesn't mean they have a relationship." I was hoping this would make him loosen his grip, hoping I could easily slip away from him as if I was sand escaping through his fingers. This was sexual and maybe he would realize that it couldn't work out between us. It did hurt me to let him go, but I was going to enjoy him while I had the chance.

"What, we actually communicated a lot before we had sex." He softened up the more I kissed his chest. "You're just too scared to leave him because you're afraid of what will occur if you divorce him. You can't deny that there is a connection between us. I don't think it's a coincidence that we keep running into each other like we do."

"I think you only feel that way because I was your first?" I didn't want to let him go, but I also didn't want a divorce.

"No, it has nothing to do with that. Sure you were my first and it was amazing, but in my life I have dated other women and you stand out," he said touching my face with his soft hands and our eyes locked on each other, "You're nubile, but besides that you are intelligent." He was running his fingers through my hair. "You are easy to talk with. I love that you are affectionate and compassionate. I wish I could be your priority instead of an alternative, but that can't happen if you are married. I hate that's the reality I have to face."

"Oh baby," I pulled him closer to my naked body, as if I wanted to be stuck to him forever. One of my hands ran down his back, as if I was brushing it. While my other hand snuck underneath his boxer briefs rubbing his penis. "Look I want to be with you, but you have to realize this isn't easy for me either baby." His head was tilted back, as I slowly rubbed him. "I wish things could work out differently for us, but this is the hand we're dealt and we just have to make the most of what we have to work with. You may feel guilty Ruby, but I know you're enjoying this, as much as I am. You're definitely enjoying this in the literal sense. You're so long I may need another pair of hands."

"Oh Bianca," he exhaled as his head was raised toward the ceiling while I could feel him getting longer. He looked as if he couldn't think straight.

"So make love to me with the time we have left. You like how my hand feels."

"Yeah, I do."

"I really like what I'm holding."

"Your hand is so warm. Oh that feels so good." He picked me up and sat me on his dresser. He was feeling harder by the second.

"This is my favorite thing about you. It feels as hard as a stone." I pulled his boxer briefs off, as he kissed me, while I opened my legs a little wider. He was kissing his way down from my neck to my waist.

I'm grateful that I was the first woman Ruben ever slept with, but there's a part of me that felt guilty. I found it admirable that his whole life he fought the temptation to not give into premarital sex. There's a part of me that wishes he could have waited until marriage and not had made me as his first.

Of course I had second thoughts as I felt his tongue lick my holy of holies for almost ten minutes. He was making me melt. My body was quivering, as he continued to lick me in a way my husband never did. My husband thought it was disrespectful for a man to do that to a woman. If this was disrespectful I didn't mind being disrespected. My nails were digging into his back, as he began to kiss my neck. As I felt him get inside me I wrapped my legs around him. He pulled me up and we fell into his bed. I was enjoying being able to share myself with him for the limited amount of time we had remaining.

Underneath this flabby exterior is an enormous lack of character

~Oscar Levant~

17

What's Up With You?

I was shocked that Michael Jackson had passed away. The world hadn't reacted to a death like his since Princess Diana. The world grieved, which resulted in an increase sale of his music including Jackson 5 products. His death was the most shocking moment in music.

I never met the man, but I felt like I lost a friend. His ability as a musician and a performer inspired me to get into music. After his death I listened a lot to his song "Man in the Mirror." He was a genius that will be greatly missed, but we all have to move on and live the life we were blessed with.

Deanna and I were on the road to Scott's house for a barbecue. Deanna's cousin was having a birthday party the same day, so we said we'd go to Scott's house first for a couple of hours and then meet up with her cousin for her birthday bash. It would be the first time I would get to meet one of her relatives.

We drove into the Helotes area where Scott lived. The street he lived on was crowded with cars. I saw a two-story red brick house covered with balloons and confetti. I figured that it had to be Scott's house. There were so many cars that Scott should have served as a valet and made himself some extra money in tips.

All I could think about was eating something because I was as hungry as a bear. I was telling Deanna that we wouldn't stay too long so we could make it in time to see her cousin. As it turned out Scott was married to Deanna's cousin. There was no need to rush.

After knocking on the door, a little Latin boy wearing a white Tony Romo jersey with a little blue Dallas Cowboys football twirling in his hands opened the door.

"Hi Deanna," the little boy said. "Who's he?"

"This is my boyfriend Ruben. Ruben this is my cousin, Logan."

"Hi," Logan said sticking his hand out to shake mine.

"How is it going," I said shaking his hand.

"Are you going to let us in," Deanna asked.

"Oh sure come on in," he replied closing the door after we walked in. I was already thinking about making some regular visits to Scott's house when I saw a navy blue pool table that matched the living room floor in what should have been a dining room table set. Along with that he had a mini bar and a small pinball machine. As we were walking on the navy blue carpet in the living room, part of the wall was covered with a 50-inch flat screen television set.

"Hey Deanna, glad you could make it out," said Scott walking out of the kitchen and into the living room with a red apron wrapped around him that read "Respect The Cook."

"You know him," I said.

"Oh yeah, I didn't know you were dating her," he said hugging Deanna. "Glad to see you Ruben," he smiled shaking my hand. "How's life treating you?"

"Not as good as it's treating you. You got yourself a nice place here. Why do you want to go into real estate again?"

"Because I'd like to keep this house," we both laughed. "Come on in y'all the party is in the back. And Ruben you can finally meet my lovely wife that I was always telling you about when we were taking our classes together."

"I couldn't pay you to stop talking about her." I looked at Deanna. "I literally paid this man five bucks to stop talking about his wife and a minute later he hands me back the five bucks and starts talking about her again."

"When you meet her you'll see why," he said. As we walked outside to his backyard there must have been 30 to 40 people enjoying themselves swimming in the pool or relaxing in the hot tub and drinking some cold ones. My mouth was watery and my stomach wouldn't stop growling seeing people eating some hot dogs or hamburgers. Luckily we walked by a table that was filled with patties and hot dogs wrapped in foil along with hot dog and hamburger buns, lettuce, ketchup, mustard, tomatoes, and onions. I grabbed a sesame seed bun, smothered it with mustard and lettuce, and threw the hamburger patty between the buns.

"Mrs. Jones could you come here please," Scott kindly yelled like Timmy calling for Lassie. I couldn't satisfy my hunger when I saw Scott's wife because my heart was pulsating. Scott's wife was carrying a red plastic cup. She was wearing a turquoise bra that were hiding her firm chest along with a silk white dress that was wrapped around her waist like a towel covering the bottom part of her two-piece bathing suit. She was walking toward us in her turquoise open toe heels showing off some toes that had just been manicured, as they had white tips on her toes. Shades were covering her eyes. She had long blonde hair that was very similar to Deanna and a beautiful cinnamon complexion. As she was walking to us the eyes of some men were locked on her like she was the belle of the ball walking in slow motion with the wind blowing in her hair, while the women looked at her in disgust as if she was the town whore. Some of them nudged or pinched their men's arms to get their attention. When she walked toward us I wanted to run for cover because I couldn't believe that Bianca was Deanna's cousin.

As she walked toward us, I casually turned around like I was checking out the place and saw a banner on their house that read "Happy 30th Birthday Olga" and another one under it that read "Congratulations Scott!" I turned back around trying my best to not look guilty. Not all musicians are great actors.

"Olga honey, this is Deanna's boyfriend Ruben Wells," Scott said wrapping his arm around Bianca.

"Well, hello Ruben, it's good to finally meet you," Bianca said taking off her sunglasses with a smile on her face. "So you're RAW."

"Excuse me," I nervously replied putting my sweaty palms in my pockets.

"Oh that's just a nickname Deanna had for you." I looked at Deanna who was just smiling at me unaware that Bianca and I knew each other. "She's always had nicknames for the different guys she has dated and she calls you RAW because those are your initials, Ruben Alexander Wells."

"Dang baby, what else have you told Olga about me?"

"Oh that you're just a good and honest man," Deanna replied wrapping her arm around mine. As she spoke I looked at Bianca who took a sip of her drink inconspicuously looking at me, as if she was undressing me with her eyes while her husband was standing there with us grinning ear to ear. "That you do right by me and so much different from some of the other men I have dated. It's definitely nice to meet a man of quality for a change."

"Wow so she's told you all that," I laughed. "Are you sure you were talking about me because that doesn't sound anything like me."

"Silly," she replied squeezing my biceps.

"Hold on to this one Deanna," Scott said.

"Yeah, you don't want him to slip away because any woman won't hesitate to grab hold of him," Bianca said taking another sip of her drink.

"Stop it, y'all are embarrassing me," I replied. "Hey Scott, I have to use the restroom. Where is the nearest one?"

"Just walk through the kitchen and it will be the first door on your left," he said. "And if that one is occupied you can go in the one upstairs. Of course don't use the one in the master bedroom," he laughed.

"I'll be back shortly," I quickly walked away as if I had to use the restroom really bad before having a flood in my pants. "Oh my, oh my," I muttered to myself, as I was walking back into the Jones' house feeling Bianca's eyes on me. When I turned around I saw that she was looking at me with a mischievous grin while her husband had an arm wrapped around her as he was speaking to my girlfriend. My heart was pounding rapidly. What if Scott and Deanna both knew that I slept with Bianca and this was just a set up? "Oh my, oh my," I said as I walking upstairs, as I saw someone walking into the bathroom near the kitchen. As I walked upstairs I saw pictures of Scott and Bianca together on the wall along with some that had them and their children. "What do I do, what do I do?" I walked into the bathroom in the hallway that was between two bedrooms, turned the light and fan on so no one could hear me talk to myself. I shut the door and locked it as if someone was chasing me.

For a couple of minutes, I had been pacing back and forth in the restroom feeling like it was judgment day and there was nowhere to run or hide. My forehead was sweating profusely. I was trying to figure things out, trying to make sense out of everything.

I understood why Scott and I clicked so well with each other. We had a lot more in common than music, movies, or career goals, but we had great taste in women, as we were sleeping with the same woman.

Why would Bianca cheat on a good man like Scott? Scott spoke highly of Bianca, as if she was a queen. He didn't sound like he was bored with her or ashamed of her. Why was Bianca tiptoeing behind his back? Why me? Did she know Deanna was dating me and that's the only reason she slept with me? Did Deanna offend her in some way and sleeping with me was her way of getting payback?

We were doing what pleased us, not taking the time to think about the people we would be hurting. There was a chance they had opportunities to give into tempting offers from other people, but they most likely resisted while we invested in a temporary encounter.

As I continued pacing back and forth I heard a knock at the door.

"I'm a little busy," I said.

"Open the door Ruben, its Bianca," she whispered. I opened the door and she walked in with a couple CDs in her hand.

"Bianca what the," she dropped the CDs on the countertop. "Do you want to get caught," I asked as she was running hands underneath my shirt across my stomach.

"You expect me to believe that if I were to leave my husband you would start dating me, while you're with my cousin."

"Stop it Bianca," I said pushing her hands away. I walked away and sat on the toilet cover seat. "Scott is a standup guy. He doesn't deserve to be cheated on. So why are you cheating on him?"

"Deanna is a good woman. Why are you sneaking around behind her back?" I was at a loss for words. Bianca grabbed a seat on the countertop next to the sink and crossed her legs. "Scott isn't who you think he is."

"Enlighten me please."

"Scott has cheated on me with different women. He expects me to just put up with it. I remember the first time it happened I confronted him about it and he acted as if it was normal for a man to cheat on his wife. So I put up with it because I had nowhere else to go and I had no other options. That is until I started pursuing an education and getting myself a job I could do where I could support two children. He's beat on me too and talked down on me, but I'm not putting up with it anymore. He may come off as Mr. Perfect, but he's not. He has everyone fooled."

"You really expect me to believe that."

"Maybe not at first, but ask Deanna she'll tell you what's really going on. There were times he would talk down on me in front of my family. They tell me I just have to live with it and not piss him off. He's even tried to get with Deanna a few times. Now as far as Deanna not giving into his advances, I don't know, but I wouldn't be surprised if she did sleep with him. It wouldn't come as a shock to me if he was trying to get with her right now."

We were quiet and the only noise being made was the fan rattling. I was watching Bianca's legs rock back and forth thinking about how much I would like her legs being wrapped around my waist. I stood up and faced Bianca, as her head was hanging down.

I lifted her chin up with my finger. "I still want you Bianca," I said leaning in closer to her.

"Then shut up and kiss me," she smiled while widening her legs and letting me in between her. I lifted her dress up and my hands rested on her thighs while she grabbed my shirt and pulled me in. As the fan continued to rattle we kissed each other not caring that our significant others were not far from us. While we kissed, her legs were wrapped around my waist and my eager fingers were tracing along the waistline of the bottom part of her bathing suit fighting the urge to pull them off so I could enter her.

She got up off the counter, as she dropped the CDs and squeezed my crotch that was feeling hard.

"Can I open my present," she asked while unzipping my jeans.

"Right here, right now?"

"Oh yeah, I have been waiting awhile to open it up."

"By all means unwrap it."

She got down on her knees, as she pulled my pants and boxers down. She pushed me up against the wall and moistened her lips. My held fell back like a pez dispenser, as I saw her mouth coming for me.

Knowing that Scott and Deanna were not that far from us got me feeling aroused. It ain't my fault if Scott can't keep his woman in line. Deanna should have known better than to leave me alone. The thought that anyone could walk in on us at this very moment was thrilling. The fact that Bianca was giving me oral pleasure in the house she shared with her husband had my heart racing. As I looked in the mirror and saw the back of Bianca's head I grabbed her head making her moan. I couldn't help, but smile at myself in the mirror. If I had been in this position a few months back I would have hated myself, but now I was proud. "Happy birthday to you Bianca," I said as her tongue was running circles on me.

"You're a sweetheart," she said looking up at me. "So sweet," she said putting her mouth back on me.

As I smiled back at myself in the mirror, I couldn't help, but wonder who this person was looking at me. Was it really me? I thought of that theme song from the opening credits of the television show "CSI." Who are you? That's what I was asking the person I was looking at in the mirror. I really want to know who are you? Tell me, who are you because I can't figure out who you are? What's up with the person I am staring at right now?

Who am I? Is this the person I should be proud of? Should I be proud to be a thief? I robbed India of her dignity. All she wanted to be was happy and feel loved and for her that meant being with me. I stole her joy that she was just beginning to find when I was out of her life.

With Bianca I am breaking and intruding on what might be a wonderful marriage. I am a man who is ruining other people's lives and I'm too selfish and self-absorbed to realize that I'm ruining my own. I'm a thief that wants what I want whenever I want it and don't care how I obtain it.

I am a parasite, a leech, sucking the life out of those around me including my own life.

After Bianca finished enjoying the gift I had for her she rinsed her mouth out with some mouthwash. She walked out with the CDs and told me to wait a few minutes. Didn't want anyone to suspect something was going on.

I waited five minutes.

"Shut up," I said to myself disgusted at what I was looking at in the mirror. I turned the light off, opened the door, and walked out of the bathroom. When I was walking downstairs I saw Logan looking up at me twirling his football. He looked at me, as if I stole one of his toys. I was walking passed him with caution like a pedestrian would a dog off his leash hoping it doesn't try to bite.

What if he knew I was jeopardizing his parents' marriage? Even though I was apprehensive I walked passed him like I didn't care what he thought of me.

* * * * *

After an hour went by, Scott pulled me aside to show me the rest of his house leaving me worried because Deanna was speaking with Bianca. I was afraid that Bianca would let it slip out that we had been with each other a couple of times or that Deanna would smell my scent on Bianca. Was Scott going to give me a death threat if I didn't leave her alone?

We walked into his study where he had a display of his hobby, model cars.

"So putting together cars is your hobby," I said. "I like to collect smoking pipes."

"I thought you didn't smoke," he replied eating some cantaloupe.

"Oh I don't, I just like to collect them."

"Putting things together helps me to relax."

"I can understand that. Scott you are truly a blessed man."

"Come on man," he said in denial waving his hand, as he fell into his leather chair behind the desk.

"No it's undeniable. You have a lovely home, have a job you enjoy, two delightful children, and a beautiful wife. You just seem to have a life that is envious."

"My life isn't that perfect or isn't to die for, but thank you. Let me show you something else I like. I had a collection of these, but when I started having kids I had to sell them. There were a couple of them that I couldn't get rid of." He rolled his chair around and went to a black safe that he had. He turned the knob a few times putting together the combination and opened it. He pulled out a silver briefcase and placed it on the desk. It also had a combination he had to put together. When he opened it he pulled out an unblemished black caliber 45. He pulled out the clip and cocked the gun popping out a bullet in the chamber. He handed it to me. "It's empty." I grabbed the gun and just felt what any person feels when they have a gun in their hand…power.

"Man, that dominating spirit comes over a man when he has a gun. I can just feel the power."

"Yeah, guns will do that to you. This other gun I have my dad gave to me." He pulled out an empty silver Smith and Wesson with a black handle. He laid it out on the desk. As I was pointing the gun in the air at his window I could feel Scott's eyes on me. I felt that Scott was examining me while staring like he knew something wasn't right about me. He looked at me as if he knew I was hiding something. Holding his cold stare it was as if he was contemplating loading his gun and emptying his bullets into me for sleeping with his wife.

"What's going on Scott?" I lowered the gun feeling a chill in the air.

"I'm just thinking about what you said." He was tapping the trigger of the gun.

"Oh, what was it I said?" I wondered how fast he was with a gun.

"Just something you said about my life." I looked up at the wall behind him. There was a wedding picture of him and Bianca where they looked younger and happier. Scott turned around and looked at the picture I couldn't take my eyes off of. "Twelve years is how long we've been together. I still can't believe it." He turned back around and looked at me while holding the handle to his shiny Smith and Wesson. "I really do love that woman. She's the one I always knew that I wanted to be with. She's the only woman I ever gave myself to, the only woman I've ever been with."

"She was your first?"

"Yep and she was my last. I know I wasn't her first, but that didn't matter to me because I loved her. We have our problems, but I still love her as much as I did 12 years ago." His eyes were watering up.

"You okay Scott."

"Yeah, I just need a minute." He let go of the gun and rested his chin on his hand looking like he was about to breakdown. "I don't know why I'm telling you this stuff, but I trust you. Olga and I have had our problems. That's inevitable in any marriage, but lately there's been a lot of tension between us. Make no mistake I still love her, even if we haven't had sex for almost three and a half months."

"Dang man," I said biting my bottom lip.

"I know, I know, but I still love her. It seems like that's not enough because those feelings aren't reciprocated." He was tapping his desk. "I've never laid a hand on her, never spoken down on her, never been unfaithful to her, but she's cheating on me."

"What do you mean," I asked leaning in a little closer looking over my shoulder to make sure nobody heard what he was telling me.

Scott bit his bottom lip before he spoke. His forehead was perspiring, as he ran his fingers through his hair. "Maybe I'm exaggerating or overanalyzing." He rested his hands on the desk and pulled his chair up closer. "If I were to catch her in the act I would want to kill the man. But if I did that it wouldn't change anything. Well things would change, our situation would be worse. There have been many times I have been hit on by women who didn't care that I was married. I was in the perfect situation where I came across a woman that wanted to just have nothing more beyond sex. I could have given into those offers many times, but I didn't because I love my wife too much. I don't know if my wife is strong enough to resist that kind of offer...that kind of temptation." He's right, she wasn't. "Deanna is a good woman. If you want what I have, but more, you take good care of her and do right by her. You have to make God the foundation of your relationship, which is something I forgot to do. I always knew to do that, but somewhere down the line I forgot about trusting in God. I'm sure Deanna will take good care of you because she has a lot of love to offer and everything else that's meant to be will fall into place. Better put these things away," he said placing the silver Smith and Wesson in the briefcase. I handed him his other gun. "Don't want my son to see these because he'll want to play with them."

* * * * *

If I were to touch the sky it looked like it would feel soft as velvet as it was mixed with tangerine and lavender making the Jones' backyard feel more like a deserted island. After eating so many hamburgers and hot dogs I was ready to fall asleep.

The sun was setting as the party was kind of winding down. Deanna rested against me in a beige chaise lounge with curved armrests. I ran my fingers through her soft and rich hair that smelled like coconut while watching Bianca swim with her daughter while Scott was playing some dominoes with some of his friends.

Looking at them both I was feeling guilty for recognizing that I might have been part of the reason their marriage was crumbling. If Scott were a jerk I would still feel guilty, but not as guilty as I felt at that moment.

"She's attractive isn't she," Deanna asked.

"What, who," I asked.

"I'm talking about my cousin."

"Well I uh," I sat up in the chair. "It seems whether or not I tell the truth I'm going to be in trouble no matter what I say so I think I'll just keep my mouth shut on this one."

"It's okay," she said tapping my leg while she looked at me. "You're a man and every once in a while, an attractive woman may catch your eye. I know you won't find anyone better than me." She kissed me on the lips and turned back around facing the pool. I'm such an idiot for cheating on her. Deanna is out of this world. It was so sexy how secure she was that she could probably make Donald Trump feel insignificant. "If there was one thing she was good at it was turning heads, so it's okay for you to be honest."

"Yeah she's attractive." I wanted to say more, but I held my tongue because I didn't want to speak too highly of her cousin that would cause her to be suspicious.

"A lot of men think Scott is a lucky man to have an elegant woman like Olga, but he would be better off without her."

"Why do you say that?"

"I love my cousin, she's my blood, but she's not doing right by her husband."

"What has she done?" Deanna's body was tensing up hesitant to say what she was about to say. "It's okay I won't tell anyone about it."

"Where to begin," she said tapping the armrest. "First of all let me just tell you that most of the people who are here are here for Scott, not Olga. Half of Scott's friends can't stand being around his wife, while the other half fantasize about sleeping with her." I can tell them what that's like. "She only has a few friends here. Some of the other people here besides family are some of her co-workers. You saw how neat and tidy the house looked right?"

"Yeah."

"You'd think they hired a maid or that she did it all herself. Well no it's only clean because Scott is the one that always has to make sure the place is in tip top shape even when they don't have company. Scott not only works hard on his job, but he works hard at being a great father and he tries his best at being a good husband, but Olga doesn't care about him."

"What makes you say that?"

"Scott does everything he can to please that woman, but it seems like she's never satisfied. She doesn't deserve him, but it's as if he's staying with her out of loyalty…almost to the point where he tolerates her. He's the one always making sure the kids are fed and doing their homework or get to bed on time. He spends quality time with the kids at night, while she's out late at night clubbing or bar hopping. I think any woman would give their right arm to be with a man like Scott, but she has her nose stuck up too high in the air to even notice it. She's been cheating on him."

I grabbed hold of the armrest as if the wind was trying to blow me away. "How uh, how do you know that?"

"She told me."

"She did what?"

"Yeah, she's been going behind his back for almost five years with so many different men. She was in San Francisco awhile back and got with some Cuban guy out there. You could say that for the last year they have been in a long distance relationship. The guy is so in love with her that she said he's talking about moving out here some time near the end of the year or early January." Do what? I remember she said she was going to see a friend in San Francisco. I guess she did more than see this friend. "Her best friend Monica," she pointed her out, "over there the tall one in the corner of the pool with the black guy." I saw Monica in the pool rubbing a Taye Diggs lookalike's stomach. "Sometimes she gets in on the action with her. My cousin tells me everything she's done as if I was her own lawyer. The two of them have gotten into some threesomes or even foursomes with each other." That explains why they're such great friends. "She's pliable. My cousin got her to join the unfaithful bandwagon. She's engaged! While she's carousing, her fiancé is in the Middle East behind enemy lines fighting to keep her alive. He's being all he can be for her. It's not right that Olga is living however she wants to live."

"If this is true then why haven't you told Scott? You both seem like really good friends."

"I love Scott, but Olga's my blood and I can't do that to her no matter how wrong she is. I know it's idiotic to say that, but I can't do that to Scott. He's even told me that he has his suspicions about her, but he has never addressed the issue with her."

"Why hasn't he addressed it with her?"

"Scott was in the military for many years and he grew accustomed to being confronted or confrontational, but he can't confront his own wife because he doesn't want to offend her and have an argument. If I told Scott everything I knew about his wife, it would crush him. And he would probably still stay with her."

"You think so?"

"Oh most definitely, because he has this problem of seeing goodness in everyone and he is under the misconception that everyone can change. It's so annoying almost to the point it's insane, but yet it's adorable."

I was fuming, like the smoke coming out of the grill. I thought I was the only one Bianca had ever slept with outside of her marriage. I knew adultery was wrong, but I felt special thinking I was the only one she made a wrong decision with. I was just another notch on her belt. Valuable like Gucci is how I felt when I was with her, but now I felt cheap and used.

I felt betrayed, as if I had been cheated on. My trust in Bianca was violated. I gave her a loving word, but in return she gave me a broken heart.

Perhaps this is karma. How many hearts have I broken with empty promises or meaningless actions? Just how Bianca did unto me, I made other women feel unique and needed. My words that would enter their ears made them feel special and loved; only to later be crushed. Majority of them I took for granted and disposed of them out of boredom.

Bianca desired a momentary thrill and I filled that void for her. She was insatiable searching for more excitement and thrills with other men.

I gave Bianca my virginity because I thought she would value it. Therein is the problem. I wanted someone else to value my virginity the way I couldn't. I gave her something that now I wish I could take back. It doesn't work that way with virginity. There's always an exchange, but never any refunds. It's a one-time only deal. Once it's given it's gone forever. So like the immortal knight advised Indiana Jones in The Last Crusade, "choose wisely."

"Scott is really in love with Olga," Deanna continued, as if she admired him. "He would take a bullet for her. If she wanted him to he would kill for her, that's how much he loves her." I could see that in his eyes when he was holding his gun, with eyes that were as solid as his revolver. "And if Scott knew that Angela wasn't his daughter, his world would crumble."

"WHAT!"

"Hey lower your voice," she tapped my leg after a couple heads turned. "There was this guy she messed around with a couple of years ago. It wasn't a one-night thing like the other guys, but their trysts continued for months, until she got pregnant."

"How do you know it's not Scott's baby," I asked while looking closer at Angela. She did have a complexion like her mother and thick, curly hair. As far as the face she didn't resemble Scott or Bianca.

"Olga's probably not the only one who has her secrets, but I think anyone can see Angela doesn't closely resemble Olga or Scott. The guy she was with was this musician who was half-Dominican and half-Italian. He closely resembled Ricky Martin, but he was just a little on the chubby side. He wore a belt buckle that had the initials AP. That's how she described him to me."

There was only one chubby half-Dominican, half-Italian musician I knew that looked like Ricky Martin who wore a belt buckle with the initials AP. Angela's father was my best friend Alejandro Padilla.

I couldn't believe what Deanna was telling me. Just to see if it was really true, I wanted to give her a lie detector test. Hopefully it wouldn't make her suspicious of me.

"This is a random question," I said. "Was Olga's maiden name Cortez as well?"

"Oh no, her maiden name is Garcia. Her first name is Bianca, but our family would call her by her middle name, which is Olga, which is why anyone who's known her from childhood calls her that. Why do you ask?"

"No reason, just curious." Question answered, Bianca Olga Garcia Jones was her full name. It's a small world after all. And in this small world almost every man has been with Bianca or should I say Olga...slut!

"In all things there are three choices: Yes, No and no choice, except in this – I either choose the truth or I am deceit." - Anonymous

Chapter 18 – Beauty Is Vain

As darkness filled the sky Deanna left with Bianca and a few of her other friends for a lady's night out continuing her birthday celebration.

After learning more about Bianca I could only imagine what she would be doing in a nightclub or bar.

Scott wanted me to stick around and watch Return of the Jedi on his 50-inch screen. I wanted to stay to see that, but to his chagrin I told him I had to leave to take care of some things. I needed to talk with Alejandro.

I sent him a text message letting him know that we needed to talk. He told me to meet him at The Galaxy where he would be reciting a poem for their Poetry Slam night held the last Saturday of every month. I wanted to meet with him in private, but I reluctantly decided to meet him there.

* * * * *

The Galaxy looked like a warehouse on the outside, as it was an old gray brick building that had garage sized doors closed. There was a large steep stairway that resembled the kind seen at Catholic churches that led to the entrance of the club. I had to watch my step because one misstep could result in a cracked skull. Homeless people lived in the older abandoned buildings that surrounded it.

Walking in it was a completely different story, as the soles of shoes were making an echo on the hardwood waxed floor. There was a bar filled with patrons and thousands of bottles stacked on the wall. There was also a collage of jazz, blues, and r & b artists filling the whole wall. People sat in roundtables with a candle lit on every table. There was a poet just finishing up, as I walked in whom everybody was applauding. While a poet was speaking there were two artists painting on an empty canvas. Some people seemed to be more entertained by that than the poets. Kat called me from the balcony where she was sitting.

I gave her a hug as I grabbed a seat next to her. She told me that Alejandro was up next.

Besides singing and playing the bass guitar Alejandro had always wanted to recite a poem center stage. This was going to be his first time to recite a poem in front of a crowd with all eyes locked on him.

* * * * *.

"How y'all doin' tonight," I said speaking into the microphone feeling nervous as my palms were sweaty, but secure underneath my blue fedora in a way serving as a shield from the crowd. I was wearing my lucky necklace that was filled with red, white, and blue beads with the Dominican Republic flag at the center. All I needed to do was paint my face blue and I could have either passed for a smurf or a member of the Crips because I was wearing a blue soccer jersey with "Italia" written on it along with some navy blue jeans and navy blue Timberlands. I needed to read this poem because I think it was something someone needed to hear. "My name is Alejandro Padilla and I wrote this poem after a…a uh…experience that shouldn't have occurred, but it did, which is something we probably all can relate to. If you've read in the Bible the book of Proverbs you might understand some of what I'm saying. Even if you don't hopefully you will still be able to feel me."

"Go on and do the poem boy," a man from the back of the bar yelled making the audience laugh. I wasn't going to look like a punk in front of this crowd. I squinted to look a little closer, as I decided to pull out my insult Tommy gun.

"Oh I know you man, you're a real ladykiller."

"That's right boy."

"Yeah, all the ladies take one look at you and die of shock."

"Ooh," the crowd yelled applauding.

"I heard your face was the perfect weapon against muggers." I made the crowd laugh. "I heard that as soon as you walked in that Haunted House Tour they offered you a job and you didn't even have to say BOO!"

"Ooh."

"Don't get it twisted. I may be a poet, but that don't mean I'm soft. Y'all came here to hear some poetry, so y'all want me to do mine."

"Yeah."

"Alright then, this is a poem I wrote called Beauty Is Vain. Enjoy!" Before I recited my poem I looked up at Kat and Ruben with a smile on my face, really glad to see that boy could come out. I closed my eyes just hearing glass cling and a couple of people coughing. It was so quiet that I could hear a cell phone vibrate. Even though I was by myself on the stage I imagined hearing a bass guitar being played remembering Olga Garcia and all the bad decisions that I made with her like it was a montage being played in a music video. I was remembering the first time we met at The Spot on the Riverwalk when I was performing. As I remembered the first time our eyes locked on each other I recited my poem speaking with my hands like I was a maestro conducting a symphony. This would be my magnum opus. "Wisdom was calling out to me, but I gave into the call of the seductress. I know that knowledge is power and possession of truth is the key, but I needed to indulge myself in one night with the temptress." I thought of that first time we introduced ourselves dancing to that timeless love ballad by 112 called "Cupid."

"I should have worn sunglasses because I had blind eyes that couldn't recognize her disguise, as this wolf in sheep's clothing had sex appeal with subtle seduction, deceiving me like the serpent did Eve in the garden of Eden, unaware that she had detoured many other guys. Looking into the hazel eyes left me hypnotized like I was under the spell of a wizard making me forget she was a hazel eyed hazard." I still left my eyes shut, but I heard some men yell "Ooh man" or "Say that" while a couple other people clapped. The first time I kissed Olga's lips that were as soft as a pillow ran through my mind. "Her kiss was sweet like honey and her words were smooth like butter, her touch was as soft as a bunny that was covering up the soul of a woman who was bitter. Leaving me without discernment, as well as lacking in sound judgment no longer embracing integrity and letting go of purity while investing in calamity." The first time Olga yelled my name when I was inside of her was in my vision while I still kept my eyes shut. "I aspired to be like Solomon and give into the call of wisdom because with it comes satisfaction, a gift from God's kingdom. She was my Delilah and I was her Samson taking my breath away softly leading me to disarray helping me forget my destiny and accompany me into misery. I was too busy trying to be a heartthrob and I ended up getting my heart robbed as God was no longer my potter because I was her molded clay. She was the predator and I was the prey." Even though he doesn't know me I could only imagine what her husband would have done if he ever found out I was the one she had a child with. "When we were caught in the act by her husband I begged for mercy, but he had a permanent frown seeing my pants down as he unleashed fury on me leaving me desiring another breath just seconds away from death. Having me think I should have listened to the commands of my father and the teachings of my mother, but I did what my parents dread and I reduced myself to a loaf of bread."

As I thought of my daughter that I would never get to know, a tear fell down my face. I opened my eyes and I felt like a preacher trying to impart knowledge into his congregation. I felt like a defense attorney making a closing argument hoping to spare the life of my client, as I really got into my poem still talking with my hands like I was using sign language hoping that what I say would reach someone. "I should have given into wisdom's call because with her there is no condemnation and there's always room for liberation. In wisdom there is trust and accountability, things that mold me into a man of integrity and lead into prosperity. She was pure and in her presence I was secure." I noticed some men who were laid back in their chairs were now leaning forward. Women were nodding their heads like they could feel what I was talking about. "Out of her mouth come words that are just, not corrupt or perverse. In all she does she pursues excellence and with her you never lose sight of purpose thus staying on course. Live and learn before you get burn. Do what works for you, but don't be led astray by your folly and remember, a woman who doesn't feel whole or isn't holy can bring agony or pain along with her beauty that is vain.

"Thank you I'm Alejandro Padilla, God bless." I blew a kiss two times like I was Sammy Sosa, as half the audience were on their feet applauding. I saw Kat blow me a kiss, as I walked off the stage.

It felt like a weight had been lifted off my shoulders when I shared my poem. Not only because it was something I had never done before, but I hadn't shared what being around Olga had been doing to me. Now I'm free.

* * * * *

It was as if Alejandro had shared the story of Bianca and I. As he spoke I was reliving everything that happened between us. I was also impressed at how well Alejandro enunciated and pronounced every word correctly.

I couldn't help, but think that none of this would have occurred if I had just walked away from Bianca the second she said she was married. None of this would have happened if I had stayed home that night instead of going out clubbing.

When Alejandro came upstairs to join Kat and I some people were patting him on the back or shaking his hand like he had just delivered a powerful presidential address to the nation. When he came to her, Kat kissed him on the lips. He then came up and hugged me thanking me for showing up. I told him we needed to step outside to talk.

"What's goin' on man," Alejandro asked walking out the door behind me.

"That poem was brilliant," I said. "Were you thinking about Olga the whole time you recited it."

"Yeah, when I wrote it I thought about all the pain that relationship brought to the both of us."

"I have something I need to tell you AP," I said pulling out my digital camera.

"What's up," he asked while I was scrolling through the pictures I took at the Jones' barbecue. When I came to the picture of Bianca and her daughter I thought about showing it to him, but instead I scrolled to the next picture of Deanna and Angela.

"When is the last time you saw a picture of your daughter?"

"It's probably been about six months since I've seen a picture of her, why?"

"I have a new one for you," I said handing him my camera. When he looked at the picture a tear fell down his face.

"Oh my, she's such a beautiful angel." He touched the picture, as if he were touching her face. He leaned back against the wall, as one of his hands was covering his mouth while more tears raced across his cheeks. "I would have taken care of her anyway I could. I was willing to be a father to her, but her mother wouldn't let me just because of the situation she was in. I would have taken her the weekends if that's what was required of me to do. If I were given only two hours a day to see her I would have done it. I was ready to be a father to my little Angelita, my Angela." His eyes were locked on the picture. "So how did you meet her?"

"Deanna is B..." I almost slipped and said Bianca, but Alejandro knew her as Olga. "Deanna and Olga are cousins."

"Is her husband a really good man or a jerk like she says he is?"

"Regretfully it's hard to hate the man. He's so innocent he wouldn't take a penny if he saw it on a street corner."

"In your opinion do you think their marriage will last?"

They would stay together only because of the kids. It would come to an end when Scott put his foot down and stand up to his wife. It would come to an end when he wouldn't tolerate Bianca's unfaithfulness any longer. "No I don't, but I'm not a marriage counselor or a relationship expert."

Alejandro wiped the tears from his face as he looked up at me. He took off his hat and fanned himself. "Did you find Olga attractive?"

"Why are you asking me that?"

"I mean; did you find her tempting. Like if you were to see her in a bar or a bookstore or even at church would you pursue her? Could you blame me for having a relationship with her?"

"No I couldn't blame you. Besides we're human and we're bound to make some mistakes. In the end there's always room for forgiveness, but that's something we seem to take for granted."

"Could you email those pictures of my daughter when you get a chance," he asked handing me my camera.

"Of course."

I followed Alejandro back inside the club.

I felt like telling him about Bianca and I, but I couldn't do it. He knew that I had gotten involved with a married woman, but he didn't need to know we were both involved with the same woman. Spouses aren't the only ones who keep secrets from each other.

Some things are better left unsaid.

Character is like a tree and reputation like its shadow. The shadow is what we think of it; the tree is the real thing

~Abraham Lincoln~

19

It's Getting Late

Monique and I were sitting down on the patio of her apartment listening to the wind blow and watching the stars connect like dots in the darkness. There were a couple of deer running through a high grass field across from her complex.

I felt like Santa Claus because she was sitting on my lap. Her arms were wrapped around me as her face was buried in my neck.

"I've always been curious about why a wedding ring is worn on the left ring finger," I said as Monique looked at me like I was killing the mood.

"So you've discovered another origin."

"Yes I have, so bare with me." I held onto her left hand as her other hand was touching my hair. "No one really knows when the tradition of wedding rings really started. But everything served as a symbol. The circle symbolized two people being together for eternity. So I guess marriage was meant to never have an end, but it seems like divorce is just too common these days." She nodded in agreement. "The hole in the center of the ring was significant in that it served as a gateway leading to events that were known and unknown. When a man gave a woman a ring it meant that their love would never come to an end. Throughout history rings were worn on different fingers, but it was believed that the Romans determined the wedding ring is worn on the left ring finger because it was thought to be a vein in the finger. This vein was referred to as the Vena Amoris or Vein of Love said to be directly connected to the heart. Scientists being the skeptics that they are had to prove this false. Regardless of what the scientists believed, the myth remains regarded by many, mostly hopeless romantics, the number one reason rings are worn on the left hand ring finger. I'm boring you aren't I."

"No Ruby you're not boring me." She was running her fingers through my hair. "I'm amazed at how much you know. Like I'm amazed and sometimes just wonder how you find out about this stuff."

"The internet is a powerful source." She laughed.

"I heard that in the early Christian marriages there was a ritual where the wedding ring would be worn on the middle finger," she said touching my fingers. "As the priest recited during the binding, 'In the name of the father, the son and the holy spirit', he would take the ring and touch the thumb, the index finger, and the middle finger, then, while uttering 'Amen', the priest would place the ring on the ring finger, which was a way of sealing the marriage."

"Girl, you just get me." I kissed her on the forehead. "You know I love you right."

"Of course I do," she replied with a smile.

"Would you mind standing up?"

"Is your leg getting sore, keep telling you you're getting old," she laughed.

"No it's not that," I said pulling a small box out of my pocket and dropping down on my right knee while looking into Monique's eyes.

"Ruben, what are you doing?"

"Look I know we've only been together for eight months, but it's been the greatest eight months of my life. I want to spend more than eight months with you. I know it's a cliché, but it's a beautiful one and I mean it when I say that you're the first person I want to see when I wake up and the last person I want to see before I close my eyes. Your hand is the one I want holding mine till the end of time. I don't know what the future holds, but whatever time I have left in my future I want to spend it with you." I opened up the box to reveal a two-caret diamond ring that was sparkling. "Monique Olivia Valdez will you marry me?"

"Oh, Ruby."

"Just say the words that will make me the happiest man in the world." Expecting her to say yes I was ready to take flight from her balcony and believe that I could fly.

"Oh Ruby I don't know; this is just too fast for me right now. Have you really thought this through? I don't know if I'm ready for this."

"What do you mean you don't know…we get along great…we love each other…"

She was laughing, as tears were rolling down her face. "I am messing with you. Of course I'll marry you boy." As she wept tears of joy, I slid the ring on her finger and it fit her perfectly. I got up off my knee and embraced Monique.

"Don't mess with me like that girl. You almost gave me a heart attack." I imagined a studio audience clapping and cheering at the announcement of our engagement like they did on Friends when Monica and Chandler got engaged. We kissed each other. As we kissed I didn't want to stop, but I knew I needed to back away otherwise nine months from now we would have a baby. "We should go celebrate. I want to tell the whole world."

"Why don't we just stay home and just cherish the moment."

"We have the rest of our lives to do that baby. Don't you want to show off your new bling?"

"You do have a good point. Let me put my shoes on." Before walking inside, she pinched my nose. "I love you so much."

* * * * *

It was two in the morning and I sat in my living room with all the lights off thinking of Monique. I've cried myself to sleep so many times thinking about the night I proposed to her.

I should have been more accommodating to her needs, but I was too selfish. She wanted to stay home and spend her first night engaged with only me, but I wanted to celebrate with a crowd. In that relationship it seemed it always had to be about me.

If I stayed with Monique, then I would have never experienced everything I'm going through now. Even though Monique wasn't a virgin she would have done everything in her power to make sure I didn't compromise her or myself. How could this great woman be out of my life just at the blink of an eye?

While I laid in the dark I received a text message from Bianca. It said that she dropped off Deanna and that she would be at my place shortly.

After all the things I discovered about Bianca, I knew that everything we were doing had to end and it needed to start tonight. Now when I see her I'll see the hundreds of men she slept with standing with her. She deceived me. Or maybe I was gullible enough to believe her stories. She probably told her fictional stories of her husband's infidelity so much that she began to believe they were true.

My phone was ringing. It was Deanna.

"Hey pretty lady," I said.

"Hey sweetie," Deanna said. "Just calling to let you know that I made it home and going to bed."

"Okay, well sweet dreams."

"I'll see you tomorrow, good night."

After getting off the phone with Deanna, I began to realize that she wasn't the one for me. Even though I was with her physically and with two other women, my heart was still with Monique.

Deanna was a good woman, but I acted like a child that hates broccoli thinking she wasn't good for me. It's not that she wasn't good enough, but she was too good for me. Monique had a way of making my heart race or made the hair on my arms stand up the way no one else could. With Deanna there was very little romance in our relationship. Just because a couple had sex on numerous occasions didn't define them as being romantic. She deserved to be with someone that would honor and cherish her the way that I could not. All that I had done with Bianca and India reminded me of that.

Bianca and I didn't deserve people like Scott or Deanna because we didn't know what it meant to stand by someone the way they did. They were loyal and would fly to the ends of the earth for us if we wanted them to. Scott and Deanna deserved each other. Bianca and I deserved to be with no one… not even each other.

As my teeth were locked on my empty pipe I was rapidly pacing back and forth through my living room, as if my hair was on fire.

Every few minutes I would look outside my window hoping I wouldn't see Scott lurking in the bushes waiting to expose my tryst with Bianca.

What if he hired a private investigator that found out she was sleeping with me? What if cameramen came barging into my place with the spotlight on me in an uncompromising position for millions to see as Joey Greco, the host of Cheaters, exposed our infidelity. Scott would then beat me down with his fists of stone. And if I wasn't knocked into a coma Deanna would be tagged for the final blow.

I went to the bathroom because I just felt like I needed to wash my hands. When I looked in the mirror I thought I saw a pirate because my face was so hairy. It had been a couple of weeks since I had last shaved my face. My breath smelled from the barbecue I ate, but I didn't bother to brush my teeth. Perhaps Bianca would be repulsed by that and not make any moves on me. Who am I kidding? After some of the things I found out about her she would probably sleep with a homeless man if he said he had a condom. It's harsh, but it's probably true. My throat was dry, but I moistened it with some mouthwash.

When I walked in the kitchen and saw that the sink was full of dishes, I realized that I hadn't washed them all this week, which I would do, everyday even if I only needed to wash a fork or a spoon.

As I turned the lights on throughout my apartment I noticed that clothes were lying around in my bedroom instead of my laundry basket, the bed wasn't made, and mail was scattered throughout my living room instead of in a filing cabinet where I would normally store my mail.

Is this what sex had done to me, made me careless? Did it make me neglect my own self-worth?

I stopped in my tracks like a deer caught in the headlights when I heard a knock at my door. It was a soft knock, but I was petrified like the cops were outside waiting to serve a warrant for my arrest.

After opening the door Bianca came in throwing her purse on the couch while I turned the lock on the door three times.

When I turned around she wrapped her hands around the back of my neck, but I pulled away from her walking to the other side of the room, as if I didn't want her spreading her germs to me.

"What's wrong," she asked.

I was trying to think of the right words to say without being offensive, but it was difficult to be tactful. "How many other men have you been sleeping with?"

"You're the only one I've ever slept with."

"Come on Bianca cut the crap. Look I know I'm not the only one. Deanna told me you've been messing around for a long time. I'm not the first. Don't you have a special friend in San Francisco you've been seeing for the last year?"

"Deanna told you I've been messing around?" I nodded my head, as she sat down and crossed her legs. "I didn't want to tell you this, but since we're being direct with each other you should know she's the family slut."

"Don't you talk about her like that," I yelled.

"I know it's hard to believe, but it's true. She doesn't know how to commit. She's a veteran home wrecker that tried many times to destroy my marriage. She even brought up the idea of us having a threesome. The only reason she told you I mess around is because she's jealous of what I have. I hate to tell you this Ruben, but Deanna can't be trusted."

"Isn't that ironic, she said the same thing about you. Maybe I should leave you both alone because it sounds like there's some kind of sick demented family rivalry happening that I'm caught in the middle of."

"You're going to believe her. You're going to take her word over my own; after all we've been through."

"Yes I am."

"I don't believe this."

"It all makes sense. It's rare to see a married woman out so much without her husband. The first night we met you kissed me and you weren't wearing your ring. I know it's wrong what we've been doing, but I'm ashamed that I'm not the first you have had an affair with." Bianca folded her arms and stared at the wall. "You had me thinking I was the first guy you had an affair with. I know I'm not the first because Scott isn't really Angela's father."

Bianca looked at me, as if I spooked her. "How would you know that?" She got up from the couch.

"Her father is my best friend. Alejandro Padilla remembers you as Olga Garcia. And of course you weren't lying to him, Garcia is your maiden name and your family calls you Olga."

"Okay you got me Ruben," she laughed. "So what do you want me to do?"

"How can you be so cold? I gave you a precious gift. You were my first. You're supposed to leave your husband. You're supposed to spend your life with me."

"Do you really think after 12 years of marriage and raising two children that I would leave my husband?" I felt emasculated while she laughed. Her words were sharp like knives cutting my heart into pieces. "Oh baby I grew up Catholic and we don't believe in divorce. We take till death do us part seriously."

"You had me thinking that I was special." I felt as if my heart was going to split in half. "I thought I was different from all the other guys in your life."

"And you were, until you decided to sleep with me. I knew that sooner or later you would show me that you were just like any other guy. I don't know I guess when I took your virginity, I lost respect for you." She walked around the living room with her hands on her hips like she was on the red carpet at a movie premiere. "No man can resist what I have to offer. I knew that one-day you would exercise your curiosity. Like a man I enjoy a challenge and that's what you were. After conquering the challenge... well maybe you'll be glad to know that you were the first black guy I ever slept with." She was looking down in my waist area while putting on some lipstick. "Brothers know how to come up big."

"Scott deserves better than you."

"What are you going to do about it? What, are you going to tell him," she laughed. "You know he'll fill you up with led or slice your throat."

"This isn't right. You just don't treat people this way. You don't play with people's hearts this way." I almost felt like laughing because I was repeating the same words India said to me. Now I know how broken her heart felt.

"Don't act like you haven't broken a few hearts. You have no right to judge me." She got up in my face pointing her finger giving me a mouth full like she was a teacher and I was her student in big trouble. She swung the swords torturing me even more. "Mister church boy thinking you know it all and are never wrong. You're no better than I am! You're going behind Deanna's back. How many women have you taken for granted? How many times have you told a woman that you love them, even though you didn't mean it? How many times have you gotten a woman's hopes up making them think they were the one, only to later break their heart just because you saw a new piece of tail you had to have or you were just bored and needed a new adventure to explore? Or you couldn't stand their flaws that made them imperfect. How many times have you put on the charm giving them a smile or that Ruben Wells smirk and not really give a woman a chance to know the real you? How many women have you hurt? Don't stand there and tell me I need to clean up, when you're just as dirty as I am."

She left me speechless. I had hurt too many women prior to seeing Bianca. I thought of my ex-girlfriends and how I looked down on them and no longer wanted to be with them just because they overstepped the boundaries I set for them or did something I didn't care for. My relationships ended because of something so trivial like me getting annoyed by one of my ex-girlfriends who would answer the phone saying "Howdy." If I knew what real love was, I would have known what it means to be unconditional.

I thought of India and how I broke her heart being a hit it and quit it guy. I told her I loved her just so I could sleep with her. What a performance I put on. I deserved an Oscar, standing ovation, and to take a bow because I had her thinking I was in love with her. I took advantage of her vulnerable heart when all she needed was a friend. I deceived Deanna making her think she was the only one for me.

"This thing we have going on is over," I turned my back on her. "As you said in the beginning, you're married Bianca."

"So, there are a lot of married people who aren't faithful."

"It's getting late Bianca; you should head home to your family."

"You're ending it with me just like that."

"That's right just like that."

"Fine, there are plenty of other men who want me." I heard her walking off toward the door. "Oh one more thing, Ruben, before I go there's something that you should know."

"What's that," I said turning my head to the side.

"I'm pregnant."

"What's that got to do with me?"

"The baby is yours." I looked at her and laughed. "What's so funny?"

"Are you sure it isn't someone else's child? I know it isn't Scott's baby because you deprived that man of sex for a little over three months. No man should have to go that long without sex from his wife. You sure it doesn't belong to someone else because I've heard that you get around. Like maybe it belongs to your good friend in San Francisco."

"My friend in San Francisco had protection. You're the only guy I've been with in the last couple of months who didn't use protection. I am a little over seven weeks pregnant."

"What, how can that be? You were on the pill? That's supposed to prevent pregnancy. It says so on the box."

"Maybe I should have taken two pills. Or maybe I lied and just told you I was on the pill so you wouldn't wear the rubber."

"I can't believe this."

"What, I like how a man feels when he's not wearing rubber."

"Heifer, you crazy!" She was nonchalant. "So what are we going to do? How are we going to tell Deanna and Scott that we're having a baby? How do you want to work this out?"

"Ruben, I'm not keeping the baby," she said looking at me like I was an idiot.

"You're going to give up this child for adoption?"

"No, I'm going to have an abortion."

"You're what?" A look of indifference covered her face, as if she had no reservations about committing abortion.

"Like I said before I'm not having a divorce. Once Scott sees me with a belly the size of a basketball he'll know what's going on. The only way to handle this is to get rid of it."

"Whoa wait a minute. This just isn't a torn up shirt we're talking about, this is a human being you're talking about. Are you serious about wanting to do this? We're trying to play God and take a life. It's not right."

"Oh please, it's a little late for a sermon isn't it. No one made you sleep with me. You could have put on a condom, but you didn't. You could have walked away or never given me your number or never had sex with me, but you did all of that. Nobody forced you to do any of that. It was a choice you made. I'm doing what I can to avoid being the single mother of three children."

"How can you be so selfish?"

"Please, it wasn't good enough for you to have just Deanna, but you had to have me also, now that sounds like selfishness to me. You're just as bad as I am, only I am comfortable with knowing that I'm a good person who doesn't mind being naughty from time to time. "She was silent for a moment and walked up to me. "Do you really want Scott to find out? I'm trying to do this to protect you because he will come after you. He will not hesitate to kill you. You have taken what is his." She touched my face. "It would be a shame to see something bad happen to you."

"This isn't right."

"I want to stay with Scott and I'll do whatever I have to do to make the marriage last."

My head was hanging low. There was no way of talking her out of having an abortion. She was so impassive about her decision. Little one, whoever you are, I just want to apologize for what we are about to do to you. "Fine, do what you gotta do Bianca."

"Okay," she said walking off. "I'll see you around."

And just like that it was over between Bianca and me.

I should have been elated that I was free of Bianca, but I still felt unsettled with everything. As I turned the lights off my phone was ringing. I didn't bother to answer when I saw India's name appear on the caller screen. I had enough drama for the night.

My child, do not reject the Lord's discipline, and don't get angry when he corrects you

~Proverbs 3:11~

20

Worth the Wait

It was Sunday morning and I didn't bother to get up for church. I called Alejandro and lied telling him that I was sick. AJ Porter was going to fill in for me to lead praise and worship.

Even though I wasn't sick I felt awful. For some strange reason it had occurred to me that I hadn't read my bible since the day I lost my virginity. I had been reading my bible every day for years and I guess I felt there was nothing that would stand out to me since I had read every chapter and every verse so many times. I remember it once being a page-turner for me like Dan Brown's The Da Vinci Code, but somewhere down the line I got complacent with it not really trying to find a deep meaning in the words I was reading.

I grabbed my bible and opened it to Proverbs chapter three. In that chapter I was reading a lot of the benefits of having wisdom in my life. Through reading this chapter I realized that I had disrespected the Lord by depending on my own wisdom and not refusing to do things I would have normally thought were wrong. But I also realized that he corrects those he loves and I was in need of some correction.

After reading my bible I decided to do some cleaning. While I was cleaning I put on an old message from Pastor Harper that I hadn't gotten the chance to listen to. It was a continuation of his sexual sin series.

"After having premarital sex or committing adultery it seems some people get into a know-it-all attitude because they've been there and done that. God doesn't want us to be ignorant. Don't you know he wants us to desire wisdom? That only comes from knowing God; you can't find it through having sex with somebody.

"The fear of the Lord is the beginning of wisdom. Rebelling against God's commands won't give us true wisdom or joy, but seeking God out like we would in trying to find a mate and obeying him will. Y'all are pretty quiet; it's not getting too deep up in here is it. Somebody call 911 because I see dead people." There was laughter. "Glad I have your attention.

"Disobedience can bring a consequence that is never anticipated. Adam and Eve didn't see banishment from the Garden of Eden coming. Prior to their sin they were living on easy street and doing just fine on cloud nine, naked, unashamed and unafraid, but after they sinned they were embarrassed by their nudity, Adam had to work to eat and Eve had to learn to submit and she also had to go through pain during childbirth. Its okay to work and to bare children, but the pain could have been avoided if they had obeyed God.

"Today couples who engage in premarital sex may have to face the consequences of carrying guilt on the wedding day. They may become suspicious of each other. They don't know how to trust each other, let alone God. They thought they knew each other well through having sex, but what they know could cause them to hold anger towards each other."

Pastor Harper went into sharing what premarital sex had done to him and his wife.

He said that after dating and falling in love with his wife, he found himself engulfed with the desire for sexual intercourse. The more struggles they encountered the less impervious they were to the temptations of sex. When they gave into sex just the cycle in building their relationship towards marriage became vicious.

They were so upset with each other that they failed in breaking down the boundaries that they had set for themselves. His wife, during that time, had a difficult time believing that God could forgive them for what they had done. When they first got married, his wife was bitter towards him because she believed that as a man, he should have had more self-control. He said that she blamed herself frequently, but she thought ultimately that the responsibility rested on his shoulders.

He went into how the enjoyment of sex wasn't present in their marriage because they had engaged in something that is one of the most anticipated acts in a marriage, but it wasn't fun for them because they had already experienced it prior to marriage.

"It took us several years to work through the guilt and anger we felt towards each other," Pastor Harper said. "Things changed once we put it behind us and truly accepted God's forgiveness. This caused us to forgive each other. After a while we began to enjoy having physical contact with each other. I say all this to say that you can decide whether or not you want to engage in premarital sex. Different strokes for different folks. My advice is that if you don't want to experience something like this you should wait until marriage and keep your mind on the things of God.

"An example of this is Jacob. One of the things we learn from Jacob is that if you want something bad enough, you have to be willing to work for it. Jacob worked seven years in order to marry his beloved Rachel, and during this time they both stayed pure. He loved her so much that this seven-year period of waiting was worth it to him. He was letting Rachel know that she was worth it, worth the wait. Church, purity works when you believe it's possible.

"In closing, church, the devil will deceive you by telling you that no one has enough self-control to resist sex, so what makes you think that you can? There are people out there who resist it, but nobody is celebrating their trust in God. As far as sex is concerned not everyone is doing it. It's okay to say no. You may not know it, but a lot of people are doing it. Let's pray."

God never gave me more than I could tolerate, but I tried to handle more than he was giving me. It wasn't God's fault for me losing my virginity, but it was my own fault because I chose to do it.

After hearing the message, I just sat in silence thinking that if I had just held on a little longer I wouldn't feel so low. But I also knew that even though I engaged in premarital sex, I could make a new start and not give into it from this point on. It would be difficult because once you've done it, it's difficult to resist because I know what to expect. Lord, please help me!

Honor isn't about making the right choices. It's about dealing with the consequences

~Anonymous~

21

She's Out Of My Life

While a Timbaland beat was playing on Deanna's stereo she was pounding on a punching bag that she kept on her patio. She looked like she was getting ready for an MMA match. Seeing her Adidas land, a front kick frightened me because that could be my chest when I was going to tell her that I slept with her cousin.

I was foolish to be forthcoming with her when she had never asked me, but I couldn't live with the lie. The guilt was throbbing at my chest as she delivered a couple of straight punches to the bag. I needed to come clean with her about Bianca and me. I wanted to be free from this lie that was holding me down.

It had been four days since the barbecue and nothing was different between us, although Deanna would tell me every so often that it seemed like I had a lot on my mind, as if I was somewhere else. I would have thought she had grown suspicious since we hadn't slept with each other for a little while, but I figured she knew that I wanted to stop engaging in sex until marriage. She was working off her sexual tension connecting one jab, cross, hook, and uppercut after another.

I was thinking of different ways I could tell her about my infidelity. I could be comical and joke that our bodies just slipped into each other. Or I could be remorseful and contrite and just start crying and be literally down on my knees begging for her forgiveness.

I'd rather be open with her then end up on Jerry Springer where I end up in a brawl and one of the girls is stripped down to their birthday suit.

I couldn't deal with what I had done and never tell her.

She sat next to me while she was wiping her sweaty body.

"Got your 12 rounds in champ," I said.

"Not even close," she replied smiling while taking her sparring gloves off. "Looks like you've been putting your own brain through a workout. Baby is there something on your mind. You know you can talk to me about anything."

She was going to regret saying that after what I had to tell her. I caressed her face, as my lips met her own. She slipped the tip of her tongue in my mouth. After I kissed her I let go of her face. It dawned on me that I probably just had my last kiss with her.

"I like kissing those soft lips of yours."

"I do have some things on my mind, but I don't know how to talk about it."

"Just say whatever comes to mind. You know that I'm easy to talk to."

I leaned forward and took a deep breath. Felt like millions of viewers were watching waiting to hear what I was going to say. While exhaling I looked at Deanna who was smiling, as she was holding my hand. "Deanna, I've done some things that I'm not proud of."

"I'm sure it can't be that bad," she said holding my hand a little tighter. "What did you do kill somebody," she jests.

I squeezed her hand while she laughed. "Please don't make this any more difficult than it already is."

"Just tell me Ruby."

"Dee." The words were determined to stay in my mouth even if it meant suffocating me. "Dee, I." This was a lot more difficult than I thought it would be. I realized at the most inconvenient time how much I really cared about Deanna. For the first time I realized how much it mattered as to what she thought about me. But, as I said, "Deanna I slept with your cousin, Olga," I knew that it was too late.

I imagined someone in an audience saying "Ohhhh no he didn't," as she let go of my hand and walked toward the window. Her towel fell to the floor, as she folded her arms. I wouldn't be surprised if she put her sparring gloves back on and knocked me out with a jab to the jaw.

Felt like a weight had been lifted off my shoulders and I was ready to move on with my life. When I saw Deanna remain as immobile as a statue, I knew it would be a while before we could move on.

It was good that she wasn't in the kitchen because that's where she kept the butcher knives and forks. As long as she didn't have any objects in her hands I would at least make it out of this ordeal alive. She didn't rip the phone cord out, so that was also a good sign.

"I am so disappointed in you Ruben," she said in a somber tone. "I thought you were above that; I expected more out of you." She turned around and broke my heart, as I saw tears falling down her face. "I can't believe that you slept with my cousin." She began raising her voice. "You slept with my own cousin Ruben. You slept with that slut. I didn't deserve this. I did right by you and I get hurt." She unfolded her arms and paced back and forth while I sat still in the couch afraid she would do something if I moved or even said a word. "I thought you had standards. I thought that you knew your limits, but I should have known that you didn't because you can never say no to anybody. I knew that you had a problem of saying yes to just about everything, but I thought you could say no to sex. This is what I get for dating a guy who always desires to please everyone. Oh, Ruben I could just kill you. Tell me this Ruben, do you love her?"

"No, baby I don't love her," I replied getting up from the couch. "It's been over between us."

"How long has it been over?"

"That's not important. What's important is that I'm trying to make things right."

"That's not good enough. Do you still want her?" I was going to say something, but she chimed in, "Be honest with me."

"The truth is that I do still want her, but I know that I can't have her because she's not what I need."

She pushed me and was throwing her hands in the air. "Are you incapable of lying? I can't believe you have a college diploma because that has got to be one of the dumbest things I have ever heard come out of your mouth." We were silent for a moment, as she continued pacing back and forth and I rested against her wall looking at the door anxious to leave the fiery furnace I dragged myself into. I don't know what possessed her to ask the next question, but she knew I wouldn't lie. "I just have one more question Ruben. Was my cousin the first girl you slept with?" When she asked me, I acted as if I was unable to speak. My eyes fell to the floor afraid to look at her. "Ruben be a man and speak up." She walked right up in front of me to where I almost had no room to breathe. "Was she...your first?"

"Yes." As soon as I replied she slapped me in the face and while yelling "Why" she was beating on my chest. I grabbed her hands and pulled her into me. I locked my arms around her making it difficult for her to escape. Thinking that she couldn't do anything, I felt how hardheaded she was, as she headbutted me. I forgot to mention that she was a black belt in Jiu Jitsu and a brown belt in Krav Maga.

The force of her head hitting mine caused the back of my head to slam against her wall. My eyes were watery and I could feel blood pouring out of my nose. Deanna just stood as still as a mannequin looking at me. I pulled a handkerchief out of my pocket and while covering my nose with one hand, I reached out for her with my other hand.

"Don't touch me," she said pulling away. "Get out."

"Are you upset that I cheated on you or that your cousin was my first?"

"GET OUT," she yelled. "We are finished. I don't want to ever see you again Ruben."

"But I'm trying to make things right."

"The only way you can make things right is by leaving me alone. You cheated on me Ruben. I will never forget what you've done to me."

"Deanna, come on, we can work this out."

"Ruben, there's nothing to WORK OUT! Just get out of here." I was walking to the door. "You hear me? I don't want to ever see you again. WE'RE DONE!" When I was walking out she threw one of her shoes at me that hit my back. It didn't bother me. "GET OUT, you selfish son of a...," I closed the door not able to hear anything more she had to say.

I waited outside her door for ten minutes contemplating going back inside hoping that she had calmed down. Seeing the blood on my handkerchief was making me have second thoughts about that. Anyway, it was pointless because when Deanna made up her mind about something, she stuck with it. I can't blame her for calling off our relationship. Honestly, could I stay with someone knowing that they cheated on me? And they cheated on me with a family member too. I would be able to forgive them in time, but I would never forget what they had done.

As I was walking to my car, I received another untimely call from India that would go unanswered. She was someone that I wish would forget about me.

The future is not a result of choices among alternative paths offered by the present, but a place that is created – created first in the mind and will, created next in activity. The future is not some place we are going to, but one we are creating. The paths are not to be found, but made, and the activity of making them, changes both the maker and the destination

~Anonymous~

22

Beautiful Girl

It had been a little over a week since Deanna left me. I called her every day, but my calls were never answered. I left messages that weren't returned. I wanted to hear her say something even if it was something as horrible as telling me to go to hell.

India hadn't called since the night Deanna and I broke up. Maybe she got the picture that I didn't want her and finally moved on with her life.

Somewhere down the road I would have to face her and allow her to get some things off her chest, but now wasn't the greatest time.

The aisles were empty at Wal-Mart, which made the shopping experience much more pleasant at 10:30 on a Thursday night. While looking at some sweat pants I heard someone yell my name.

"Ruben is that you," a woman said leaving me speechless. I couldn't believe it; she looked like she went through a transformation.

"Rosa Barnes, what's going on girl," I said, as we hugged each other. She went from a moptop look to now having her hair run down passed her shoulders and it wasn't as dark as the night anymore, but she went back to her original saucy red hair look. Her fair skin was still immaculate and her green eyes still made me think she was Cleopatra reincarnated. "You're looking good Red, how have you been?"

"I've been doing well. I'm just doing some late night shopping."

"Yeah, best time to do it because there's less of a crowd here."

"So how have you been?"

"I can't complain. I'm doing some freelance work for Prevalent and I recently passed the real estate exam, so I need to find a realtor I want to work with."

"That's great."

"What are you doing these days?"

"Well believe it or not, I got a job as a teacher."

"Really, get out of here."

"Yeah, I'm going to be teaching mathematics at Hobby Middle School. It's different, but I think I'll enjoy it. I am looking forward to having all that time off during the summer and holidays. The pay may not be up to my standards, but I like to think of the time off I get as a perk. My parents moved down here from Corpus Christi and I'm doing some freelance work as a graphic designer until school starts."

"That's good, making some money with those talents of yours."

"Yeah, well look I don't want to keep you and don't want to be out here all night, it was good seeing you and I'll see you around."

"Yeah it was good seeing you." As she walked off I couldn't let her leave without me saying one last thing to her. "Hey Rosa, wait a second."

She turned around. "Yeah."

"It may not matter now, but I just want to say I'm sorry for making things harder than they needed to be when we dated."

"It's okay," she smiled. "Ruben, you've always been a good person. There's just been some times where you made a couple bad decisions." I didn't expect her to say that, but it was something that I needed to hear. "You be good Ruben."

I waved, as she walked off. Her slim frame was looking good in those Apple Bottom jeans. I wanted to ask her to come to my place, but I knew what that would lead to. Was she dating anyone? Even if she wasn't it's not like she would easily take me back. She was stronger than that. If she did take me back, we would go back to the way things were as if we never broke up and neither one of us would be happy.

In a brief amount of time I had grown accustomed to having sex. Now that I was going through withdrawals I was a fiend in need of a fix. It was tough resisting the temptation. I thought it was tough to resist sex when I was a virgin, but it was even tougher now that I knew what to expect.

As I was looking around I saw Rosa walking back my direction with a plastic bag in her hand.

"Hey Ruben," she said.

"Yes Rosa," I replied.

"You want to come back to my place."

"Yeah sure," I said pushing my shopping cart aside. It wasn't like I needed paper towels and dish washing liquid right this minute.

* * * * *

As I was following Rosa to her place, which was only five minutes away from my apartment, I was getting an erection just the thought of touching her soft vanilla skin. At the same time, I was thinking I should just take a detour and go home, but I was going on the straight and narrow path to Rosa's place.

As we pulled into the parking lot of her apartment complex my heart was rapidly pounding, my mouth was dry, and my palms were sweaty.

As I pulled up next to where she parked and got out of my car my legs started feeling heavy. She smiled while she got out of her car. As she was walking to her apartment I stood still.

Rosa was the first woman I dated after my relationship with Monique ended. She wasn't a virgin or a Christian. At the time I was a virgin she respected that and wouldn't do anything that would cause us to go any further than a kiss. Making out was the most I had done with her. If I had done anything more she probably would have been my first.

Remembering how soft she could kiss had me anticipating how warm she would feel in bed. If I told her that I wanted to have sex, she wouldn't reject me, but I was trying to turn over a new leaf. It's a struggle to try to make things right.

She turned around and walked back towards me, as I was frozen in my tracks.

"You okay Ruben," she asked.

"I can't do this Rosa," I replied knowing that if I walked in her apartment there was no turning back. I would be walking out of her place when the sun rose. There would be consequences waiting to visit me.

"I'm not asking for you to start dating me again. I just want some good old-fashioned casual sex."

"I can't do this Rosa."

"Come on I know you're curious. I know you want me. I saw how you were looking at me in the store. Once you step into my apartment your curiosity will be laid to rest."

"I'm sorry Rosa, but I just can't do this." I backed away and unlocked my car door.

"What is your problem?" I opened my door.

"This is not right."

"Are you afraid if you sleep with me that you're going to turn white?"

"I can't." As I pulled out Rosa was left standing there with one of her hands rested on her hips while she was throwing up the middle finger with her other hand.

As I was driving I knew I needed to call Bianca. I was reluctant to call her, but we needed to talk.

Hopefully it wasn't too late.

"Hello," she said.

"Bianca don't have this abortion," I yelled. "You can't do this. Our baby deserves a chance to live."

"I took care of it a couple days ago."

"What do you mean you took care of it?"

"What do you think I mean?"

"Bianca what have you done?" I pulled over into an empty car wash lot. "No, no, no, why did you do that?"

"You really think Scott would believe the baby was his if the child has a dark complexion, come on Ruben. My complexion isn't that dark, so he could put two and two together. It's bad enough that he thinks Angela is his own, this is one that won't slip passed him. Not to mention we haven't had sex for over three months. I still have a marriage to maintain."

"More like you trying to make everyone think you're the perfect wife, when deep down everyone knows that you're not. You just want to prove everybody wrong."

"Don't you start with me! Besides it's not like you wanted a child...right." She was right on the money because I didn't want to have a child this way. Having one after marriage, not before is the way I preferred to do it. I should have fought Bianca harder in preventing her from having an abortion. Bianca should have heard me give her some options if she didn't want this child. Give it up for adoption or just give the child to me for full parental rights, but the last thing I ever wanted to do was end someone else's life. Some people might say we did nothing wrong, as a life wasn't taken, but I have always believed that human life begins from the moment of conception. I was Bianca's accomplice by letting her do what she wanted.

"This is wrong Bianca."

"We can't all live right, now can we Ruben. Well good night." She hung up, as if she had been through something like this before. I was astounded as to how apathetic, how indifferent she was with this situation. A human being was killed and she acted the way most people do when they step on a cockroach. No guilt or sorrow, but continue on our merry way.

After speaking with Bianca I pulled my keys out of the ignition.

"I'm so sorry," I said burying my face in my hands. "I'm so sorry." That's all I could say. We robbed a being of having a chance to experience life.

I imagined this child being a girl. I don't know why, but I imagined that this girl would have my complexion and Bianca's long curly hair. She would have hazel eyes like my own and a round nose like her mother that wasn't too big or too small. I thought of her being the vocal and active type that would possibly do more than her mother or myself had ever done. As I looked out in the street I could see this little girl running to me with a smile on her face, but just like that she vanished, as an 18-wheeler drove by.

Bianca and I were in an adult situation that handled it like selfish children not caring about whom we would be hurting. This child could have done so many great things and impacted the world in ways that I couldn't have imagined, but now we'll never know.

Every beginning is a consequence. Every beginning ends something

~Paul Valery~

23

Gone Too Soon

Monique and I celebrated our engagement for a couple of hours at Arturo's shaking our hips and moving our feet to some salsa and merengue music. When we would dance to a bachata song I would hold her tight, as her head rested against my chest and her arms were wrapped around my neck.

At the end of every bachata song I danced with her I would always give her a slow dip and bring her back up at that same tortoise pace. She was going to be my dance partner for life and that felt so right to me.

Alejandro was there along with Torres and Roland and a couple of Monique's friends as well. If we weren't near each other in the club sometimes we would look at each other and just scratch our noses with our left ring finger as our way of saying "I love you."

As we were walking out to the car I had to stop Monique and just look at her.

"What is it," she asked.

"Nothing," I said touching her face. "I just want to hold on to you forever and never let you go."

"It's a little early for the vows Ruby Wells."

"It's only a preview."

"You're silly," she said kissing me on the lips. As we kissed I pulled her in tight, as she rubbed the back of my head. "Mmm, but I love that you're silly." She pinched my nose.

When we left I was too tired to drive, but Monique was delighted to drive, as she was still ecstatic from being engaged and to one day share my last name, as well as share the rest of our lives with each other.

We pulled up to a red light listening to our favorite song by Musiq Soulchild called Never Change.

"Monique Wells," she said. "I love the sound of that."

"I can't wait to spend the rest of my life with you," I replied.

"I love you so much Ruben. Tonight you have made me the happiest woman in the world."

"I love you Monique."

The light turned green and my eyes were getting heavy. Monique put her foot on the accelerator and we were cruising. As we were crossing the street my eyes were easily lifted and my heart was rapidly pounding, as we both heard tires screeching and saw two headlights of a Dodge Ram pickup truck coming quickly towards us on her side. I didn't have enough time to trade seats with her or be her shield. We just looked at each other and grabbed each other's hand.

The pickup truck rammed into us like a linebacker sacking a quarterback. The truck must have been going 90 mph because the impact of it was so powerful that it had our car flipping over and over again. After three flips I lost count.

When the car finally stopped flipping I was amazed that I wasn't unconscious or dead. I was feeling nausea, especially since we were hanging upside down. My legs and all my body parts were in their rightful place. There was pain in my right arm, but I was more concerned about Monique since the driver hit her side.

Monique had never let go of my hand.

I was telling Monique we needed to get out because I thought I could hear gas leaking. I unbuckled my seat belt. Monique didn't say or do anything. She didn't reply when I asked if she was okay. She didn't squeeze my hand when I squeezed hers. I panicked when I realized she was motionless.

"Monique, come on baby we gotta go." I looked at her and her eyes were closed. I felt for a pulse on her wrist and neck, but couldn't find a pulse. "Oh God please no. Come on Monique."

I unbuckled her seatbelt and was able to kick open my door. I pulled her out and carried her about twenty feet away from my vehicle. I placed her on her back. When we got to a safe spot I checked for a pulse again in her neck and wrist, but still couldn't find one.

I pulled out my cell phone and dialed 911.

"Hello," an operator answered.

"Yes, I need an ambulance," I replied. "There's been an automobile accident on Broadway and 410. Two cars were involved."

"Is anyone injured?"

"Please send someone out here quickly because my fiance doesn't have a pulse."

As I hung up the phone I could see that Monique wasn't moving. I tapped her a few times to wake her up, but her eyes remained shut. I placed my left hand on her chest with my right hand interlocked on top of it. I gave her multiple compressions. She didn't wake up. I tilted her head back and lifted her chin. Pinched her nose, took a normal breath, covered her mouth with my own and blew out my breath hoping to see her chest rise. After breathing into her, her chest didn't rise. "Oh God no, please God, not like this." I gave her multiple compressions again and there was still no response from her.

I kept on breathing into her and pumping her chest for the next three minutes until the paramedics arrived. I remember when I heard the sirens that it felt like a rescue was in store for Monique. If I couldn't save her, maybe they could.

Of course I was keeping them from doing their job because I wouldn't stop trying to save Monique. One of the firefighters had to pull me away from Monique and hold me back, as the paramedics were trying to resuscitate her. After a few minutes of trying to resuscitate her they had shaken their heads realizing that it was hopeless and there was nothing more they could do, but let her go.

I begged them to try again. My cries were louder than the sirens like Sean Penn in Mystic River screaming over his daughter's dead body.

We were supposed to have a life together.

The police had come and arrested the man who was behind the wheel. He had been beyond drunk, as he was also high on meth. They were asking me questions about what I witnessed in the accident since I was the passenger, but I couldn't focus on anything because I had lost my fiance.

I wanted to kill the man with my own hands, but that wouldn't bring Monique back. All I could do was cry over losing her, as I watched the paramedics cover her body with a white sheet.

* * * * *

For the longest time I had blamed myself for Monique's death. It was my idea for us to go out and if we had stayed home we would have never been in a car accident. What if I was supposed to be in the driver seat where the impact was most felt in the car accident? What if we had left just an hour or a few minutes earlier? Her family didn't blame me, but they said she lived a full life. They were sad she had to go, but they knew she was in heaven where they would one day reunite with her. I don't know why, but even though nobody blamed me, I continued to punish myself with guilt.

I dropped by the Mission Park cemetery where she was buried. One day out of every month I would visit the cemetery to see Monique's gravesite, but I hadn't visited since March.

When I came to her tombstone I knelt down and brushed the leaves off that were surrounding it. Her tombstone read 'Monique Olivia Valdez, January 4, 1980 - January 23, 2007. A proverbial woman who is irreplaceable, Proverbs 31:12.'

"I know it's been awhile," I said feeling like she was sitting in front of me. "To make up for lost time I brought you some fresh roses." I pulled a bouquet of fresh red and pink roses from behind my back. I placed them next to her tombstone. "I'm sorry I haven't been out here. I know that you expect me to live and go on with my life, but I can't forget about you Monique."

I took off my sunglasses and pinched my nose like she used to always do to me. As I touched her marble tombstone I imagined I was touching her smooth face. Tears fell down my face.

"You were a good woman Monique. You were the love of my life and it will be awhile before anyone can take that title away from you." I was looking down at the grass, ashamed of everything that I had done in the last few months. I felt Monique was talking to me and telling me to pick my head up. "Monique I'm sorry that you've seen me act the way I've acted for the last few months. That's not the man you fell in love with. You knew me as honest and generous, not deceitful or selfish. Somehow I lost sight of who Ruben Wells was." More tears were falling down my face. "I've done so much wrong and hurt people who didn't deserve it. I hurt people who wanted to do nothing, but love me. Lord I'm so sorry. I feel like I've slapped him in the face too many times. When I lost my virginity I felt like I violated my relationship with him, as if I cheated on him. Instead of leaving Bianca alone I slept with her, having her break a promise to a good man. Slept with Deanna and cheated on her with Bianca. Slept with India and avoided her afterwards, giving her a reason to make her feel like she wasn't of value. Bianca had an abortion. None of this would have happened if I had just stayed home so I could be well rested for church. I wanted to be with someone so bad that I stopped depending on God. It got to the point where I abandoned my relationship with him. I'm so sorry Lord; I want to make things right the best way I can. Right now I don't need to be with anyone." I pulled out my shiny silver trumpet from the case I brought with me. "Monique I remember that you enjoyed hearing me play any instrument, but I know you enjoyed the trumpet the most. So I thought I would play you a medley just like old times."

I closed my eyes and began playing the trumpet. As I played the wind blew causing leaves to fly away and the weak branches of trees were swaying back and forth. I continued to play as I stood up and slowly walked around Monique's tombstone like kids pacing themselves in a game of musical chairs. I was remembering all the good times we shared. I was blowing hard into my trumpet, as if it were magical like it would resurrect Monique. Maybe just maybe I could wake her up one more time.

Each of us needs to be willing to look at life realistically, see ourselves as we are, and come to terms with what's true

24

You Are Not Alone

On August 13, I celebrated my 28th birthday. My family and close friends threw me a surprise birthday party at The Tower of Americas, which is San Antonio's own version of the Empire State Building.

Alejandro and Kat lured me in by having me go with them to what I thought was a new jazz spot. There was some jazz music being played. In attendance were my parents, as well as my uncles and aunts, Raquel and her boyfriend Saul, Torres, Roland, Buster, and Shiloh.

My Aunt Stella and Buster acted as if they had never met before, especially when he saw that her 13-year-old looked more like an adult standing next to him, as he had to literally look up to him.

I was happy to share my birthday with family and close friends because that was also the night I decided to tell them all that I would be moving to Dallas in a few weeks to pursue my dream of winning a record deal. To make some money I had already secured a job with a real estate agency and I would also do some freelance writing for magazines and newspapers in Dallas.

A few people were sad to hear that I would leave, but everyone understood I was pursuing a dream and they supported me.

San Antonio is one of the largest cities in the United States, but walking around the tower deck made me realize that. From 100 stories up I could feel the wind blowing fast. The city's lights were shining bright. I am going to miss this city. I had some of my greatest moments in San Antonio like getting engaged. I was getting a chance to create more great moments in a new city.

My parents walked up to me while I was overlooking the city.

"I always knew that you would leave San Antonio," my mother said. "But even though I was prepared for it, it's still a little difficult to take in when you hear the news." She tightly wrapped her arms around me.

"Mom, I'll be leaving in a few weeks and I'll only be four hours away," I replied.

"Honey let him go," my father said touching my mother's shoulder. She let go. "I'm proud of you son. You're taking a chance on something new. I know you'll do well out there. Whenever you come back for a visit bring me a Dallas Cowboys jersey. I know he's retired, but I prefer Emmitt Smith."

"You got it," I said sticking my hand out to shake his hand.

"Put that away," he said wrapping his arms around me. I hugged him back. When he let go he patted me on the back.

"It's getting late," my mum said. "We're going to go now because we can't hang with your young people. We need our rest."

"Alright, I'll see you guys later. Love you."

"Love you too Ruby."

* * * * *

Torres and I were in the restaurant talking while other members of my party were outside on the tower deck.

"Can't believe you're leaving," Torres said with a toothpick hanging out of his mouth.

"It's time for a change," I replied.

"I can understand that."

"How are you and that girl, what's her name?"

"Iris."

"Yeah Iris, how are things going with you two?"

"Things are good right now. I can't complain."

"Are you still a virgin?"

"Yeah I am," he laughed.

"Good, that's good T. Do you carry any rubbers with you?"

"No."

"Well that's not a bad idea. It helps you to know that you won't put yourself in a situation that you won't be able to turn back from. If you carry one that will let people know you're open to doing it. That's the mistake I made."

"You're human and we all make mistakes."

"I know, but if you want to wait until marriage then do that and do what you can to avoid the temptation or resist it. If this is something you desire the most there will be all types of things thrown your way to make you lose it. Like you told me it's a one-time only deal, once it's given it's gone forever."

"Yeah, well don't forget about us little people when you make it big."

"I better see a book by Torres Russell on bookshelves within two years."

"Probably going to hear you on the Steve Harvey Morning Show," he laughed.

"Whatever."

Alejandro and Kat walked in and sat with us.

"So you feelin' good about this move man," Alejandro asked.

"You know I am," I said.

"Well if you're there longer than a year I'm movin' out there with you."

"Whatever," I said incredulously.

"I'm serious man, who else is goin' to watch your back out there."

"Ali, you a fool," Kat said kissing him on the cheek.

"Y'all think I'm playin', but watch y'all gonna see."

"So," Kat said sitting next to me. "Big brother, you have any unfinished business you need to take care of before you leave?"

I thought about it for a minute and felt everything in my life was settled that needed any kind of resolution. "No, I think everything is taken care of."

"Are you sure about that?"

"Yes I am."

"Really, what about…" She mouthed Deanna's name.

"Oh."

"You know you have to at least try to resolve things between the both of you. If you're going to leave you have to leave right. You know that."

"I know that you're right. I do."

* * * * *

As I stood outside Deanna's apartment I thought about the first time we met and how things flowed so well between us. I was the problem that restricted it from moving forward. I thought about not knocking on the door, but I couldn't leave without at least apologizing to her.

When I knocked on the door I was surprised that Scott answered. I saw his kids sitting on the floor eating some fast food.

"Hey," I said.

"Hey Ruben, how's it going brother," he replied.

"I'm doing alright. I just needed to talk with Deanna."

"Oh, of course." What the heck is going on? What is Scott doing here?

"Hi," Deanna replied standing outside closing the door behind her. I noticed that her apartment was almost empty. It was filled with boxes.

"How are you?"

"I'm fine."

"Your place looked empty. Did somebody rob you?"

"Oh no, I'm moving out. I ended up getting that job in Chicago. It took them awhile to call me back, but I got it."

"That's great. When do you leave?"

"I'm leaving in three days. I've been doing a lot of packing the last few days. Scott and some of his friends helped me move out the heavy stuff. He stuck around to help me pack up some things, save some time with two people instead of one person doing it all."

"Is there something going on between you two?"

"What do you mean?"

"Is there a relationship or are you sleeping together?"

She slapped me in the face. "How dare you, you have no right." Her slap stung a little. "There is nothing going on between us," she said while folding her arms. "Unlike some people we know how to keep our hands to ourselves. His wife is out somewhere doing God knows what. He asked if I needed some help and I told him I could use his help. Wait a minute why am I explaining myself to you. And even if I was with him what does it matter to you? We're not together anymore."

"I know that, but Scott is still a married man."

"Yeah and he's still faithful to his woman. I respect his marriage." She stepped closer and whispered, "Wish I could say the same for you."

"Does he know about me," I said getting closer to her and lowering my voice.

"No, he doesn't know."

"You're not lying to me are you?"

"I'm not like you Ruben I know how to be honest even while under pressure. He doesn't know. He just knows we broke up because we both wanted different things. Now what are you doing here Ruben? It's not like you really have any reason to be here."

"Yeah I know."

"Well can you hurry this up please because I'm really tired?"

"I'm going to be moving to Dallas in a few weeks. I'm sorry for what I did to you. I'm sorry that I slept with another woman. You deserve better than that."

"You're dang right I do. I was patient with you. I was willing to always stay by your side. I gave you my heart and you repay me by sleeping with my slut of a cousin. She's a slut, but she's still my cousin." She was looking behind her hoping that Scott didn't hear what she was saying.

"I forgive you Ruben, but I can't forget what you've done. You…" She bit her bottom lip, as if she would say something that she would regret. She closed her eyes for a second. "What did you think would happen after you apologized?"

"I thought that maybe…"

"You thought that maybe we could be friends. That maybe while I'm in Chicago and you're in Dallas we would stay in touch and then somewhere down the line turns into a couple again. This isn't one of those movies you critique Ruben. This is real life where there are no cuts, but you only get one chance to prove yourself to somebody. In this life you and I will never be friends. What you did was unforgettable. You have my forgiveness, but you will not have my friendship. It's getting late and I'm extremely tired. So now the only thing left to do is to say good night. I wish you the best in Dallas."

Before I could even utter a word Deanna closed the door on my face.

The only problem with turning over a new leaf is that some people can't forget what you've done, which means they may not choose to accept the new you. This is a part of my life I have to choose to accept. We all have to choose this day what we will do with our lives because after all everything begins with a choice.

25

State of Shock

It wasn't until twenty minutes later that I finally went home. It was half an hour after eleven and it was quiet outside my apartment complex. Not that there was usually noise around this time of the night, but it was just too silent for me to be left alone with my thoughts.

I wanted some kind of noise to distract me from thinking about Deanna and how I had done her wrong. I needed a distraction the thought of how much I had hurt India. I needed something to take my mind off of Bianca having an abortion. Some kind of distraction to keep me from thinking about the life we spoiled.

As I walked into the apartment I closed my eyes and leaned against the door. My apartment was filled with boxes as well since I would be moving in a few weeks. Once I got my bearings I turned on my television to see Frasier and his brother Niles having some philosophical debate that had their father rolling his eyes. As I threw my keys on the couch I heard a knock at my door. Were my neighbors complaining about the volume and needed me to turn it down.

Before opening the door I didn't bother to see who it was like I normally would. As I opened the door all I saw were some beautiful legs standing in white stilettos. As I continued to look up I saw a white dress and white blouse to match it exposing a lot of cleavage. I was shocked to see India outside my place with a smile on her face.

"Hey you," she said resting one of her hands on her hip, while her other hand was holding a little white purse. "Are you going to let me in?"

"India what are you doing here," I asked.

"Came here to see you silly, why else would I be here," she asked slowly pushing the door back and walking in my apartment.

"But why are you here? I told you we're done." I slammed the door after she walked in.

"Please don't take that kind of tone with me." She was walking through my apartment as if she owned it. "What is with the boxes?"

"I'm moving."

"Are you moving to another side of town?"

"No I'm moving to Dallas."

"So you're just going to leave me." Her back was to me. I don't know if she was crying or if there was a scowl in her expression.

"I guess so. That was the last thing on my mind, but yeah I'm definitely leaving you behind."

"So I guess I'll have to do this the hard way."

"India what are you talking about?" I could hear her unzip her purse. She turned around with a photo. She handed it to me. It wasn't just a photo, but it was a sonogram. If I had a glass in my hand standing on a hardwood floor it would have fallen and shattered on impact with a floor. Needless to say I was shocked. "That was my child...our child. I know that you would think it's impossible since

I'm in my 40's and scientists believe women can't get pregnant in their 40's, but sometimes science can be proven wrong."

"What do you mean our child?" I couldn't take my eyes off of the sonogram.

"You're the only man I was with recently."

"I meant what do you mean when you said *was* our child?"

"A few days ago I suffered a miscarriage. Nothing strange happened; it just had to do with my age. While it's not impossible for a woman in their 40's to get pregnant, it is more difficult for them to have children." While India spoke my mind drifted away. I got Bianca pregnant, but she had an abortion. I supposedly get India pregnant and she suffers a miscarriage. Was I not meant to bring kids into this world or was I not meant to be a father at this point in my life? While I was pondering that, something India said caught my attention. "I figured since all of us are here...you, me, and our baby, I thought we should all be together one last time."

"What are you..." I looked away from the photo and saw India standing calm and collective like a Bond girl while pointing a .357 magnum at me making me throw my hands in the air so she would know I won't make any sudden movements, as she dropped her purse. "India, what are you doing?"

"No man has made me feel worthless like the way you did. You made me realize that I'm of no value to anyone. I felt like I was the luckiest girl in the world to be your first, but you disrespected me like a whore. You gave me a gift, planted a seed in me. When I found out I was pregnant I felt my life had an even greater purpose. But then the miscarriage happened. So since I can't have a child or have you what's the point in going on because my life is meaningless." A tear fell down her left cheek. "Isn't that what you think?"

"No, no India that is not what I think."

"Then why did you treat me the way that you did?"

"I don't know, I was with someone else and I didn't know what else to do."

"Get down on your knees." She walked a little closer, as I got down on my knees while her hand was steady holding the gun.

"You could have done the honorable thing by telling me you were with someone and left me alone."

"I'm sorry I didn't mean to lead you alone."

"Oh but you did." She was standing very close to me. All I could feel was the cold steel of the gun on my forehead. "You had me remember what it was like to feel butterflies. I was really feeling you. I definitely thought it was mutual after we made love."

"It was more like we had sex."

"Shut up," she yelled punching me in the face. Her face felt like a sledge hammer making me spit out blood on the carpet and the impact was so strong it made my eyes watery. That's two women now who have either slapped or punched me in the face. This is not something I want to get used to. Assuming India lets me live.

Oh dear. I could actually die tonight. This is not a movie where the gun isn't a prop and it's not filled with blanks, this is the real thing. If she fires the gun blood will gush out of my body. That's unpleasant. The thought of lying motionless wasn't welcoming either. The more I thought about death the more my hands trembled.

I like to be in control and know what's coming. I definitely didn't see this coming. It's ironic that when I played music I just went with the flow no matter what. Life is like jazz at times, out of our control and unpredictable.

"Please let me make it up to India. I'll do anything you want. Just put the gun down please."

"You'll do anything?"

"Yes anything."

"Make love to me," she smiled with her eyes wide open. "What better way to go out then to go out with a bang."

"What?"

"Before I kill us both we are going to have sex one final time." She got down on her knees so we could be on the same level.

"No."

"Don't tell me you don't want me." She grabbed one of my hands and put it against her chest. "Squeeze my breast." I pulled my hand away. "You're not going to touch me. You don't find me sexy." She leaned in to me. "Kiss me." She pointed the gun on my chest. "KISS ME." She grabbed the back of my neck and was pulling me towards her while I was pulling away from her. "Why won't you kiss me? You don't think I'm desirable." Her eyes got even wider. "TOUCH ME." She punched me in the face again. Maybe this will turn out like the movies where the incorrigible bachelor gets saved by the ex-girlfriend or the one that got away. So maybe any second now Deanna will come barging through that door and go Laila Ali on India.

"No."

"You don't tell me no." She pointed the gun at my face. I was staring at the barrel of the gun that looked as big as cannon.

"Oh God, please forgive me." I couldn't believe this is how my life would end, black on black crime. "Please forgive me Lord." I couldn't remember the last time I prayed. And how convenient is it that I decide to pray when I'm in trouble or need something. I closed my eyes and folded my hands in a tent shape.

Bianca and I spoiled a life. We tried to play God by not letting someone experience life. We never gave this child a chance to experience a first taste of ice cream, ride a bike, walk, crawl, all the things we experience. We were selfish by destroying another life. "Stop this India, please."

"What am I not attractive enough for you?"

"India you're scaring me."

"What?"

"I find you frightening."

India lowered the gun. She looked as if she had just been told that she was diagnosed with leukemia. She stood up, as her mascara was messy with tears running down her face. "What am I doing?"

"India please put the gun down and we'll talk."

"No we're done talking. I'm done talking." She was still crying.

"Please India." I was about to get up, but she pointed the gun at me.

"You see what you did to me Ruben. Look at what you did to me. I just wanted to be loved. All I wanted you to do was love me. I just wanted to be loved. That's all I ever wanted…was to be loved."

India put the gun in her mouth.

"INDIA NO!"

My arms weren't long enough to pull the gun out of her mouth. Before I could even get up she pulled the trigger and blood had splattered on my wall. Her white dress was now crimson covered with her blood. My body was shaking as she was lying motionless in my living room.

This was my fault. India's death was on me. I didn't tell her that she was loved. I didn't make her feel secure that she was precious.

I neglected to show her God's love. I was remiss in not letting her know that his love for her is everlasting and he would never abandon her. All she needed was his love.

Isn't that what we all want…to be loved. We can choose whom we give our hearts to, but God's love is always made available to us.

Epilogue

All I could do was thank God that I was still alive. The police had arrived at my place within ten minutes. They were in my place for hours questioning me, dusting for prints, and investigating India's body. It had taken awhile, but I was clear and it was ruled a suicide. I had nothing to be guilty of, but I did feel accountable for India taking her own life.

I do weep for India. All she wanted was to be loved. I took advantage of her, when I should have been the one to tell her that God's love was always there for her and that was the first step in feeling fulfilled.

A year had gone by before I stepped in San Antonio again.

While I was away I saw my family in Atlanta where we celebrated Thanksgiving. Kat and my parents visited me in Dallas for

Christmas and New Year's Eve. Alejandro seemed to come to Dallas every other month. The last time he visited I saw him with a For Rent Magazine for the Dallas area.

I came back to San Antonio because my cousin Raquel was marrying her NBA-superstar fiance, Saul Russell.

It was fun catching up with the rest of my friends. It seemed almost everywhere I went Alejandro was there with me. I miss him also, even though I know neither of us will say it.

The wedding ceremony was beautiful. I couldn't help, but be envious of what Raquel had with Saul and that seemed to be completion. They don't ever have to wonder if someone is out there for them. I know that it won't be easy and they will have to work to keep what they have, but for them it will be worth it.

I'm still single and I don't know where the one is that the Lord has for me, but I know that he's preparing us both for the divine moment when we both cross each other's paths. Who knows it could be someone I already know. Whether she's a virgin or not makes no difference to me just as long as I know she's the one God has for me, I know she'll be everything I need.

I stuck around for the reception, but I didn't stay too long.

After I left the reception I went by Nocturnal where I first met Bianca. It was the place where my whole life changed. The club was no longer called Nocturnal, but it was now called The Pyramid.

The place was completely remodeled, as it looked posher than run down when it was Nocturnal. They had a live salsa band playing, but there were very few people dancing because they weren't playing booty shaking music like they did when it was Nocturnal. There were more tables to sit at and more lounge areas to relax in. It was classy, but if I want classy I can go down to Magee's. This is what I decided to do.

When I walked into Magee's some of the people that worked the door greeted me with a hug and didn't bother asking me to pay a cover charge. Tucker Magee walked up to me and hugged me like I was a prodigal son returned home. I sat by the bar and listened to the band play, which was led by a black woman backed up by an all-white band that was playing with some soul and funk like they were a reverse KC and the Sunshine Band. They just got done singing No Ordinary Love.

One of the white guitarists stepped to the mic.

"This is another oldie, but goodie," he said. "This is Me and Mrs. Jones."

When I heard the song played I was frozen in my seat.

Bianca raced through my mind as I heard the song. It's funny, but no matter how hard you try it's impossible to forget your first. After Deanna rightfully dumped me I never had sex again. So I guess I've become a born-again virgin, if that makes any sense. I was afraid to see Deanna the night of my birthday, but I'm glad I did.

There are times that I'm upset she cut me off, but Deanna made a wise choice in deciding to do that. Even though I've decided to make some changes sometimes there are no guarantees.

We have to choose whom we accept to be a part of our lives. Deanna decided that I was to no longer be a part of her life. She had every right to make that choice after the things I did to her. Hopefully she's doing well in Chicago.

As I was taking in the atmosphere I saw Mari and her husband sitting in a booth together. They really looked happy with each other. His left arm was wrapped around her. She looked like she was lost in his embrace, as her head rested on his shoulder. He looked like he was a man in love, as he kissed her forehead. I thought about saying hello, but I didn't want to interrupt their date night especially if they were rekindling the flame.

Sometimes I wonder how Bianca is doing. Has she done right by Scott or is she still doing wrong behind his back? Maybe I should ask her since I just saw her walk into Magee's.

Whoa, wait, what?

She walked into the club with a smile on her face. She still had dirty blonde hair, but it was straight. She was standing in some open-toe silver stilettos showing off her manicure along with black pants and a black top to match it that exposed her chest looking a little bigger than the last time I saw it. Monica and two latin guys walked in behind her. The guys were busy digging through their wallets for five or ten dollar bills at the door while Monica was watching the band play and Bianca was looking at me with a smile on her face.

I stayed in my seat and noticed that her left ring finger wasn't covered with any kind of ring.

We both looked at each other, as she was smiling bright and I was trying to think of what I should do, say hello or ignore her.

I thought about the conversation we had and how cold hearted she sounded about getting rid of a child that we both could have had. And of course I couldn't help forget how angelic she was when I first met her.

So there I was intrigued while also disgusted with her. I couldn't believe that I was having a hard time wondering if I should go talk to her or act like I had never known her. I'm sure to most people the answer was an easy one, but I was making it more complicated than it needed to be.

Everything begins and ends with a choice.

Made in the USA
San Bernardino, CA
28 January 2017